LOVING THE SISTERS

PAMELA R. HAYNES

COPYRIGHT

CONTENTS

Loving the Sisters   V

Foreward   VI

Loving The Sisters Poem by Nina Simão   VIII

Dedication   XI

Acknowledgements   XII

LOVING THE SISTERS   1

1. Patti   2

2. Charmaine   18

3. Rose   34

4. Patti   48

5. Charmaine   63

6. Rose   72

7. Patti   81

8. Charmaine   87

9. Rose   95

10. Patti   107

11. Charmaine   115

12. Rose   128

13. Patti   137

14. Charmaine   145

15. Rose   151

16. Patti   155

17. Charmaine   164

18. Rose   170

19. Patti   176

20. Charmaine   186

21. Rose   191

22. Patti   196

23. Charmaine   201

24. Rose   206

About The Author   213

LOVING THE SISTERS

Pamela R. Haynes

FOREWARD

My first encounter with Ms. Pamela R Haynes was in 2017 at the Miss Barbados UK pageant in my previous role as Deputy High Commissioner for Barbados to the United Kingdom where she was a guest. I was delighted to hear that she had published her first book "Loving the Brothers" and chose to have her book launch in Barbados in 2019.

I was honoured to be the featured speaker at The book launch which was held at Chattel House Books in Fontabelle in Bridgetown, where her proud parents were in attendance. Sadly, Pam lost her mother in September 2020 and this book is lovingly dedicated to her.

The theme of domestic abuse which this book confronts is close to my heart as I have personally seen it first hand in my neighbourhood growing up as a child. The book therefore, resonates with a lot of persons internationally to raise awareness of the stigma of domestic violence, which in most cases is hidden in plain sight.

The year 2021 was a very difficult one for Barbados with the trifecta of adverse events namely, hurricane Elsa, ash-fall from La Soufrière volcano in St. Vincent and of course the lockdown due to the Covid-19 pandemic. During this period Pamela showed empathy by offering words of comfort and support as she has done all her life both in a personal as well as a professional capacity.

Pam's extensive research of victims of Domestic Violence has led her to become a mentor to families who have been affected negatively by this endemic. She previously worked as a Senior Probation Officer with the UK government for 26 years. She is now poised to assist victims in documenting and sharing their own stories anonymously. Pamela always felt that the theme of her stories was universally pervasive and therefore appealed to persons of different cultures. Pam never gave up on her dreams to write and publish these stories.

She is now a mentor to other women in the UK diaspora who want to express themselves in writing their own experiences. In addition to this, she has been made an Ambassador for a Charity based in Barbados called "Advocates Against Domestic Abuse".

I look forward to celebrating the publication of Loving The Sisters with Pam when she next visits Barbados'

Senator Alphea Wiggins; BSc; J.P

LOVING THE SISTERS POEM BY
NINA SIMÃO

Can we not we not just love & understand each other?
Can't we just love & understand each other?
Have my back, & I for sure, will have yours
We were tight, like, brother's and sister's
once upon a time, an all black cast
meant to last, through all obstacles, being thrown at us
& our history, goes, way back, when,
we were, we still are,
the main targets, of hate,
but little by little, we're losing our powerforce!
They 've tried, everything!!
To make this our fate, is it too late?
For us, to succeed?
In this, world full of, so much hate, & greed
How do/did we even find ourselves, in this sad & sorrowful state?
Now at loggerheads, & at war with each other
Why do our kings not protect us, honour us, enough, to respect
us
& to not lay their big, manly hands on us
Oh sisters! We've cried, far too many tears
for far, too many years
thus, we've hardened, maybe, more than we bargained, for,
been made to be strong, carried the weight, way too long
Alone, on an ever winding & treacherous path, where, very few
last, & make it through, unscathed
So much to bear, & yet heavily burdened, like carrying, big
boulders on our shoulders

Yet we have become, use to it, in some way,
reducing our femininity, in some way,
some may say, aggressive & LOUD!! Or maybe, just proud!
Worn as a shroud, to protect us, like armour, for our own
defenses
Can we not find a little comfort, & have peace,
even behind, closed doors?
Not have wars,
where there should be no, battles fought
We have been molded, conditioned & taught.
to be the strongest,
Certainly not through choice, and of our own doing, really, not
our fault at all
Can't you see! I am the reflection of your mirror image,
so do not hate me
love me, as you would love, your mother or sister
Don't treat me like something, from the bottom of your shoe
For I am not the slave master, and neither are you!
Don't beat up on me, else, I will fight back!
Even if there leaves no skin left on my back
from the lashings, you happily, dish out daily
verbally, mentally, physically, emotionally, even, sometimes
financially
but let's just call it as it is, you're a BIG BULLY!
Not fully, a man
In my eyes, you are not worthy of that given name,
Such a crying shame!
More so, for me, please!!! I beg for some help! To break free!
Of my now, a reality, in a caged insanity, mixed in misery,
Go!!!???? Huh! No easy task, at all, to say it yes,
but to do it. is so, sooo questionable??
Really, not at all, as simple as you may think
Coz, within a blink of an eye, (fist punch hands or thump mic on
chest)
another woman, lays down, & dies
You don't dare wind up, a narcissist, with their psycho-pathic
minds,
as empathy, really, really does leave them blind
Theres no chance to ever be as one? On the same levels, instead,

ix

like a whirlwind, resembling the actions of some frenzied,
Tasmanian devil/s
When the constant barrage of torments keep coming,
again, the shame, the pain, and even more blame
Do not raise your clenched fist at me, else I must flee,
and do not hunt me down, when I do leave
Don't dare to cry, for then, the milk has long been spilled
it will be a long & arduous task to ensure, my life returns, once
more
but my life, is my life & I choose to do as, I please
As you are neither my mum, nor dad, or, some dictator, just a
raging/bleep,bleep Fucking/ Hater!!!
For you did not care to hear, my cries, as part of me, and my spirit,
twisted, turned, inside out & died
you did not care as you sucked the life-force, from me
to feed your own inadequate, deficiencies
Just love up a sister, will ya! Or let her be, free!!!
To restore and hold her head up, high, again, with some
resemblance of dignity
have peace & harmony, restore back to, within/her vicinity
First! Shhhhh! Quick, quick, hurry hurry! Walk out the door,
meanwhile, ignoring the shouts that you're a whore, note to self
don't dare go back, guaranteed for more attacks & even then, to
leave, there are no guarantee's
Please be ready & worthy for the love, deserving of a strong,
beautiful, & fearless queen, don't tear her down, to wear a frown,
instead replace it with the crown, that she so deserves
If not, simply, let someone else, adore her, that can, a real man!!!
That does not treat her any lesser, brother's just cherish love, &
bless her
As you would, or should, have love, for your own, blood sisters
ninasimão2020

DEDICATION

In memory of my beautiful Mother
Genetha R Husbands
Meet me by the river, Someday.

Acknowledgements

Special thanks to my loving Husband Neville and our children.
My Dad Ronald W Husbands
My reviewers,
Janette Pierre, Carlene Forbes and Petra Baptiste.
Poet Nina Simão.
Events Manager Lorraine Noonan.
Supporters Karen Small, Valari Mitchell Clarke, Cheryl Braithwaite and Marvine Harewood
Advisor Pastor Grace Ellis-Goodridge.
Editors Michelle Patu, Sade Knows
My lovely publisher Stacy Brevard-Mays and team at Hear Our Voice LLC
To all the NHS staff at Whipps Cross Eye Treatment Centre.

LOVING THE SISTERS

Pamela R. Haynes

CHAPTER ONE

PATTI

To begin telling you the story, I have to go back to Jamaica at my hen party, where Rose and Charmaine dropped their bombshells and made a whole heap of serious allegations against their husbands that made my jaw literally drop to the floor. I could not believe what Rose was telling me; she wasn't holding back, and Charmaine kept chipping in and telling Rose to "Allow it. Allow it." When I met them at the homegoing service, Marcus did not give me the impression that the two women were so close.

I felt cornered, and I wanted to get away from them. I made my way through the hotel lobby, with Rose and Charmaine in tow. Rose was going on about me being sent to "save" her, or some crock of shit like that, and I didn't want to hear it. My head was hurting me, and I just wanted to go up to my hotel suite and lie down. Even as the lift doors were closing, Rose was being held back by Charmaine, but her final rant would haunt me for the rest of the night.

"You think loving these brothers is easy? Well, I'll tell you it's not. You'll see. You'll see. It takes one signature to get married, but a whole heap to get divorced."

I was shaking so much I couldn't quite press the lift button to take me up to my floor, and when I got to my hotel room, I couldn't find the key card for the door. So, I ended up throwing the contents of my clutch bag on the floor. When I finally got in the room, a wave of heat hit me like I had walked into a brick wall. I switched on the air conditioning, kicked off my high heels, and discarded them in the middle of the room. I pulled my maxi dress over my head and threw it on the floor along with my Spanx girdle.

I sat down on the bed to take off my bra, instinctively holding my breasts, as they were released from the constraints of my brassiere. I rubbed under my breasts where the underwire had dug into my skin, then moved up to the shoulders to remove the bra straps one by one and massaged my shoulders. They were sore and aching from lying in the sun too long without applying enough sunblock.

If Marcus were here now, he would have massaged some lotion into my skin. I almost reached out for my mobile phone to call him, then I remembered he was out and about with his friends and his brothers; the two wife beaters. I laid back on the bed and I cried my eyes out. I wanted mum to reassure me but given her position on my up-and-coming nuptials, this new information would have added fuel to her fire. I almost called Antoinette, but she wasn't a fan of my decision either and I wanted someone to be on my side.

The only person who was exclusively in my corner was Marcus. Manley and Junior are his brothers. How exactly was I supposed to raise this issue with him? How was he going to react? I have never seen Marcus angry or cross before, and I wasn't going to be the one to upset him. Rose's words were swimming around my head in a loop. 'You think loving these brothers is easy? You think loving these brothers is easy? You are sent to save us Patti.' Just who did Rose and Charmaine think I was? I'm a Senior Probation Officer, not a bloody superhero!

I may be perceived as a strong black woman, but I'm no Wonder Woman. Rose even spooked Charmaine, who was as drunk as fart, and cussing off Junior like a sailor. I spent the rest of the night tossing and turning, willing myself to sleep, but sleep was evading me. Was I doing the right thing? Was Marcus my soul mate? I must have drifted off at some point, because when I woke up feeling cold and I rose to switch off the air conditioning unit on the other side of the suite, Yolanda was lying next to me, sleeping blissfully. We agreed that Marcus would crash in her room after he got back from his stag do and Yolanda would bunk in with me.

I glimpsed at my watch; it was four in the morning. If I fell asleep now, I could potentially get three hours of sleep before I had to get ready for my wedding. I got back into bed under the covers and closed my eyes. It felt like only a few minutes later when there was a knock at the door. Yolanda wasn't budging, so I put my dressing gown on over my naked body and answered the door. It was the concierge delivering a bouquet of tropical flowers with a card from Marcus.

"I love you, Empress! M"

The porter was hovering around the doorway, so I grabbed my purse and gave him a US dollar. Looking pleased with himself, he wished me congratulations and blessings on my wedding day. I had just enough time to make myself a cup of coffee when the door knocked again. I opened the door expecting a member of the hotel staff from hospitality, who had come to run through the finer details of our wedding day, or the stylist who was coming to do my hair, but to my horror, when I opened the door, it was Manley and Junior.

"Can we have a word?" asked Manley, stepping into the room uninvited. Well, it was more of a command than a question. I held the door open for them to walk through. It was obvious they had just returned from the stag do. Junior appeared to undress me with his eyes, and I drew my dressing gown closer together to cover my exposed cleavage. Manley's eyes darted around the suite in disdain before making eye contact with me.

"I'll cut straight to the point Miss Scotland," he paused for effect.

"You're marrying our brother in a few hours and although we think it's a big mistake, marrying a stranger, he's an adult, and it's his mistake to make. But when you involved our mother, you crossed the line. She just lost her husband and you're dragging her into this mess. What were you doing begging my mother for her emerald ring?"

Again, it was a statement rather than a question.

"Yeah," added Junior, "that ring has been in our family for generations and it's worth a lot of corn."

Junior was pacing on the spot, and I felt instantly intimidated by them both, but I soon found my voice.

"I didn't beg your mother for anything," I replied staring down at the ring on my left hand. "That's a matter between her and Marcus. So, I suggest you take it up with them."

"But we're taking it up with you, you old witch!" Junior was coming up in my face. "I bet you did some African juju or obeah shit on him to make him turn fool fool! And you're old as fuck! you can't even give him kids!" Junior said spitefully.

"Get out the pair of you," I said, raising my voice.

When I looked towards the queen size bed, I could see Yolanda stirring on the other side of the room.

"I'm warning you, so listen to me good," Manley retorted in a whisper, pointing his threatening index finger in my face, "I don't care how you do it, but you call off this farce and give my mother her ring back."

They then stormed out the door. I closed it quickly behind them, put on the chain, and locked it. Moments later, I was still behind the door crying silently and shaking like a leaf. I was so scared with what just happened, but I was also angry with myself for allowing them to scare me as they did. Who did they think they were speaking to? During my career, I managed 'bad' men, and I even recalled dangerous men back to prison without fear of reprisal.

Yes, at work, I am a 'badass,' I reminded myself. I have been regularly called downstairs by staff to deal with service users kicking off in the reception area and I have restored order without calling the police. On one occasion, not that long ago, I attended a parole board meeting at HMP Norwich in a room smaller than Yolanda's bedroom at home.

So small, the inmate could reach out and touch me, or in the worst-case scenario, give me a right hook before any of the prison officers could rescue me. During the proceedings, the chair asked if I was going to recommend the prisoner's release into the community. I looked the prisoner in the eye fearlessly and I told him I wasn't supporting his release, knowing it would be twelve months before he would be eligible to apply for parole again. Yet, a few nasty words from the 'blues brothers' had caused me to have a free fall meltdown.

"Pull yourself together, Patti," I said to myself over and over until I was calm.

Marcus isn't anything like them. Just the other day he was doing ballet in your bedroom!

I hugged myself. A hot flush swept over me as I walked across the room, so I switched the AC back on again. I then sat on the chair at the desk and dialled Antoinette's room.

"Get over here girlie, I need you."

When I looked through the spyhole, Antoinette was on the other side of the door dressed in pink silk pyjamas, matching dressing gown and headscarf, with a stern look on her face. She was pacing outside.

However, when I opened the door, she didn't rush inside.

"Shall I just kick off this kiss my ass room door right now?" she raged, pointing with her mobile phone to the door that led to the suite Marcus was staying in with his brothers.

I tried to pull her inside to quiet her down.

"Ssshhhh!!! Yolanda's sleeping..." I said, pointing to the bed.

"But what de rass doh nah? How dare they threaten you, Patti! Just say the word. I know people who know people right here in Negril who can sort them out, Hun. And for free too. 'Cause they owe me a favour!"

Antoinette was angrier than I was. I laughed nervously but nothing was funny. Antoinette sucked her teeth as she entered the room.

"You think I'm joking, Patti? Last year, my chambers represented some big time Jamaican gangsters. They were facing 'Mandela time' for people trafficking, and we got them off; not guilty. But we couldn't stop them from being deported back here though. They are well connected with law enforcement and politicians in Kingston, all I have to do is make a couple of phone calls...just say the word!"

I could imagine The Gleaner's front-page headline, 'Bride Sends Gunmen to Shoot Groom's Family.' I shook the thoughts from my head.

"No, Antoinette. That's quite alright. I can handle them, they just caught me off guard," I said. "Especially after the crock of shit I heard last night."

I made more coffee and proceeded to fill her in on what Rose and Charmaine had told me.

"Well, you know I 'had to go' last night?" said Antoinette.

"Oh, yes. What was that about?" I asked quizzically.

"I remembered Charmaine from a court case not that long ago."

I gasped, placing my hand on my chest clutching my imaginary pearls.

"Yep. I represented Junior Morgan up at Snaresbrook Crown Court. I don't think his wife remembers me, but I remember her!"

"Well, she was half cut last night," I interjected.

"Well, that Junior is one very violent fucker. I think he has a screw either loose or missing up in his head.

Seriously! he beat up a man, and a woman, breaking her nose. I think the woman was expecting a baby, but don't quote me on that!"

She gulped her coffee before asking, "Didn't Marcus say anything?"

I shook my head. "He was at court supporting Junior."

"Why didn't you say anything?" I chided and gave her a mock slap on the back of her hand.

"I was going to when I met him at Levi's, then he started pulling out flowers and plane tickets for you and my god daughter to fly out here so, how could I rain on your parade? You were so happy."

We sat in silence, sipping our coffee, and letting that sink in.

"What did Junior get?" I asked.

"I can't remember off the top of my head, sorry."

"So, my soon to be brother-in-law is a service user?" I sucked my back teeth disappointedly.

"I know right, I strongly suggest you tell your people as soon as you get back."

This time, both Antoinette and I kissed our teeth in unison.

"Stupse! Out of the two of them, you know who scares me the most?" I whispered.

Antoinette hunched her shoulders.

"Manley," I continued, "you should have seen how he was getting on at the homegoing barbecue they had for their father at their family home. Most people came over to say hello, but not him. And when Marcus finally introduced us, Pastor Manley paid more attention to the jerk chicken he was cooking on an old oil drum than to us.

"Yolanda turned to me saying, 'Who does he think he is, Desmond Tutu?'"

Antoinette and I both laughed loudly, then we remembered Yolanda was still sleeping.

"Seriously though, the look he gave us, it was almost like he doesn't like women..." I trailed off.

7

"Misogynistic!" said Antoinette.

"Yes, misogynistic, that's the right word Antoinette."

We both sat quietly, reflecting, and sipping our coffees.

"You know we're going to have to help those women," Antoinette stated.

"Rose and Charmaine?" Antoinette nodded at me. "Yes, I know it's the right thing to do," I said reluctantly.

"But don't watch dat today, you enjoy your wedding day. I'll set up a meeting for the four of us, probably our next Westfield Wednesday when we get back."

"Westfield Wednesday!" I exclaimed. "That's our day," I moaned.

"I can't take anymore time off Patti, I have a big trial coming up at Blackfriars Crown Court when I get home and adoption leave to take. Anyway, Rose and Charmaine joining us shouldn't arouse any suspicion from their husbands because it is something we've been doing since Westfield opened."

"True," I concluded.

We finished our drinks in contemplation, until Antoinette broke the silence.

"Patti, one thing I'm sure about. Marcus is nothing like those two brutes! You've got the best of the bunch there. Go ahead and get wed, my darling," she said, rising to give me a long hug. "I'll be back in an hour or so with your pageboy. We'll get dressed in here with you and Yolanda. In the meantime, have a long soak in the tub."

"OK," I said, escorting her to the door. "Please don't say anything to my mum or Marcus; Veronica would actually take them out!" We both laughed. "And I don't want Marcus upset on his wedding day."

"Your secret is safe with me. Now lock the door behind me."

~~~~~

I turned the taps on the bath and poured in all the complementary bubble bath, running the liquid under the hot water until the bottles were empty. I stirred the water with my hands, creating a tidal wave of white bubbles on the surface, and I turned the cold water tap down slightly when I was satisfied that the depth was sufficient for my bath. I stepped in, grabbing a face towel from the side rail to fashion a makeshift pillow for my head.

The water was hot, and the steam had already fogged up the huge mirror residing above the bathroom sink. Over the next half an hour, I topped up the tub with more water and let the hot water wash over me. It was so therapeutic that by the end of my bath, I could barely lift my own body weight out of the tub. When I came out of the bathroom wearing the hotel bathrobe, Yolanda was up and on the phone.

She covered the phone's mouthpiece to whisper 'Good Morning' to me and completed her order by giving our room number to the restaurant staff.

"How are you doing, Mum?" she said on her way to the bathroom.

"I'm good. Thanks, darling. I'm getting married today!"

"I know, Mum!" Yolanda shouted excitedly from the loo. "How do you feel?"

"Errrrm, I'm nervous and excited at the same time I suppose", I replied.

I could hear the loo flushing and Yolanda washing her hands. When she came out to join me at the table, she gave me a big hug.

"Mum, there really is nothing to be nervous about. Marcus is a good man and he's blessed to have you as his wife. I love you and I'm happy that I can go to university knowing that you have Marcus now and you won't be lonely."

Our mother and daughter moment was interrupted by a knock at the door. I was trying to get there before Yolanda, but she told me to sit down and relax. I watched nervously as she opened the door to Antoinette.

"Good morning, Yolanda. Good morning, Patti," Antoinette shouted, suddenly bringing energy and excitement into the room. "Wait do na, you order my breakfast yet? I'm so hungry, even my hungry is hungry!"

We all burst out laughing, Antoinette had certainly brought the joyful atmosphere I needed.

"So, where is my godson?" I asked Antoinette.

"With his fadda. He's real vex with you!"

"Oh, why so?"

"He said he wanted to marry you when he grew up, but now you're marrying Uncle Marcus!"

We all laughed again; my godson was one funny little boy. There was another knock on the door. I tensed up; I couldn't help it. I looked at Antoinette as Yolanda raced to open the door again. In stepped a young woman in her early thirties, I think. She was very tall, dressed in a purple beautician's top with customised gold buttons and black trousers. On her head, she wore an elaborately tied purple head wrap. Her make-up was exquisitely applied, and it only enhanced her high cheekbones. When she smiled, she had the cutest gap between her front teeth and she introduced herself as Sydnee, the hotel's beauty technician.

She stood leaning on her beautician's trolley, which was also purple. "Good morning. Congratulations on your wedding. I can see you are going to be a beautiful bride. I'm here to pamper you a bit by giving you a few treatments. This morning I will be giving you a manicure, pedicure, facial, and doing your hair and make-up. Are you ready to start?"

Well, I couldn't say yes quickly enough. She had that kind of spirit that made you take to her immediately.

"Well, alrighty," she said, smiling again. "May I use the bathroom to get some water to fill my foot spa and wash my hands?"

"No problem at all," I said, indicating to Yolanda to show her where the bathroom was.

Antoinette looked at me, inquiring with her eyes whether I was OK and I nodded reassuringly. Before I knew it, my feet were enjoying all the bubbles from the delightfully warm foot spa. Sydnee was making a start on my manicure when the door knocked again. She felt my hands tense and asked me if I was OK, but I kept my eyes trained on Yolanda as she answered the door. This time it was Veronica already dressed for the wedding. She entered the room like she was Miss Barbados 1979, all regal, dressed in a white kaftan with pink shoes and a matching pink clutch bag. Yolanda took my wedding dress from her and lay it across the bed.

"Good morning, everyone," mum said nonchalantly.

"How are you feeling now, Mum?" I inquired.

"I'm not too bad. I feel a lot better this morning, thank God. I'm hungry though."

"Yes, we all are," said Antoinette, "the people better feed we soon!"

Mum took a seat at the table and kicked off her new shoes. There was another knock at the door, but I didn't go rigid at all this time because Antoinette and Mum were here, and they weren't about to let Manley and Junior threaten or intimidate me in anyway. This time it was Beverley who looked a little worse for wear, like she hardly got any sleep at all. She was carrying a hat and shoe boxes which she placed on the bed next to my wedding dress.

"Well, come on then. Show us the shoes. They better be red at the bottom!" I shouted excitedly.

"Of course, they are! Good morning, everybody," Beverley said a little sheepishly as she brought over the shoebox and removed the left shoe.

It was beautiful, I didn't know that Louis Vuitton shoes came in white, and I was wondering if the shoe would fit as my feet had swollen with the heat, but I knew I could manage the heel quite easily.

"It's perfect," I said to Beverley. "Thank you so much. I can't wait to try everything on."

I noticed a twinkle in Beverley's eyes, and I looked at her inquiringly, but she didn't rise to my bait. I put two and two together and I couldn't contain myself.

"So, tell us Beverley. What happened between you and the hotel manager you were dancing with last night?"

Everybody looked at Beverley.

"Come on," said Antoinette. "I can tell you got some. You got that satisfied look on your face."

Beverley tried to stay strong, but a smile eventually plastered on her face, and she giggled like a little girl. Sydnee was trying to be discreet while she finished my nails, but I could tell she was listening attentively. Bored, Yolanda took her phone and went out onto the balcony.

"Well, Derrick is a very smooth dancer, and you know what they say about men that can dance!'

We all roared with laughter, except mum.

"Now that's where you are lying Beverley," mum interjected. "That nice young man didn't sleep with you." Everybody looked at mum. "Because Mr Derrick spent the entire night in my room!"

"Mum!" I shouted, raising my hands, forgetting my fingernails were still wet.

"Way to go, Miss Veronica! This is precisely how Stella got her groove back." cackled Antoinette.

"Stop it, Antoinette," I said, feeling embarrassed.

"Well, why not?" mum said, fist bumping Antoinette, "I'm old, not cold!"

They continued to laugh like two old fisherwomen. This time Sydnee and Beverley were laughing, too. When the laughter subsided, mum explained that she had not been feeling very well last night when she called the concierge. Derrick, the night manager, came to her room and waited with her until the doctor came. He was there most of the night.

"Mum, why didn't you call me?" I said, suddenly feeling ashamed.

"Well, you know me. I don't like to make a fuss. The doctor confirmed I definitely caught a chill on the plane. But as I said before, I'm feeling much better this morning. So, who did you get off with last night?" Mum said, giving Beverley back centre stage again.

Beverley was trying to be coy before she blurted out her story.

"Well, after you stormed off with those two mad women running behind you, and Yolanda was hanging out with the band after their last set, Derrick was called away and now I know why. The party fizzled out, so I sat at the bar and had a few cocktails, watching basketball on the screen behind the bar, when this charming man came up to me. He said he was a reggae artist staying at the hotel but was living in the UK. I must confess, his face looked familiar, like someone I saw from back in the day. We must have been chatting for hours because the bar started closing, so I suggested we go back to my room for coffee."

"You dirty dog you!" mum said.

"I don't even remember when he left the room, but I doubt I'll see him again. He was checking out today."

"So, what's his name? You do remember his name, right?" asked Antoinette.

"Of course, I do," replied Beverley feeling offended. "What do you take me for?"

I shot Antoinette a look and she closed her mouth.

"His stage name is Sweet Boy, his real name is Carlos, but everybody calls him Junior," Beverley said innocently.

My jaw hit the floor whilst Antoinette and mum were banging on the table and making a whole heap of noise.

"Cheese on bread, man! Cheese on bread! what is dis ya telling me this good, good morning?" Mum said, crying with laughter.

I couldn't speak.

"'Murder!" Antoinette piped in. "Girl, you realise who you slept with?"

"Can one of you please tell me what's so funny? I don't understand?" asked Beverley.

"One smart dead," exclaimed mum.

"At two smart door!" her and Antoinette said in unison.

That was Veronica's favourite Bajan saying and even I knew what it meant. Just as you thought you were being clever, someone out there is cleverer than you.

"Can you stop talking in parables and fill me in? You're frightening me now!" said Beverley.

"And so, you should be!' responded Antoinette.

"All I'm saying is, when that heifer comes for you, and she will, I'm not coming to rescue you, Bev!"

"Whatever are you talking about?" Beverley stood up.

"Calm yourself and sit back down," Antoinette cautioned, motioning to Beverley to take a seat. "Remember that big fair skinned woman at the table last night at the hen party, I think her name is Charmaine?"

Beverley searched her memory to try and recall the events from last night.

"Yes, her and the other woman were shouting at Patti right at the end?"

"Right, well you slept with her husband," Mum said before Antoinette could deliver the punchline.

Mum and Antoinette laughed; all I could do was stare at Beverley disapprovingly. She looked genuinely shocked at first, then she tried to justify her actions.

"Well, I didn't know he was married. He wasn't wearing a ring," she said calmly, but I could tell she was embarrassed.

"When has that ever stopped you, Beverley!" Antoinette said, spoiling for a fight. "You would have slept with him anyway!"

Antoinette was right about Beverley, the party had to go on and on and on. I remember that club night we went to in south London. Beverley ended up dancing with this guy to some slow jams. At the end of the night, she wanted to go home with him. How many times have Antoinette and I been in this scenario with Beverley, standing outside nightclubs trying to convince her not to go off with strange men that she only just met? Beverley broke the only cardinal rule we had set ourselves, which was, 'if you go out together, you must come home together.'

I had not yet told Antoinette how she behaved at the conference last year either. Not only did Beverley sleep with a solicitor (another married man) after the dinner and dance, but she also openly came out of his room and sat with him in the same party clothes at breakfast the following morning.

"Calm down. Calm down," said mum, "I strongly disapprove of Beverley's behaviour but what's done is done. The most important thing is that Charmaine doesn't get to find out! I won't have anyone spoiling Patti's wedding. Agreed?"

We all nodded in agreement when the door knocked again, and this time we all jumped. Beverley opened the door. It was Derrick, the hotel manager, and four members of the hospitality team. They brought in extra tables, covered them with white linen cloths, plus all the crockery and cutlery required for breakfast. On the desk, they placed several chafing dishes of breakfast items, a large basket of tropical fruit, cold drinks, and an urn of hot water at the end.

"Good morning, everyone. Good morning, Miss Beverley," Derek said. "Miss Veronica, how are you feeling today?"

"I am much better thanks," Mum said in her posh voice. "Thank you so much for taking care of me last night."

"Just doing my job, Miss Veronica. So glad to hear you're feeling better. Ladies, if there's anything else I can help with, do let me know." And as quickly as he came, he left the room with his team, closing the door behind him.

"Alrighty, then," said Sydnee, "I'll leave you to eat and come back in about half an hour."

"Aren't you hungry?" I asked.

"I'm fine," she replied.

"Nope, if we're eating, I insist you must eat with us, too."

"OK then. I'll just wash my hands."

Veronica got up and she called Yolanda inside to get herself something to eat. Yolanda lifted each chafing dish telling everyone what was underneath.

"OK we got ackee and saltfish. We got sausages and bacon, scrambled eggs, plantain, hard food, and baked beans. The pastries look delicious. And there's loads of toast too. I'm going to put some music on."

Breakfast was eaten in virtual silence, each woman mulling over what had been discussed earlier and listening to Jah Cure's latest album. 'That Girl' is easily my favourite track on the album. Sydnee opted for a plate of fruit and was delicately demolishing a ripe mango.

"Miss Patti we really need to speed up now. I still have your hair and make-up to do," she cautioned me. "12 o'clock is going to come before we know it."

"Thank you for the reminder, Sydnee. Come on ladies let's get our skates on."

"Well, I'm ready already, all I need to do is clean my teeth and put them back in again."

We all laughed; Mum knew how to lighten the mood.

"Well, I've bathed already," said Antoinette

"Me, too," added Beverley. "All I need to do is slip on my dress."

"Cool, I'll jump in the shower now then,'" said Yolanda.

My hair didn't need interlocking, so Sydnee tidied up my locs around my hairline and gave me an updo hairstyle to compliment my birdcage hat. Sydnee kindly tied mum's pink scarf into a head wrap, which was just as elaborate as her own; Mum was delighted. The girls helped me get into my mermaid dress, which fortunately fit me perfectly. I stepped into my shoes before Sydnee placed my hat on my head and turned the veil down. I checked myself out in the mirror whilst everybody 'ooooed' and 'ahhhhed'.

"You're gorgeous, mum." Yolanda's eyes were moist with tears.

"Yes," said mum. "I never thought I'd see the day... I'm so proud of you!" She came over and gave me a hug.

"Girl, you look good enough, too sweet!" said Antoinette, her Barbadian accent more prominent.

Beverley burst into tears, but I wasn't quite sure whether she was crying over me or crying over the latest predicament she had gotten herself into.

"My work here is done," Sydnee said, packing away her stuff.

"I'd be honoured if you joined us to celebrate my wedding," I said, extending an invitation to her.

"Are you sure, Miss Patti?"

"I'm positive," I replied. "My day wouldn't be the same without you. Go on, you've got half an hour to spruce yourself up."

Sydnee left the room, wishing everyone the best and said she would see me later. Yolanda took a selfie of the four of us together, promising not to upload it onto her social media until after we were married.

The next half hour was a blur. Antoinette and Beverley left the room to go downstairs and join our other guests. Olivia, the manager from Wedding Services, came to deliver my bouquet and escort us from our room to the wedding venue outside, on the hotel grounds. On our way through, everyone was giving us their best wishes and congratulations. Thank goodness the hotel was air conditioned. Olivia came to a halt at the entrance of the private gardens, she told us to pause and wait for a cue from her before walking down the aisle. Then my all-time favourite song, "Tell Me" by Omar, pipes through the nearby speaker.

"We still doing this fancy walk?" mum asked, smiling at me.

"Yes, Mum. Let's do this."

I looped my arms through mum's and Yolanda's and took my bouquet from Olivia. I listened to Mum counting us in. 'left together, right together, left together, right together'. When we turned the corner, there were a few rows of white chairs covered with pink silk bows. Everybody was wearing white except for Mrs Morgan, who is still in mourning. Everybody was smiling our way; at three generations of strong black women. I looked completely through Manley and Junior like they weren't there, focusing only on Marcus, who then proceeded to walk towards me like we rehearsed.

As I slipped off my left shoe, Mum and Yolanda took their seats. Marcus went down on one knee, on the pink coloured runway, and he expertly placed my foot back in my shoe.

"A wah gwan Empress," he said, smiling at me.

We walked towards the marriage officiant together. A few moments later, we exchanged vows, we jumped the broom, and I became Mrs Patti Morgan. It was such a wonderful day which ended with Marcus and I going for a photoshoot on the beach, still in our wedding attire. I was relieved to take my shoes off and enjoyed the feel of the sand in between my toes. Despite rolling up his trousers, Marcus got himself soaking wet, by the incoming tide and he didn't even care! We found a hammock, and after several attempts, we both managed to get in. Marcus and I cuddled up nice and cosy.

"Are you happy Mrs Morgan?" Marcus asked, looking me dead in the eyes.

"Yes, I am, my darling, my husband!" I lovingly replied. I could see Marcus smiling as the sun set, gold tooth and all. We looked up at the stars as Marcus pointed out a constellation, three stars in a row called Orion's belt, it took my breath away.

~~~~~

I chuckle as I recalled poor Marcus carrying me over the threshold of my house when we returned to London yesterday.

It wasn't romantic like in the movies. It was more like a fireman's lift and Yolanda could not stop laughing. Marcus moved in with us until we decided where to live in the long term.

Oh shoot! I had better hurry up and get ready for my first day back on the plantation. I ran up the stairs and knocked on Yolanda's bedroom door to wake her up for college and then I made my way to my ensuite.

I turned on the shower and removed my dressing gown, hanging it on the hook behind the door. I sighed, looking at my reflection in the mirror, raising my right arm above my head. My breasts felt heavy. I used my left hand to examine my breast again, just below my armpit. Yes, it was still there, a lump about the size of a new 5p coin. I am not going to be able to keep this secret from my husband for much longer.

CHAPTER TWO

CHARMAINE

I was home shivering, drinking a cup of English breakfast tea, and wishing I was back in Jamaica. Don't get me wrong. I missed my kids terribly, especially when I broke my phone, and I couldn't speak to them. I went from speaking to them and my mum daily to not hearing from them the entire last week of my trip. I was looking forward to picking them up from the nursery this afternoon.

I already missed the sunshine and the heat. London was bleak, cold, and grey. When I got back this morning and emptied my suitcase on the kitchen floor, everything had a funky smell, so I decided to wash my clothes again. I separated the whites from the coloureds, and I sat at the breakfast bar watching the dark clothes in the washing machine spinning around the drum. My mum is going to want a full update of my first trip abroad and given mum was still angry with Junior about the Mandy situation, I will have to filter what I tell her.

If she knew just half of Junior's antics, she would be in his skin, and I do not need the additional aggravation. I will start by telling her about meeting Mother Morgan for the first time and how lovely she was to me. Our mothers did speak on the phone a couple of times after the twins were born; I like to believe they would get along. I will definitely tell mum about how big the family home was, describing all five bedrooms in detail and the large kitchen with the island, the huge living room, not to mention the sleeping quarters for her "helpers" Medina and Lennox.

I must tell mum all about the nine nights event; the food and drink, the singing and praying and although I never met Overseer Morgan I cried, along with everybody else, it was so emotional.

She will laugh her socks off when I tell her that Junior made a show of himself by threatening to jump in the grave and his brothers had to hold him back. I will tell mum all about Rose and the bruises I saw on her body when she fainted in church. I had better leave out the fact I swore in church, my mum wouldn't be impressed. The parishioners who overheard what I said were more upset with me swearing than they were with Manley being exposed for beating his wife. The hypocrites!

Medina and Mother Morgan took turns to look after Esther while Rose recovered. I managed to creep into her bedroom and keep her company most nights; we were both so lonely. Rose opened up and shared what was happening in her marriage, how Manley had found her contraceptive pills and he had beaten her up and I shared with her what was happening with me. The dimly lit room made it easy for me to tell her about my life with Junior Morgan, the violence, the weed, and the women. Tears rolled down my face when I told her about Junior's outside woman being pregnant. I was still trying to wrap my head around that one.

~~~~~

Everything kicked off at Patti's hen party. Rose was adamant she was going, so we dressed up, and Lennox dropped us at the hotel. To think, all this time, Marcus' girlfriend and her daughter were staying at a five-star hotel just a few minutes' drive away from us. The Cliff Hotel was so impressive, just as impressive as the hotels along the beach that I had jogged behind; it was a treat to go inside. The hotel staff treated us like royalty, even though we rocked up in a beat up bright yellow school bus. We were escorted through the hotel lobby into the outside area of the hotel.

We quickly found Patti and her daughter Yolanda, and we were greeted warmly by them. Poor Rose looked like a fish out of water. She stared around the complex like she had fallen asleep and woke up in Sodom and Gomorrah. She sat upright in her chair, clutching her handbag to her, like it contained the ten commandments. I had never met anyone who had never drank alcohol before, so when she asked the waiter for water, I decided to hit the hard stuff for the both of us. After all, when was I going to get another chance to try all these elaborate cocktails? And for free too?

An hour or two later, I was well on my way to getting bladdered and it felt good letting go, allowing the alcohol to take hold. I swayed to the music in my seat. The in-house band was so good, I even got up to have a boogie on the dance floor with Patti and her mate. I was on my last cocktail, a 'Sex on the Beach', when Rose went into flip mode.

At first, I thought she was joking so I continued to sip my drink, but then she blurted out my business too! I was so shocked and so drunk, I ended up dragging Rose away from Patti and pushing her into a taxi. She was talking gibberish about angels and demons and Patti being "The One"! She spooked me for sure. When we got indoors, I helped Rose into bed, putting her in the recovery position.

It was my opportunity to practice what I had learned in the first aid course I completed as part of the Positive Parenting Programme. Rose, who had exhausted herself, complied. My intention was to go back to my bedroom and put myself in the recovery position, but on my way to my room, I saw Medina waiting in the living room with the comb and hair grease.

"I'm coming, Medina, I'm just going to wash my hair."

Medina nodded.

She had promised me a new hairstyle for the wedding the following day. I washed my hair quickly and rushed back, drying it with a towel.

"Oh, let me do that for you Miss Charmaine."

I sat on the dining room chair while Medina stood and tenderly dried my hair before parting it and applying coconut oil to my scalp. She combed through my hair several times until she dealt with the shrinkage and my hair increased twofold in volume. My scalp was so tender headed, but Medina used a drop of Jamaican black castor oil, and she gently massaged my head. She applied pressure around my hairline and down my neck and shoulders. It felt so good. I felt as though I was being loved and looked after. About half an hour later, Medina tied a bright yellow du rag around some very tight plaits, promising me a lovely curly afro in the morning. I went to lie down, and I fell asleep exhausted.

~~~~~

Despite the head massage, I woke up the following morning to a banging headache. I promised myself I'd never drink alcohol again. I wasn't up for jogging, and when I presented myself at the breakfast table, Medina had made a pot of cornmeal porridge and homemade ginger tea, I could have kissed her.

Mother Morgan was feeding Esther and she asked how the party was. I thought it was safer just to answer fine. After breakfast, Medina pulled out my plaits and coaxed it into an afro bun style, complete with a gold-coloured Alice band. I gave her a big kiss and a hug and rushed to get ready. Patti and Marcus' wedding was themed, and all the guests were invited to wear white.

I overheard Mother Morgan clearly saying that while she was happy for Marcus, she had buried her husband of fifty years only last week, and she intended to wear black until the good Lord told her otherwise. Medina had responded saying, 'Amen'. I threw almost everything out of my suitcase onto the bed looking for something white to wear.

The closest thing I had to a white dress was a bandeau style maxi dress my mum had thrown into the case at the last minute. It was a bit too long for me with giant pink flowers on it. I had to wear it with gold flip flops and a small gold, long strap bag that Medina had kindly loaned me. It was just going to have to do. *I came to Jamaica for a funeral, not Marcus' wedding.* I heard Lennox beeping the school bus horn, so I slipped the dress over my head and rushed out of the door. When Rose joined us on the bus, I thought we would sit together for the short ride, but she sat nearly at the back of the bus fussing over Esther.

OK, Rose, I thought to myself. She had thawed a little towards me once we were walking through the hotel grounds and we took our seats in the shade.

Rose smiled and passed Esther to me, whispering in my ear,

"Please don't say anything to anyone about last night."

She sounded terrified.

"Something happened last night?" I answered, smiling back.

The Morgan brothers looked so handsome in their white outfits, even Junior, although I hated to admit it. With his dreadlocks tamed into a ponytail, he looked a lot more like Marcus. The groom came over to thank us for coming and he complimented me on my hair.

"Charmaine, fab hair darling, if you weren't already married to Junior and I wasn't marrying Patti, you'd be a contender for sure!"

He kissed me on both cheeks before turning his attention to Esther. I blushed, feeling warm and fuzzy inside. Junior had not even acknowledged me. I was amazed at how Patti and Marcus had organised such an elaborate wedding on such short notice, it was certainly better than my wedding.

When Patti slipped off her shoe, her designer shoe I might add, Mother Morgan explained that the couple had met earlier this year when her shoe had fallen off at the station. Then they jumped the broom. It was a broom like the one Medina had used to sweep the veranda. It was made of straw, but this broom was covered with pink and white tulle and ribbons. Mother Morgan shared the idea behind the tradition. Apparently during slavery, the enslaved were not allowed to legally marry, so the next best thing was to 'jump the broom' from single life to married life. More and more black couples had chosen to embrace the tradition as part of their wedding day.

~~~~~

The hotel band played at the end, whilst the new Morgan's signed the register, and we had a refreshing glass of champagne. Everything was beautiful. I wished my phone was working so I could share the day with my mum, she would have loved all of this. Rose promised to send me her photos when we returned. The wedding celebration room was breath-taking with pink and white everywhere, including tablecloths, napkins, and balloons.

After the wedding breakfast, there were only two speeches, one from Patti's mum and the other from Marcus. I did not realise that Patti was adopted until then, her and her mother looked so much alike with similar complexions, build and height. Both even covered their mouths when they laughed, too. Marcus ended his speech by saying:

"My wife and I...." he paused because all the guests were cheering, "invite you to join us on the dance floor for our first dance."

The DJ, as if by magic, played the first bar of the song as the couple entered the dance floor. Luther Vandross' dulcet tones piped in singing, *If this World Was Mine.* Suddenly Junior was in front of me, smiling with his arms open, requesting me to dance with him.

I actually looked around me, thinking he was asking someone else. Mother Morgan took Esther from me, and I joined Junior on the dance floor, followed closely by Manley and Rose. Cheryl Lynn then piped in, singing the second verse, *'If this world was mine, I'd make you a King...'* and her words resonated with me. I closed my eyes and found my head resting on Junior's chest as I fell in step with his rhythm.

Junior was giving me a slow wine and I was completely in the moment, captivated by the setting and the love in the room. By the bridge of the song, Junior was grinding into me, I felt his erection and it felt so good. We had not been intimate since he got arrested, so I was excited at the thought of it, and I pushed back into him. He held me tighter.

These days I could hardly raise a smile from Junior, much less anything else. Luther and Cheryl were screaming out the ballad and I held on to Junior as we rocked forwards and backwards and dipped down low. I thought to myself, 'I could be the bigger person and speak to Mandy when we returned to the UK'. I'd make sure her child was financially taken care of, and the children knew each other.

I looked up to speak to Junior to tell him I knew all about the baby and to inform him of my decision. I realised he was not there with me; he was not present in the room with me. Junior was looking towards the bar. When I looked in that direction, I saw one of Patti's friend's smiling back at Junior. The look she gave him told me all I needed to know.

Have you ever been in a club and the wrong man pulled you for a dance? Then the DJ decides to play the record from the start or the EP version of your favourite song? Well, that's exactly how I felt, stuck. I tried to pull away from Junior, but he had me on lockdown. He held me so tightly that I could not move.

I went from hating Junior to loving him to hating him again in four minutes. When was this song going to end? *'Give me pretty lovin', baby. Give me pretty lovin', honey...'* I was here in paradise wishing Luther and the woman would shut the fuck up!

At the end of the song, I stepped away from Junior, I snatched up my handbag and placed it over my shoulder in one scoop. As I headed to the bar, I took out my earrings, placing them down my bra. I made brief eye contact with Patti's friend, who was dancing with her husband.

She tried to pull away from her husband, telling me, "Don't do it!"

That was confirmation. When I got to the bar I smiled at the woman, and I took her in. She was about the same complexion as me, a size 18 squeezing herself into a size 14 dress. Her breasts were literally hanging out of her outfit, it was that tight. She was a bit shorter than me, wearing the tallest heels in the place and sporting the most horrendous curly weave. She was a joke. I decided I could take her.

"What would you like to drink, madam?" The bartender asked, wiping down the bar.

"Hey, Neville," I said, reading his name tag, "I'll have a glass of whatever she's drinking." I paused, pointing at the woman with a fake smile, "For my husband!" I added as I watched her smile fall apart. "I'll have a double Baileys with lots of ice for myself."

Neville smiled as he busied himself with my order.

"There you go, madam," Neville said as he presented the drinks.

I said thank you to Neville and placed a US dollar on the plate. I picked up both drinks and threw the glass of red wine right in the woman's face yelling,

"Stay away from my fucking husband, you tramp!"

I then turned on my heels, wishing I had worn high heels instead of flip flops, and went out of the nearest exit. Poor Neville looked like he didn't know whether to laugh or cry. I sipped my drink as I stomped through the hotel like I owned it. Lennox was standing up, chatting to the other taxi drivers. He was very surprised to see me but took me home, nonetheless.

~~~~~

Once I got inside, I took off my flip flops by the front door and walked on the cold marble floors through the house to the bedroom, where I retrieved my emergency bottle of Baileys. I went into the kitchen to find that Lennox had opened the shutters and windows. He had put my glass on the counter.

I took a plastic container out of the freezer which, once upon a time, had contained vanilla ice cream but now contained a block of ice. I used an ice pick to chip away a few shards of ice and dropped the pieces into the glass. The ice made a cracking sound when I poured the warm liquid over it. I was just about to put the container back into the freezer when I heard a tapping noise coming from the sink. I was scared shitless and froze like a statue. A few seconds later, I saw a small green lizard trying to escape through the kitchen window. It took me a couple of minutes to get my breath back, then I took my drink into the lounge and switched on the widescreen TV in the corner using the remote control.

Looking through the channels, I settled on watching back-to-back episodes of NCIS, hoping to catch a glimpse of my idol LL Cool J from NCIS Los Angeles. He did not disappoint me. I wondered if I had the balls to kill Junior like the people on the telly. I thought about poisoning him but quickly decided against it since I no longer cooked for him, his suspicions would arise straight away. Secondly, Junior often fed the twins from his plate, and I could not risk poisoning them too.

I thought about drowning him in a bath of acid like the man in this episode did to his wife, but I was confident Ebay would not deliver the amount of Hydrofluoric acid required to completely dissolve his body, so where would I store his carcass in the meantime? The bath would be the ideal location, but how would I bathe the twins? Nope I was going to have to think of something else. I took a long sip of my drink. I could shoot him for sure. I filled up my glass with more of the alcohol, and gulped down the contents draining the glass. How much would it cost me to get hold of a gun? If I bought the gun, could I afford the bullets? And where would I buy a gun from?

I thought of my local pub and laughed out loud at the idea. It was hardly the Blind Beggar in Mile End where the notorious gangsters, the Kray twins, hung out back in the 1960s. Nope, The Lamb was a cosy West Indian public house a few streets between me and my mum's homes in Plaistow. Me and my crew use to go in there on a Friday night to cadge drinks off the older men, before going clubbing. On Fridays, the landlords' daughter cooked up a Dominican feast.

If we could find a pensioner to buy us a plate of food, our evening was set! The only fight I ever saw in The Lamb was over someone losing a game of dominoes. The cussing was in Dominican patois, so half the pub had no idea what they were arguing about. But with the promise of free drinks, the kerfuffle ended as quickly as it started.

My quest to kill off Junior wasn't going very well. I decided against pouring myself another drink, so I washed out the glass. The fireflies were busy making patterns outside the kitchen window. I walked back into my bedroom, swaying like I was on the deck of a cruise ship, finally throwing myself across the bed, putting myself into the recovery position. I fell into a deep, deep dream. In the dream, I was back at Patti and Marcus' wedding. I was dancing with Junior, who was wearing a flashy white suit. I was wearing a tight fitted gown that was flown in from America, with red bottom shoes, nicer than the ones Patti was wearing. Junior and I could not keep our hands off each other. This time we were so frisky. I whispered to Junior, 'Let's try for another baby!' Junior looked at me with delight and held me closer.

'Seriously?' he asked.

'Why not? The twins start school next year, your latest album is doing well?'

He nodded in agreement.

'We could move,' I continued.

'What if we had twins?' he joked, we both laughed. 'When?' asked Junior. I looked at him, puzzled. 'When can we start trying?' He said with a broad smile.

'How about we try now?' I replied in a sexy voice.

I could tell Junior was turned on immediately. We discreetly left the wedding party dancing and made our way to the beach like two naughty schoolchildren. Once at the beach, Junior carried me so I didn't have to take my shoes off. We got to a secluded part of the beach, and he placed me gently on a beautiful four poster bed, covered by a pergola adorned with white drapes. When Junior reached down to open a bottle of champagne, I realised that this had been his plan all along!

'Well, I thought I might get lucky on our last night here.' He smiled. 'Here's to making more babies, who are beautiful just like their mother!'

'I'll drink to that!' I beamed, and we clinked our glasses.

Junior climbed onto the bed next to me and we held hands in the dark. There was a comfortable silence between us as we gazed out into the darkness and listened to the waves crashing against the shore. We could have easily been on a deserted island; it was all so serene.

'Thank you, Charmaine, for coming out to Jamaica to support me. I just want you to know that I love you very much and I want to spend the rest of my life just loving you.'

'Awwwwww babes, I love you too,' I said, reaching for him in the dark.

Junior took my glass with his and placed them both in the ice bucket. He moved in to kiss me slowly on the lips. I instantly felt a tingling sensation all over my body. His tongue broke through my lips to explore my mouth. I greedily sucked on it, and I heard him moan. I became breathless as he kissed my neck and I fell back onto the bed; the pillows catching my fall.

Junior pulled off his suit jacket and shirt then resumed kissing me. We didn't speak. I didn't want to break the spell. My nipples became hard, longing to be caressed, squeezed, or sucked. I was willing to submit to whatever Junior needed from me. Junior pulled down my dress and he threw it to the bottom of the bed. I tried to pull off my shoes, but he told me to keep them on! I was lying there in my Rigby and Peller underwear, whilst Junior took me in.

The moonlight lit up his handsome face and he looked famished like he was about to devour me. It felt so sensual to be desired by my husband. Junior teased my breasts out of my bra and massaged them tenderly. I gasped, reaching for him to pull him closer to me. I tried to stifle a scream of pleasure.

'Go ahead and scream baby, no one can hear you!' Junior said as he licked and sucked my right nipple.

So, I let go and screamed. Junior then reached between my legs and his touch felt like he'd switched on all the lights at the same time. My legs parted without any resistance whatsoever. Junior paused to undo his belt and pull down his trousers and boxer shorts, enough for what he wanted to do next. His penis bounced on my thigh; he was rock hard. He pulled my knickers to one side.

'Girl, you're so wet! Are you ready to make another baby?'

'Stop!' I shouted. 'Stop, Junior!' I demanded.

'What's wrong, Charmaine? Are you alright?'

'No, I'm not alright' I said, trying to sit up.

'Hun the hotel said we would not be disturbed if that's what you're worried about. Couples on honeymoon use this spot all the time!'

I could sense the frustration in his voice.

'Junior, none of this is real!'

'How do you mean? We're in Jamaica together at this beautiful resort, aren't we?'

I could feel him losing his erection.

'No, Junior. I'm dreaming. This is all one sad dream. I am going to wake up in a minute and the reality of you and your affair is going to crash in!'

'But I want you, Charmaine. I need you!'

Junior was pinning my arms down, now, hurting me.

'Let me go!' I shouted.

'As I said earlier, no one can hear you screaming out here!' Junior said in a sinister tone.

I started screaming with fear and I reached out to scratch his face.

"Rathid, Charmaine! Are you okay, wake up!"

Junior was beside me, looking worried. I was disorientated for a few moments. I was no longer on the beach, I was in my bedroom back at the house, with the morning sunshine pouring through the gap in the curtains. I tried to catch my breath as Junior rattled on.

"Girl, you were fighting someone in your sleep! That was one bad dream!"

"Dream?" I finally responded, "more like a fucking nightmare!"

"Seen! What was it about?"

"Nothing I want to share with you!" I said spitefully, turning on my side away from him.

"Sorry I spoke...but now that you're up, do you fancy a bit?"

I didn't bother to respond; he soon got the message and went back to sleep. I was too scared to sleep just in case I went back to that dreadful place. I decided to go for my last run on the beach. By the time I ran up to the hotel, I had shaken off that bad feeling. But how sad and lonely was I? The only way I can be intimate with my husband was when I was dreaming about him! Well, no more, that was the last time.

~~~~~

On the way back, I said goodbye to a few of the vendors, and one gave me a couple of tee shirts for my children. When I reached the main road, the old dutty ras was sitting in his usual place, cutting a knobbly piece of wood with his cutlass He called to me.

"Dawta! me have something for you."

Had he not used the term of endearment 'daughter' I would have probably run across the road and pretended not to hear him, but I was intrigued about what he had for me.

"I over stand that you are going up to foreign today?" he enquired.

"Yes, that's right" I replied.

"Carry dis for de two yout dem," he said, handing me a small black carrier bag.

Inside were two handmade leather necklaces, each with a jagged tooth at the centre. I looked at him.

"Not my toot," he explained with a laugh. "dats a shark toot."

"Ah thank you," I said, I knew the twins would love these.

"Have you ever tried sugar cane before?" said the Ras.

"No," I said nonchalantly.

"Here, take this and bite down on it."

He handed me a square piece of cane and watched me as I bit into it.

"It's the very last of the crop," he said proudly.

It was like biting into pure honey. The juice ran down my chin. I licked my lips and bit into the cane again so that it released the juice straight into my mouth.

"Good, isn't it?"

"Mmmmm," I respond, closing my eyes.

"Take another piece?" he offered, and I accepted.

"Once upon a time I would chew sugar cane all the time. I can't do dat anymore, no teet!" he cackled, I laughed too. "Promise me you'll bring de two pickney with you next time you visit. Mek de youts know Yard before Babylon tell them lies," he commanded.

"I would love to come back next year; they would love the beach. Anyway, we'll see."

I spat the remaining trash out on the floor and just as I was feeling comfortable in his presence, he made the following unsolicited remark.

"Why is it every time I and I see you, my third hand wants to greet you too?"

He was licking his lips. I spat out the trash.

"What the fuck?" I said backing away. "You dutty old man, I'm old enough to be your daughter, granddaughter even!"

I was vexed now. As I looked for a gap in the traffic to safely cross over, I heard him saying, "I can't eat sugar cane anymore but there are other things I can suck."

I was utterly disgusted with him and annoyed with myself for letting him insult me again.

~~~~~

Once I returned to the house, there was the usual rush to eat, shower, pack and get ready to leave. Medina had given me loads of food items that I was sure I wasn't allowed to bring back to the UK, but I didn't protest. Most of the stuff I could buy at Wenty's Caribbean shop on Upton Lane or in the world food isle at the supermarket. Saying goodbye to Mother Morgan and Medina was so hard as we boarded the yellow bus for the last time. When we got to the check-in desk, Marcus, Patti, and the others were in line checking in. I couldn't spot the woman I threw the red wine on. When it was our turn to check-in, we were informed that one of us was entitled to an upgrade to upper class. Without hesitation, I snatched the boarding pass from him saying, 'thank you' and glared at Junior, daring him to say something. After finding my seat I was drinking champagne with Patti and Marcus a couple of rows in front of me, they look so loved up. Once the aircraft was on its way homeward bound, we were served a three-course meal with a choice of wines.

Afterwards I watched a couple of movies. I wanted Baileys but they didn't have any, but Bailey's cousin went down very well. I went to the first-class loo to change into my pyjamas and when I returned, my seat was converted into a bed. I smiled at the thought of Junior cramped up in cattle class. I had the best sleep ever.

Do you remember the Wizard of Oz, when the first parts of the movie had been shot in black and white, then Dorothy wakes up in glorious Technicolor, but when she finally returns home, it goes back to black and white again? That's exactly how I sum up my return to the UK. London is devoid of colour and heat. Everything was grey, cold, and miserable. None of the other passengers were happy either, especially when the pilot announced that it was 5°C outside the aircraft. Junior looked dishevelled in his crumpled-up jacket. He was still vex with me too, but I ignored him. I stopped briefly in duty-free to buy two bottles of Bailey's liqueur on special, one salted caramel flavour and the other orange truffle. Both looked divine. At the arrivals gate, Junior's friend, Stepper, was there to meet us, and thankfully, he had brought us our puffer coats, and boy we needed them. I was shaking with the sudden drop in temperature. . He is the only person allowed to drive Junior's precious BMW. It is an old series, but Junior has kept it immaculate, ensuring the car was serviced at the right time and was hand washed. Stepper greeted me first with a kiss on each cheek and then he fist bumped Junior.

"Welcome Home!" he said with a smile.

He grabbed my suitcase and headed towards the exit. Stepper is one of Junior's oldest friends, one of the first people to befriend him at the recording studio when Junior first came up from Jamaica. I liked him too, he didn't talk shit like the rest of the hangers on in Junior's crew. Stepper was Godfather to our twins. And he was the only person who corrected Junior when he was out of order, so I consider him to be an ally. So much so, if Junior said he was in the studio with Stepper, then I believed him. Stepper was the first amongst his friends to marry his woman and they have one child together. He was a family man and fiercely loyal to his wife. Once we located the car I settled into the back seat. We were quickly on the M23 heading towards London when I asked Stepper to turn the music down a touch because I wanted to have a nap.

"No problem, Mrs M," he replied. I pretended to sleep.

"So how is Mother Morgan?" Stepper asked.

"She's good you know, alright under the circumstances," Junior replied, being as vague as ever.

"And the funeral?" asked Stepper without missing a beat.

"It was good you know!"

The two men were silent.

"And your brothers?"

"What is this with all the questions? You is a detective?" snorted Junior.

"Pardon me for showing an interest, you've been away for four weeks, and you didn't return any of my calls."

Silence again.

"Yeah, sorry about that, I had a few problems with my phone. Anything happen while I was away?" enquired Junior. "Don't worry about her, she's fast asleep."

"OK. I checked in on the fam like I promised. I even took the kids out for a burger!"

"Nice one, nice one. I really appreciate that, Stepper. And the other thing?"

"Yeah, I went to see her over at her yard. A right shithole, Junior, if you don't mind me saying. The flat was so nasty, the kind of place you wipe your feet on the way out. I don't know how you could cheat on Charmaine with dat! What were you thinking Big man?"

Junior was silent now.

"Well, in my opinion, she looks even worse now. I wouldn't call her a mampy because she's with child, but she's well on her way to becoming a Legobeast!"

I shuffled in my seat at that one. I had not heard anybody use the word 'legobeast' in years. Mandy must have really let herself go and piled on the weight.

"OK, keep your voice down nah, man!" Junior said in a whisper.

"Sorry, sorry, sorry...well everything's on her is swollen. Her legs, her ankles, even her face! She ain't blooming at all. Mate, how did you breed dat?"

I could hear the disgust in Stepper's voice.

"Well, I was wondering if the yout was even my child at all. She was sleeping with that African man and all."

"You can always ask for a DNA test once the yout is born, which by the look of her, could be any minute now. Does Charmaine know?" Stepper enquired.

Again, Junior was silent.

"Breddrin!" Stepper chided, "She stood by you during the court case, surely she'll stand by you now."

When Junior finally spoke, he said, "I really can't handle all of that now...Charmaine wasn't putting out and Mandy was. I wasn't expecting her to get herself pregnant! What am I going to do Boss man?"

"You step up, tell your wife and take care of your responsibilities, that's what you do." That was clearly not what Junior wanted to hear and the two men didn't speak for the remainder of the journey.

~~~~~

The second load of clothes were now in the washing machine. When I went out into the garden to hang out the first load of clothes, both Stepper and Junior put out their spliffs. The last thing I wanted was cannabis ash blowing onto my clothes.

"Coffee anyone?" I asked.

"Yes please," they both responded.

I broke the seal on my new jar of Blue Mountain coffee and decided to open the mountain of posts that had greeted us on the doormat. One was for Junior, and it looked like it was from Probation. I opened it, Junior had the first session of the domestic abuse programme tomorrow and every Tuesday and Thursday thereafter until Christmas. There was the usual junk mail and a letter for me! Who would be writing to me? There was no clue on the back of the letter. I make the coffees and cut two slices of the cake that Medina made for me.

"Cheers Charmaine," says Stepper.

"You're very welcome. There's a bottle of rum inside for you. Thanks for picking us up today."

We looked at Junior.

"Ya Mon, respect every time!"

I went back inside and nursed my second cup of tea. The next time I went to Jamaica, I was going to bring my own teabags, their red label wasn't cutting it and my preferred brand of tea was too expensive over there. I looked at the letter which appeared to get bigger and bigger in size on top of the breakfast bar. I needed to open it, so I did. I was blown away! I was well chuffed! I managed to land myself a job interview with Primani!

CHAPTER THREE

ROSE

I had been back in South London for the last seventy-two hours. I was kneeling in the dark, wishing I was anywhere else in the world except for where I was now. The floor was cold, and I had been on my knees for what felt like hours. Manley was leading in prayer...sigh. The house was so cold, I'm positive it was warmer outside.

When we bought this property, with the deposit that Uncle Samuel gave me, Manley promised he would do it up before our first baby arrived. To be fair, he made a good start by renovating the property downstairs with the kitchen and the small lean-to conservatory. Manley gave me access to the larder and chest freezer in the conservatory once a day to retrieve items to cook, otherwise it was kept under lock and key. When he was renovating the kitchen, he let me choose the kitchen units and the tiles; he and his friend Deacon Maurice made a very good job of it. The front and back reception rooms only required decorating and they did well with putting up wallpaper and painting the skirting boards.

Yes, I was pleased with the work they had done but little did I know it was all for show. The food cupboards remained empty most of the time and the front room was only used to host parishioners from the church. Upstairs hasn't been touched, and I am fed up with asking for a new bathroom suite. Manley claims we don't have any money, even when he once had a small windfall at the bookies. I tried to make the best of it, especially for my girls. I bought a cheap can of pink paint and painted their bedroom.

~~~~~

I was in my bedroom, still kneeling, trying to stay awake and focus on my own silent prayers. I was exhausted! The girls were asleep, even baby Esther. Manley has been giving me the silent treatment since we got back from Jamaica. The only time he talked to me, was to bark orders at me or chastise me for doing something wrong. He even started to undermine me in front of the girls.

This was his way of punishing me for all the things that happened in Jamaica. Now he was praying for my disobedient soul. I suppose he's right to punish me, this was all my fault, and it served me right. When I fainted in church and exposed my bruises, he was embarrassed. His mother and her housekeeper kept me safe from further harm during the rest of my stay.

I stopped wearing my wigs and sported my natural hair, which Manley was also cross about. Whilst everybody else said the new hairdo took years off me, Manley couldn't disguise his disapproving sneer. He was going to keep me on my knees every night until I learnt to take my wedding vows seriously and obey him.

~~~~~

My mind drifted back to my last few days in Negril. On the night of the hen party, Manley warned me not to go. To be more precise, I was forbidden from attending. He described the hotel as an abomination full of drunken Americans who had too much money. He even went as far as quoting 2nd Corinthians 6:14: 'Do not be equally yoked with unbelievers', but he was going to Marcus' stag do!

As soon as he left, I got Charmaine, we dressed up and Lennox took us to the hotel. I wasn't interested in Patti's hen party per se, but I wanted to observe her up close, maybe have a one-to-one conversation with her. When I was recovering from the fainting incident at the funeral, Charmaine had come into my room to sit with me.

At first, I thought she was interfering, but she soon disclosed that her and Junior's marriage was plagued with fights and emotional abuse. She told me about Junior's court case and his affair, and I was mortified. Charmaine thought we would trade stories, but it took a while for me to open up. But a few nights later I eventually told her what was going on. I thought she was about to knockout

Manley herself she was so angry. I told her about Grace and Gabriel, but I didn't tell her who they were. I wanted to, but I found it difficult to believe it myself.

I made Charmaine promise not to say anything to anyone especially Mother Morgan, Manley is her favourite son. Yet at the first opportunity, I lost it and told Patti we wanted to leave our husbands. Charmaine was too intoxicated to care. Poor Patti, she must have been so scared as she left, and I ran behind her screaming. I totally disgraced myself and I wasn't looking forward to going back to the hotel for Patti and Marcus' wedding. I felt ashamed and I was worried about what might happen if Manley found out that I disobeyed him. Everything that happened after that was a blur.

~~~~~

I don't know how I got home or how I ended up in my bed in my underwear. I woke up at 5 am and got down on my knees to repent. My knees hit the cold tiled floor and I should have reached for a pillow, but I wanted to punish myself. How could a Pastor's wife carry on like that? I asked for forgiveness, and I prayed for my girls. I asked for health and strength to get me through the next 48 hours in Jamaica and travelling mercies for when it was time to get on the plane to go back home.

I prayed for Patti and Marcus and a sign that I had not imagined what occurred at the funeral. I was hoping Patti was the woman who was going to help me. I felt light when I stood up and opened the curtains to let the warm Caribbean sunshine into the room. Mother Morgan knocked on the door and came in with baby Esther, passing her to me for a feed.

"When you're ready, come and get some cornmeal porridge, it's going to be another long day," she said, smiling tenderly as I attempted to breastfeed Esther.

She was fussing to latch on, pulling at my nipple and hurting my breast. After nursing five children in a row, I discovered that I did not like breastfeeding at all. It wasn't that magical bonding experience like it was in the beginning with Mary, the babies came too quickly, it felt more like a leech sucking the life from me.

When Esther was satisfied, I changed her nappy, put on my dressing gown, and ventured outside. Charmaine was getting her hair done, which reminds me, where was my wig? Did I have it when I went to the hotel? I sat at the table and greedily ate my porridge, cradling Esther in one arm. She was growing rapidly, almost ten weeks old now. The sun had accelerated her ebony complexion and she was as dark as Manley. I smiled at her.

"If you hurry, I can do your hair too," Medina offered, "go and wash it and I'll blow dry it for you," she continued.

Charmaine held out her hands to take the baby, but I pretended I didn't see her and placed Esther in the baby stroller near the door.

Fifteen minutes later, I emerged with a large bath towel wrapped around my body, my damp hair under a matching hand towel wrapped into a turban. Medina shared that she had been a hairdresser back in the eighties with her own salon in Negril, but things did not work out. People did not want to pay her, and Lennox suggested that she pack it in. She shared that her granddaughter had taken an interest, but she had gone to beauty school, she was a beautician at the same hotel where Marcus and Patti were getting married in less than an hour.

Medina had worked miracles and my hair was bone straight and resting on my shoulder blades. She trimmed the ends and flat twisted the front to finish.

When she handed me the mirror I was delighted, the style had somehow made me look younger. Charmaine gave me loads of compliments and offered to do my make up, but I declined. Lord knows what Manley was going to say when he saw me. I didn't want to make it worse by wearing red lipstick, looking like a Jezebel! I thanked Medina with a big hug and a kiss, then I retreated to my room with a sleeping baby to get ready for the wedding.

~~~~~

The next time I saw everybody was when I got on the school bus. Charmaine had motioned for me to sit with her, but I kept moving. I sat near the back and gazed out of the window. I can't even tell you why I was acting so cold towards her since I chose to go to the hen party. Charmaine didn't force me, and she did not make me get on bad like that either. I breached her confidentiality when I shouted out her business to Patti, and probably the entire population of guests at the hotel. I suppose I was highly embarrassed, and I didn't want Charmaine to get into an argument with me about it. As the hotel came into view, I felt I was going to my own funeral, not a wedding. I was frightened that someone was going to expose me. I needn't have worried; nobody batted an eyelid.

The hotel foyer was busy and full of activity like it was last night. Even more so, as guests were checking out and some were meandering at meeting points, waiting to go on tours and organised bus trips to nearby attractions.

My mum would have adored the setting and the theme of the wedding. My mum organised most of the events at church, she loved arranging the flowers and making bespoke bouquets. My dad grew the flowers in the back garden for mum to use, but this extravagant display was an attack on all my senses. The tropical flowers bore witness to God's handiwork, every shade of pink imaginable.

The scent from the flowers consumed my nostrils with their fragrance. The decorative little posies of hibiscus and the kiss-me-over-the-garden-gate on the back of every chair, transported me to my childhood, running through the grounds of the plantation house where my cousins grew up. As you can imagine, Manley and I were invited to lots of weddings over the years, more so when he became an ordained minister. He is dying to officiate his first wedding. Whilst he's sat on the rostrum with the other menfolk, my mum would sit with me.

We'd playfully rate the wedding venue, decorations, and food then give our overall verdict. Silver platter is exactly what this was, a plush venue, with canapés and champagne served by attentive waiting staff and fine dining produced by outstanding caterers. At the other end of the scale is what mum called 'Pudding Pan', the horrid church hall with the stinky loos. Not a flower in sight except for the bride's bouquet and a balloon arch! And you were sitting and waiting for an age for your table number to be called for a buffet of Auntie's homemade rice 'n' peas with jerk chicken or escovitch fish.

Nope this wedding was going to exceed them all, I could tell. Even if they served Jamaican food, it was going to be authentic cuisine, not something drowning in scotch bonnet peppers. For heaven's sake, not everybody liked jerk everything! I sat next to

Mother Morgan and Charmaine in the second row on the groom's side.

Marcus, Manley, and Junior all looked very smart, dressed in white. I laughed when the little boy threw pink petals all over the place and his mother dragged him to sit with her, he clearly wasn't happy about something. Patti took my breath away when she made her grand entrance and Marcus was beaming away. I have never seen him so happy.

After the first dance, we said our goodbyes. Manley retrieved our luggage from the back of the school bus, and we took a taxi to Kingston. I was sad to leave everybody behind having a good time. Antoinette introduced herself to me again and she gave me her number right in front of Manley, suggesting I joined them for a girlie evening when we got back to exchange photos and stories of the wedding. I wanted to cry; her kindness touched me. I could tell Manley wasn't happy but he's never happy unless he's preaching fire and brimstone from the pulpit or hanging out with Deacon Maurice once a week.

~~~~~

The drive to Uncle Samuel's home on the outskirts of Kingston was long but the taxi driver had the decency to keep the air-conditioning on and we made the journey in good time. As we turned into their estate, a thousand happy memories of Summer's past came back, and I was about to reminisce when Manley rudely reminded me of our objective.

"Remember, if he offers you any money, say yes, then give the cheque to me. Do I make myself clear?"

I slipped out of the taxi holding Esther and climbed the porch stairs, before I could ring the bell, Uncle Samuel and Auntie Myrtle opened the door. Uncle Sam stood there with his award-winning smile and jet-black hair. He now dyed his hair and that was the only vain thing about him. Auntie Myrtle looked regal with her long snowy white hair in two plaits resting on her shoulders.

"Ahhhh, welcome home, come in the three of you," Auntie said warmly.

"Hello Pastor Manley," Uncle said, grinning and shaking Manley's hand as Manley grinned back. "So sorry to hear about the passing of Overseer Morgan. He was a great man."

We were quiet for a few moments as Manley's face fell apart and he needed a few moments to compose himself.

"Oh, let me see the baby, why she's your twin Pastor Manley!" Auntie exclaimed.

She ushered us to sit down. I wanted to pause to take my shoes off, remembering the house rules when I had stayed in their home as a child, but Auntie was having none of it.

"Don't worry about that, it's not like you've been working in the fields all day treading in mud."

She chuckled and I laughed with her.

"Let me look at you though. You don't look like you just had a baby," she chided, "a little on the thin side to me."

Auntie gave me a look of concern, but I lowered my gaze.

"Leave the woman alone Myrtle, she looks fine to me." Uncle proclaimed and when I looked up, he winked at me. "Can I fix you a plate of food you two?"

Manley answered for the both of us.

"No, thank you, sir. We ate at the wedding."

"Of course, but that was this afternoon, surely, you're hungry by now?" inquired Auntie.

"How about a hot cup of cocoa tea?" Uncle asked smiling at me. "Come on, Rose. You help me and Pastor can fill Myrtle in about the wedding."

~~~~~

In the safety of the kitchen, I sat at the table and watched Uncle making the tea.

"There's bun in the pantry," he whispered. "We bought it especially for you! Cut me a slice too, but don't tell Myrtle, she's got me on a diet. I had gout in my ankle earlier this year, the pain was excruciating. She has me cutting back on everything I like."

"Because she loves you, Uncle Sam!" I interrupted.

"Yes, I know, Rose, and I wouldn't have it any other way, just every now and then I fancy something sweet." He paused, "I'm 91 years old now." He straightened up and turned to face me, "Old enough to see that you are so unhappy Rose. What's been going on?"

The tears fell silently between us. Uncle Samuel turned off the stove and joined me at the table. Seeing the bread knife in my hand, near my wrist, he took it from me. He was crying too as he spoke.

"God, forgive me, but I could go inside the front room and stab him right now!"

In all my thirty-five years on God's planet I have never seen Uncle Samuel upset, angry, or even cross. He was scaring me now. Seeing the startled look on my face he calmed.

"Rose," he said, taking me by my hands. "He was never good enough for you in the first place, leave him."

"What about the children? The church?"

I was breathing so hard I thought I was going to have a heart attack.

"I have some money to give to you," he reached for his chequebook in the kitchen draw. "It's made out to you.... not him," he said coldly. "Take the children and get away!"

Uncle used an old biro and scrawled his signature at the bottom of the cheque.

"Here take this!"

I didn't.

"Uncle Sam, I cannot take it. If I don't hand the cheque over to him, things will get worse for me."

I burst into tears.

"Now, stop the crying, Rose. You have my mother's middle name, and she was a strong Jamaican woman. And so are you. Your grandmother was a vendor in the market selling fruits and vegetables. Where do you think Jamaican women kept their money to keep it safe?"

Uncle blushed. I took the cheque, whilst Uncle poured our drinks into his best China cups, I slipped the folded cheque into the cup of my bra. We returned to the living room all smiles.

"Manley, I hope you don't mind but I have a cheque for you and the family..."

"No no no Elder Samuel, we're OK," Manley pretended to object.

"But we insist," said Auntie Myrtle. "You have had a lot of expenses recently, at least hold on to it, just in case, and put some money into the children's savings accounts."

"Very well," Manley said, examining the cheque my uncle gave to him. I could see his pupils enlarging at the amount. "Yep, ten thousand pounds will go a long way. I will put a grand into the girl's accounts when we get home, thanks again."

I looked at Uncle Samuel again and he winked.

"Thank you for your generosity but I am shattered, I need to get some rest. What service are we going to tomorrow?" I asked as I got up and took baby Esther from Auntie.

"We're attending the six o'clock service," Uncle answered.

I nodded and walked towards the bedroom. When he thought I was out of earshot, I heard Manley speak.

"Thanks again Elder, the money will come in handy with another mouth to feed. Rose hasn't worked since we got married and she has run up a whole heap of catalogue debt...it has been so hard on me."

I wanted to run back in the room and say, 'Liar! Liar! Pants on fire!' but instead, I bit my tongue. So, our financial problems were down to me? I don't have any catalogues let alone run up any debt and you're there gaslighting me to my family? I put my baby in the middle of the bed and retrieved the cheque from my bra. 'God is good,' thank God for Uncle Sam, twenty thousand pounds is going to change my life.

~~~~~

No sooner had I put my head on the pillow, it was time to wake up again. Manley had baby Esther, giving her a bottle.

"Good, I was waiting for you to wake up! Elder mentioned last night that I will be expected to preach today. We have got to put on a united front, I need your support."

"OK, Manley."

When I joined everybody at the table, the first thing Auntie did, after saying good morning, was speak to me.

"Rose, you're not wearing that wig to church, are you? You'll be way too hot! Tell her Manley."

"I agree with you! She's beautiful just the way she is."

There he goes again, lying like a cheap rug! I kept my wig on. We left baby Esther with the helper Suzanna, and Uncle drove us to church. Even though it was a fifteen-minute drive, it took Uncle half an hour. He was that slow now and I had feared we may have had an accident. I really thanked God we arrived at church safely. I planned to ask Manley to drive us home later. As I expected, Uncle Samuel escorted us to our seats at the front and Manley up the stairs leading to the pulpit. Manley greeted the Pastor and other members of the church board. I looked around the church beaming at the work completed so far in restoring the building. The congregation was one hundred per cent Jamaican. Very different to our church in Battersea, which is so diverse in comparison.

We had members from all over the world who brought their way of worshipping with them. We also had a large cohort of young people who loved incorporating modern drum beats and rapping into praise and worship. As choir mistress, I have embraced the 'Double Double' song, even adopting a Nigerian accent and singing 'Double O' like my fellow Nigerian sisters. I can appreciate the song "Blinded by Your Grace" by Stormzy, but I must confess, I was looking forward to the old fashioned, Pentecostal revival gospel from yesteryear.

I wasn't disappointed, from the introduction to "Down on My Knees". I grabbed the nearest tambourine and did a shuffle. By the next song, I was singing "From the Rising of the Sun" and Auntie Myrtle was jumping and skipping, praising the Lord. She's eighty-nine years old, acting sixteen. I was sweating like a pig, but I didn't care!

"Brother Arthur come on up and bless us with a chorus," shouted the lead pastor.

He boasted the microphone to a young brother, who I understand is from Prospect, in St Elizabeth. When the baseline started, I expected to hear him sing "Murder She Wrote" by Chaka Demus and Pliers, well known reggae artists. To my delight, he sang "Cornerstone", an original song he'd written. I followed the words on the overhead projector—the words resonated with me so deeply. Psalm 118 verse 22 describes how I have been feeling for a long time, rejected by my own husband, someone who was supposed to love me. Now I know who I am, I am head of the corner. Brother Arthur marched up and down the altar, accompanied by members of the choir and I joined in gladly. I felt empowered and on a spiritual high. The whole congregation was rocking and worshipping. Auntie Myrtle tapped my shoulder and I blinked back at her.

"Rose, they just called your name! Go on up to the rostrum."

I was escorted to the top of the stairs by a very proud Uncle Samuel. Manley had a fake smile on his face, he looked like he had been chewing doodoo. I had a word with the moderator then I started with an apology.

"Good morning, Saints! Greetings in the Mighty name of Jesus!"

"Greetings!" the congregation bellowed back.

"You know when you're getting your praise dance on and it's so good, you don't hear your own name is being called!"

Everybody laughed.

"Pastor Manley and I would like to thank you for the warm welcome and your condolences during this time and a special thanks to my aunt Mother Myrtle and my uncle Elder Samuel for inviting us to spend our last Sunday in Jamaica with you. I have been asked to say a few words before the preacher delivers the word. Please turn your Bibles with me to Ecclesiastes Chapter 3."

I pause for the congregation to find the chapter in their Bibles.

"Let's read together, verses 1-8:

To every thing there is a season,
and a time to every
purpose under the heaven:
A time to be born,
And a time to die;
A time to plant,
And a time to pluck up that which is planted;
A time to kill,
And a time to heal;
A time to break down,
And a time to build up;
A time to weep,
And a time to laugh;
A time to mourn,
And a time to dance;
A time to cast away stones,
And a time to gather stones together;
A time to embrace,
And a time to refrain from embracing;
A time to get,
And a time to lose;
A time to keep,

And a time to cast away;
A time to rend,
And a time to sew;
A time to keep silence,
And a time to speak;
A time to love,
And a time to hate;
A time of war,
And a time of peace."

I paused again, the congregation was silent, expectant.

"Amen, church?"

I get an amen back.

"There is something profound about believers standing and reading the Word of God together." I continued. "Saints, these eight verses sum up my life right about now and I am hoping you are encouraged by my testimony. Ten weeks ago, I gave birth to a beautiful baby girl..." I paused as the congregation applauded, "but what you don't know is, saints, I almost died."

I shared my testimony about Esther's arrival and linked it to Overseer Morgan's passing. I worked my way through the verses, linking them to recent events in my life, ending with a time of war and a time of peace.

"And I am here to tell you that we are at war saints, husband against wife, brothers against sisters, children against parents. But I am here to tell the devil, if it is a war him want with me, it is a war him going to get!" I said it in pure Jamaican patois. The congregation was clapping like we were going into battle right there and then.

"We cannot have peace until we win the battle to win back our family life. For the devil is out like a roaring lion, seeking whom he may devour."

The congregation was standing by now and applauding. I backed away from the microphone, but the home pastor tells me to carry on preaching, so I did, for another fifteen minutes. I talked about the war wounds which will happen along the way and ended by throwing off my hat and wig and singing a rendition of the chorus,

'Although the battle may be hard, and the conflict sore, though rocky the road, as you travel along. Hold out a little longer, take

Jesus at his word and he'll carry you through, right through to the promise land.'

Exhausted, I stood down from the platform and I handed the microphone back to the lead pastor who carried on singing where I left off. Manley was slow clapping as I passed him while the other ministers congratulated him as though he'd schooled me.

I returned to my seat to hear the head Pastor say, "The Preacher man has a preaching wife! Hallelujah. Saints who missed this service will be asking for a recording of this sermon for sure, for the Word of God is sharper than a two-edged sword. Amen church of God?"

The congregation agreed by clapping and the first service of the day was dismissed when the home pastor proclaimed the benediction with his hands held high. "Now may the saving Grace of our Lord Jesus Christ, the love of God and the communion of the Holy Spirit be with you all now and forevermore. Amen!" I am sure I greeted every person at church, with either a holy kiss, a handshake, or a hug.

People came up to me to talk about the themes I raised in my sermon, like the impact of social media on our young people, gang violence in Jamaica and the UK, the transgender agenda in education, and the infiltration of occult embedded into video games. Some parishioners were threatening to dash the family game consoles on the road, much to the dismay of their children.

The people were certainly fired up for sure. Auntie Myrtle laughed out loud when Brother Arthur asked to take a selfie with me without my wig. Of course, I obliged and invited him to visit us in the UK the following year, Manley was seething. The home pastor, who introduced himself as Pastor Mackenzie, offered to pray for us both. At the altar, the senior board members laid hands on our shoulders and our heads and prayed over our lives and the lives of our children.

One of them began to speak in tongues and I understood every word. ***"You are a warrior, not because you will always win, but because you will always fight back."***

~~~~~

Now back at home, reality hits me like a sledgehammer. I was dragged out of the empty wardrobe by my matted hair. I had to blink several times to adjust from the darkness of the closet to the light. I guess it was probably about 6am on Tuesday morning, but I was not sure. Pain shot through my legs, seeing that they were cramped from me kneeling all night, my bladder hurt as I desperately needed to pee. But I was defiant as I stare him down.

"If you would just obey me woman and know your place, none of this would be happening to you!"

I was naked. I tried to cover my breasts and private area with my hands.

"Get on the bed and assume the position, it's time we tried for a baby boy."

With that, he grabbed me roughly by the arm and threw me onto the bed. I don't protest, as I welcomed the warmth and comfort of the duvet. I peeped into the cot but I could not see baby Esther.

"She's in with her sisters in the Moses' basket," he says, reading my thoughts. "Come on then Preacher woman." he mocked.

"No!" I say as bravely as I can and launched an attack. I reckoned I can get a few good punches and kicks in before he overpowered me.

CHAPTER FOUR

PATTI

M y first day back on the plantation, that is the Camden office, dragged a bit, but it wasn't as bad as I thought it would be. I spent most of the day trying to log back into the system. My colleagues staffing the IT helpdesk got me back online swiftly, then I spent the remainder of the day catching up with Jerome and Steve, the managers who kindly looked after my team in my absence. They were both happy with the bottles of Appleton rum I gave them.

All was quiet on the western front, team wise, but we are pressing full steam ahead, preparing for another inspection. I decided to spend time with each team member, bringing them Tortuga Rum Cake, or wedding sponge cake for the team members who did not imbibe alcohol. After the catch ups, I returned to the laptop and deleted volumes of emails. One email caught my eye and concerned me at the same time, because it was from Chief Executive, Lillian Duncan.

She was known as a leader with a velvet cosh and for being a bit of a diva. But when I was a newly qualified probation officer, she was a brand-new career driven Senior Probation Officer. She mentored me and we had always got along. What did she want to speak to me for? Human Resources had already sent me the written feedback from my last Assistant Chief Officer interview. I was in a different space now, about to start married life; I didn't want to rehash all that negativity again. The following day, I made my way to the headquarters as instructed, leaving home at 8am. I got the number 123 bus to Blackhorse Road Station.

I stood on the tube until Seven Sisters station where I was chuffed as I got a seat and I soon alighted at Victoria station.

HQ was a few minutes' walk away. In all fairness, it was a straightforward journey taking about forty minutes. After passing through security, I took the lift to the third floor. I was delighted to see Claudette beaming back at me from the reception desk.

"Hey! Good morning. First day back? Oh, you caught the sun, didn't you? You look so well. Where did you go?" Claudette made me laugh. So full of chatter. A right gossip, but very good at her job.

"I got married in Jamaica," I said proudly, showing off my ring.

"Oh, Patti!" Claudette gasped, reaching for my left hand. "'I'm so happy for you! That's a beautiful ring too, looks like an antique. You should get that valued."

It didn't occur to me that the ring had any monetary value, just sentimental value, as it was worn by Marcus' mother; then I remembered Junior saying it was worth a lot of money.

"Heads up!" Claudette nudged me from my thoughts. "Look sharp, the Woman in Black is heading your way!"

I turned around to see Lillian strolling towards us and she looked pissed. My heart dropped to my boots. I thought to myself, was there a SFO heading my way? A Serious Further Offence is when a probationer we're supervising on a court order or licence, goes on to commit a more serious offence, like murder.

It's one of the worst things that can happen to a probation officer. Fortunately, it never happened to me when I was a practitioner, but I saw it happen to my peers. The case file would be seized, and all the records scrutinised to see if the case was managed well or not. As a manager, I sat with members of my team when they were being interviewed by the Serious Further Offence unit. Although it was a learning exercise, I saw many probation officers buckle under the stress. I even stepped in once when I felt the interviewer was being a tad heavy handed with team members, almost as though my staff was to blame for what the service user chose to do. But I kept up to date on the news in London whilst I was away, and I did not recall a significant incident or terrorist event occurring. I would learn why the woman's face was so sour in good time.

"Patti, let's go out onto the mezzanine so we can talk."

Now I was vexed. It is the first time she's seen me in two weeks, and she can't open her mouth and say, "Good Morning?" Some people really have no manners. I followed her through the glass doors, shooting Claudette a look that I hoped said, "You see this rude woman?" Veronica would tell her straight, something like, "Did me and you sleep together in the same bed last night?"

Lillian sashayed around the mezzanine until she found an empty corner with two barrel chairs. This wasn't a dressing down or the commencement of disciplinary proceedings, as I first thought. Lillian would not dare do that in a public place. So, what was it?

"It is so good to have you back, Patti," she confessed.

I should have replied it's good to be back, but I'd be lying so I stayed silent.

"Let me bring you up to speed," she said, clearing her throat.

Everything about Lillian was corporate. Her shiny blond hair was set in a loose bob on her shoulders. She was wearing a black shift dress with a matching dress coat. Her high heels were on point I twisted my engagement ring on my finger nervously.

"We have a Thematic Inspection coming up the last week in January."

I nodded to let her know I was aware of that.

"We also had a team of HR consultants in, reviewing our recruitment processes."

I pulled a funny face wanting an explanation.

"Yes, concerns were made at the Ministry of Justice about the transparency and fairness of our HR processes, especially the last recruitment drive for directors."

OK, I thought to myself, Lillian was going to give me feedback on my last job interview. This would be thorough as she was on the interviewing panel. I braced myself for feedback, grasping the sides of the comfy chair to give the illusion that I was open to receiving criticism. The truth was, I was over it. It had bothered me before going to Jamaica, after several attempts, but I was in a better place now and I didn't want to pick at those old wounds again.

"The upshot is, Patti, the consultant who reviewed your interview notes felt your answers were underscored in comparison to the other candidates, an unconscious bias I hasten to add. I hated the term unconscious bias, my experiences of discrimination, racism and microaggressions especially in the workplace had always felt like conscious biases to me."

She paused to give me eye contact but this time I held her gaze, nonplussed.

"Your scores were revised, and I am delighted to let you know that you are appointable after all!"

She smiled, satisfied with herself but it soon faded.

"Patti, do you know what that means?"

I opened my mouth to speak but the words did not tumble out.

"Congratulations, Patti!"

~~~~~

After the meeting, I rushed to the loo, pulled the lid down and sat on the seat. *What the ass just happened back there!* I thought to myself. *You just told the chief exec that you needed twenty-four hours to think about accepting a promotion and she looked like she was going to wrestle you to the ground!*

There was a lot to think about. Did I need the stress associated with such a high-profile job? At one time not that long ago, a promotion like this was all I ever wanted. I would be the first black woman among my peers to break into the senior leadership team since the new organisation was formed. What if they were setting me up to fail? What if the lump in my breast is malignant and I have to take time out for treatment? I would go home and discuss it with my husband. I'd tell him about the lump and the promotion, so he could support me properly. I managed to dodge Claudette, exited the building swiftly and made my way to the Camden office. If I accepted the post, this would be my last week at that site. Lillian wanted me to take over the Redbridge and Waltham Forest teams. My number one objective was to lead the units through to a successful inspection the following year. A tall order given most teams across London were grossly under resourced with an over-reliance on agency probation officers.

As I walked through the main entrance, the waiting room is chock-a-block with service users and poor Leah is staffing the reception area alone. I used my fob key to enter the general office.

"Hiya, where is Bev? Has she gone to lunch?" I enquire, checking the time on my smartwatch. It is already after 1pm.

"Off sick," she whispered, covering the switchboard phone with her hand.

"OK, I'm going to ask Toyin to arrange someone to cover immediately, it is ridiculously busy down here!"

I take the stairs wondering what was wrong with Beverley. I promised myself I would call her this evening for a girlie catch up. Upstairs was just as chaotic as the reception area.

News had obviously hit that we are facing another inspection. How will I tell my team that I am abandoning them too? I went to my room and closed my door. Most of my team knew not to disturb me unless there was an emergency. I called Toyin, the office manager, to arrange more cover, she said she would go downstairs and assist herself. I asked for Beverley but all she said was, she has an upset tummy, but she was expecting her back at work tomorrow. I am reassured by that comment and hang up the phone. My laptop took an age to spring to life, so I went to my tray to retrieve the cases transferred in from other areas and now residing in my borough.

Once the applications were loaded, I allocate the cases to Probation Service Officers across the unit. There were a further thirty cases to distribute via the system, so I decided to work through my lunch hour to get the work done. The clock had already started ticking on when the new assessments needed to be completed and there is no room for delays on my part.

After allocation, I saw there are several assessments to be countersigned. The assessments are mainly from the newest members of my team and may involve me sending the work back to them to amend due to omissions and/or errors. It was all very dull but a necessary part of my role as a middle manager.

In between, I took a few bites of the salad Marcus had made for me: lettuce, cucumbers, spinach, beetroot, and avocado. It tasted divine. I checked the time; it was already past 3pm. To switch things up a bit, I started the agenda for my performance meeting and sent it out by email to my team, along with a copy of the minutes from the meeting four weeks before. I had arranged for a speaker from HQ to update the team on the new alcohol treatment requirement that we would be piloting. On the agenda, we had our Christmas party to discuss. If I took the new position, I would need to tell my team tomorrow. I had made it a habit, since becoming a manager, to move away from my desk and walk the floor to find out how my team was coping.

It was also a good time to check if all those newly released from prison have reported to see their probation officers as required.

In case of a no show the officer would make inquiries with the releasing prison. There could be a myriad of reasons why somebody failed to report, from being released late, transport problems or being arrested on release. Once the facts were established the probation officer and I would then make a decision about whether or not to recall the offender. If the decision was to recall the offender, an officer had exactly one hour to complete the paperwork, including getting me to sign it off. I was relieved to hear that the three men who were supposed to report to the office straight from prison had done so without any issues and returned to my room to call Mr Man, aka my husband. It still felt weird calling Marcus by his new title.

"Ah Wah gwarn Empress?"

"A straightforward day on the plantation, I should be home around six, maybe earlier," I said with confidence. "And, where are you?"

"I'm home already, going to jump in the kitchen to prepare some food for my good lady wife!" Before I can reply, he said, "and you can get some too."

We both laughed.

"OK, Hun. I'll catch you in a few hours."

As I hung up the phone, I heard a knock at the door.

"Come in!' I shouted loud enough for the knocker to hear. In came one of my Trainee Probation Officers Femi, she is all flustered. Femi had been in my team for five months and she is fast becoming one of the rising stars within the organisation. A straight 'A' student at Hertfordshire University.

Her parents originally hailed from Nigeria, but Femi and her sisters, Yemi and Kemi, grew up in Nottingham. Femi got a first-class honours degree from Nottingham University, a prestigious Russell group uni and much to her parents' disappointment she did not want to become a doctor, lawyer or accountant. She moved to London to study to become a Probation Officer and live with her boyfriend.

"Sorry for interrupting you, but I'm not sure what to do..."

"Take a seat, Femi." I ushered her to one of my comfy chairs. "What's happening?"

"Well, I got a call from the court duty officer at Havering Magistrate's Court. One of my service user's Mr Jackson, was arrested last night and appeared in court today charged with common assault."

I took note of the salient points as she spoke.

"It looks like he assaulted his partner, and her four children were present," How scary for her children I thought.

"He is on licence to us. He was only released eight weeks ago for ABH on his wife,"

I pulled a face.

"Yes, not the same victim," Femi said reading my expression. "He is on licence until the end of December."

"So, the NPS are only informing us now?' I asked.

"Yes, an uber busy day in court apparently, worst still, the court didn't know he was on licence, so he got a fine, he has just been released...the police are going to accompany him to the address to collect his belongings, but based on his previous pattern of offending, he presents a significant risk to his former partner and her children."

I had the answer, but I deliberately stayed silent, giving Femi time to think on how she should proceed.

"OK, Femi, what are your thoughts? How has he been responding to supervision?"

Femi took a deep breath.

"Mr Jackson has kept all his appointments since his release. He engages very well in supervision, especially with the one-to-one building better relationship sessions. In my opinion, he would have benefited from completing the domestic violence programme, but he received a custodial sentence which wasn't long enough for him to complete the programme inside."

I nodded in agreement.

"Given he is now NFA and he's a risk to his former partner and her children, I think I should recall him."

I look at the clock and see it's already 4.45pm. Even the most experienced PO could not complete the recall paperwork in time, so I took charge now.

"Femi, do we have a copy of his licence?"

She nods, I drummed this into my trainees from the beginning of their training, 'No licence no recall!'

"You start the recall, call the police non-emergency number, and explain what your concerns are for the victim and her kids.

Call Mr Jackson to find out where he is going to sleep tonight. If there is a phone number for the victim, advise her of his release and give her the CAD number."

This time Femi pulled a face.

"Computer Aided Dispatch reference number," I explained, forgetting she would not be familiar with all the acronyms we use in probation. "Give her the CAD number, she must dial 999 if he turns up at her address mouthing off, and I don't want him sofa surfing at another women's house. If he's homeless, there are some new night shelters opening in the borough for Christmas. Not ideal but it's a start until we can refer him to our housing partnership. Report back to me at 5pm."

"Thanks, Patti, I'll make a start now."

Femi rose and scurried off to make a few calls. When she comes back, all that was outstanding was the recall paperwork and unfortunately, Mr Jackson has not yet answered his mobile telephone.

"Thanks for the update, Femi. Complete the remainder of the paperwork tomorrow and I will call the out-of-hours recall team."

"Sorry, Patti..." Femi said apologetically.

"Nonsense, Femi. You did really well with the late notification of his release from court and you carried out all of my instructions."

Before I left the office for the evening, I called the out-of-hours recall team and sent a text message to my line manager to notify her of my decision. At some point, she will have to countersign the recall documents too, but the clock was ticking from now. As I signed myself out on the whiteboard in the reception office, I remembered that Bev was ill. I should call her when I get home.

~~~~~

As soon as I get indoors, I kick off my shoes and pad across the parquet floor to the kitchen. Marcus looked fine as ever in his grey gym sweats with his socks and sliders. He was listening to jazz music blasting through the JML boom box. I surprised him with a wet kiss on his cheek.

"Ya find ya way home, Mrs Morgan?" he smiled.

"Hey, love," I replied. "Unfortunately, my day isn't over yet. I have some work to finish off. When is dinner going to be ready?"

"I just need to fry the fish and make the gravy...let's say 20 minutes?" he asked, turning back to the stove.

"That should be plenty of time, see you in a minute."

My spare room has a day bed in it and a reclaimed mahogany desk set up in the alcove of the bay window facing the road. I quickly set up my laptop and reply to a couple of emails whilst I waited for the duty officer from the recall team to call me back. Even though I was expecting the call, I still jumped when the phone finally rings.

"Hello?"

"Hello, this is Sonia ringing from Recall Team One. May I take your name, please?"

"This is Patti Scotland calling from London."

We went through the details on the phone and even Sonia was surprised that the court released the offender without checking his status.

"So, finally, Patti, can you tell me the reason for immediate recall this evening?"

"Yes, sure, Public Protection," I said confidently.

"Thank you, we will begin processing the revocation order in the next few minutes. Please ensure the remainder of the paperwork is sent tomorrow morning."

"No problem at all, and thanks."

I hung up the phone, hoping that the service user was picked up quickly and the woman and her children were safe. I updated the database with details of our professional discussion plus our decisions. I sent Femi a reminder to fast track the paperwork and update her assessment tomorrow morning. I placed the laptop back in the bag and put it all in the bottom drawer of the filing cabinet in the corner of the room, in accordance with the new information security guidelines.

Locking the cabinet always reminded me of the social worker who went to the pub for a drink with police following a Multi-Agency Public Protection meeting and her handbag was stolen with the MAPPA minutes still inside. She ended up being prosecuted for breach of the data protection act. I was also reminded of the police officer who left her notes from the Prolific and Other Priority Offending meeting on the dining room table and went to bed. When she woke up the next day, the house had been burgled and amongst the items stolen were her confidential notes. Well, that was not going to happen to me on my watch. At any meeting which I chaired, I collected copies of the minutes and placed them in the confidential waste sack as soon as I got back to the office. I also ordered a two-drawer filing cabinet to put my work in if I had to work from home.

I freshened up and changed into a pair of grey tracksuit bottoms and a white t-shirt, then joined Marcus downstairs. He was singing along to Jill Scott, so he didn't see me approaching. He stopped when he spotted me and smiled shyly.

"Perfect timing," he said, plating up.

I sat two placemats at the table and two glasses. Yolanda went to stay at Veronica's to give us some space. I smiled to myself, feeling content as I took my place at the table, curling my right leg under my bottom. I was getting everything more regularly now; regular homemade meals and regular sex. I didn't need a man to make me happy, I was responsible for my own happiness, but I was content and fulfilled. I thank Marcus for the bowl of food, and I loved the way he presented it. There was cassava, pumpkin, chow-chow, sweet potatoes, spinach, fried sea bass and fiery red onion gravy. I was speechless when I saw Marcus add Encona hot sauce to his food. We ate in comfortable silence until Marcus asked about my promotion.

"So, Patti, did you decide what you want to do? Are you going to accept the promotion?"

Now was the time to tell him about the lump in my breast, but I didn't want to change the energy in the room. I knew Marcus would instinctively want to look after me, but suppose there is nothing to worry about? I'm not going to tell him until I knew what I was dealing with.

"Of course, I'm going to take the job, Hun!" I exclaimed, pushing the bowl away. "I have been chasing that promotion for years! Thank you for having my back though, Marcus. And thanks again for cooking up another bowl of fantastic food."

I rose to clear the table.

"Well, you've got Mother Morgan to thank for teaching me to cook," Marcus explained, stretching and putting his hands behind his head. "When she did night work at the hospital, she would cook for us before she went to work, but when she did the day shifts and my dad was at work, too, she would leave the meat out for me or Manley to season and cook before she got home. It all came in handy when I worked away in Beijing years ago. I quickly got fed up with takeaways and dining in restaurants. There was so much fresh produce in the markets there, loads of fruit and vegetables that I had never seen or eaten before and I had no idea how to cook them. We must go there one day, Patti, so you can experience it for yourself."

I was still finding out new things about this man.

"How long did you live in China for?" I wiped down the kitchen tops and began loading the dishwasher. It was only fair, he cooked so I tidied up.

"Eighteen months!"

"Oh, wow! What an opportunity! Was that to do with your work?" I ask.

"Yes, I had just started out as an engineer. We were working on the pyrotechnics for the Beijing Olympics in 2008."

"Impressive!" I said, walking back into the living room.

"Speaking of working away, Patti, I signed up to work this Christmas in Paris. Obviously, this was all agreed upon before we got married. I'm working Christmas Eve and Boxing Day," he sighed heavily, looking unsure of how I would react.

What he doesn't know is I'm not a big fan of Christmas anyway. Of course, I made a fuss for Yolanda when she was little, but she spent many of her Christmases with her father and his family. I either went to Antoinette's or Veronica's. I always volunteered to work between Christmas and New Year and took my annual leave in the New Year. I hadn't given much thought about Christmas this year.

"Babes, don't cancel work on my account, we'll sort something out nearer the time."

"OK, if I can get back for Boxing day I'll try."

With that, he reached for the remote control and scrolled for the sports channel.

"You know you better tell Veronica about your promotion?"

"I know, you and Antoinette already know, and I swore Yolanda to secrecy. I'll call her in a minute before it gets too late."

I grabbed my bag from the front door and sat with Marcus on the couch. As I looked for my mobile phone, it rang, and it almost rang out to voicemail.

"Hello?"

"Hi, Patti, it's Pippa. So sorry for the lateness of my call. Can you speak?"

I whispered to Marcus that it's a work call and I repositioned myself back at the dining table. Marcus turned off the music and turned down the volume on the TV so I could hear her.

"Of course, it's fine, how is life in RISE treating you, Pippa?"

Since the probation service split between the private and public sectors, RISE was a brand-new mutual comprising of staff who deliver accredited group work programmes. Pippa was one of four managers who was responsible for leading teams of programme facilitators. I was one of their sessional bank staff who helped out from time to time to deliver the domestic abuse programme.

I instinctively held the phone under the crook of my neck to search for my diary and a pen. I have always gotten on with Pippa and I valued her feedback on my performance when my sessions were observed and scored. This was to ensure programme integrity, but the turning point that cemented our working relationship came when we delivered a session together at Reed House in Hackney. She had been unable to find cover for the group, so she ended up volunteering to run the session with me. We prepared the session in good time and the men filed into the group room at 6.30pm. I read the mood of the group as being quite low, but that wasn't unexpected. There was an FA cup game on that evening and some of the men would have rather been anywhere else watching the football than here with us.

We had a round robin exercise right at the beginning of each session where each man has to mention their partner's name. How old their children were, if there had been any arrests or incidences since we last met, and have they imbibed alcohol in the last 24 hours. Pippa did not know any of the men, but I could see she was making notes as the men introduced themselves. One bright spark decided he wasn't going to mention his partner's name because he was angry with her about contact arrangements with his children. We decided to 'roll with resistance', a motivational interviewing technique, and move on with the session.

It was no big deal, he had eighteen months of the programme to complete. Later on in the session, Pippa accidentally called him by the wrong name, and he went ballistic. She apologised and she tried to correct herself, but he was having none of it saying, 'Now *it* won't let me speak!' Well, I went in, telling him that Pippa had just stepped in, and she had to learn fifteen new names this evening and if she hadn't stepped in, the group would have been cancelled. 'She made one mistake and look how easily the bad names came flying out of your mouth. This is why we ask you to say your partner's name right at the beginning as it focuses the mind. Now what is your partner's name?'

Well, he looked to his peers for support, but they used imaginary shovels telling him he had dug himself into a hole. 'Colette,' he replied. 'Thanks for that,' I said, rising to update the whiteboard with my purple marker. 'Back to you, Pippa!' Poor Pippa had gone bright red, but she was able to recover enough to continue until the break. I know I was discussed with her colleagues because after that session, I was contacted by other programme managers all over London to cover groups for them, but I remained loyal to the unit in East London.

Now, Pippa is sharing how she was carrying a lot of sickness in the team. They had recruited new members, but they were not expected to be up and running until after Christmas. I could hear the desperation in her voice.

"So, I need cover until Christmas week, are you available, Patti? If it helps, the group will be at the Ilford office, you'll be running the group with Gemma."

Well, that sold it for me. I loved working with Gemma. She was a highly experienced programme facilitator, bubbly born again Christian. The kind of young lady, when she walked in the room, God walks in the room with her. Also, Gemma's mum makes the tastiest jollof rice I have ever tasted, and she would send a Tupperware dish for my dinner.

"Pippa, it's going to be tight, but I can help until Christmas, we are prepping for an inspection in January."

"Oh, thank you, Patti! Phew!" I could hear her exhaling.

"Please, let Gemma know," I said.

"Will do!" she replied.

After the call, I update my diary, the extra money will come in handy.

"I'll pick you up after the group" Marcus volunteers.

"Thank you, babes," I give him a smile.

"I'm going up, are you coming?" he said, yawning.

"Yes, in a minute. Let me call me mum first."

"Okaaay"

He disappeared upstairs. It was already after 10 o'clock but I tentatively dialled her number. I figured if she didn't pick up after three rings, I'd call it a night and ring again in the morning. Veronica picked up after the first ring.

"Who dead?"

"Pardon me?" I asked.

"I said who dead?" mum replied.

"No one as far as I know!"

"Well, why are you ringing me in the dead of night? And I'm nearly seventy-five years old and all my friends are deading off!" This was true, I should have called her in the morning. "And I dreamt about my grandmother on Monday night. She came to me in a dream wearing black and holding lilies."

Here we go, I thought to myself.

"Well, I don't know about that Mum, I'm ringing with good news."

"OK, den. Who's pregnant? I dreamt about fish last night!"

Oh, for goodness sake, this woman and her dreams. However, this one I would pay attention to. Veronica was never wrong about babies and fishes.

"Well, it's not me and it's not Yolanda!" I say defensively.

"No, it's not Yolanda. She was here lying down on the sofa complaining of stomach cramps. Don't fret she's OK. She's downstairs now working on her UCAS form."

Poor Yolanda has suffered really bad period pains from the time she experienced her first period when she was eleven years old. Several hospital appointments later, she was diagnosed with endometriosis. But if Veronica said somebody was pregnant, I would have to look closer at our circle. I am really praying it is Antoinette. Antoinette and Malakai had been trying for years to have a baby of their own. Wouldn't it be a miracle that once they adopted Elijah, they fell pregnant with a baby......

"So, what's your news then Patti?" Veronica asked impatiently.

"Mum, I got a promotion at work!!!!"

"Jesus Mary and Joseph! I've been praying for you, Patti! Congratulations! I am so proud of you! Where are they posting you?"

"Redbridge and Waltham Forest," I replied.

"On your doorstep!"

"Yep, I'll be based at Clements Road, but I plan to be quite visible at both offices."

"Good, good, good. What did Marcus say?"

"He's happy for me, mum"

"And Yolanda?"

"She knows, tell her I'll catch up with her in the morning."

"Alright den.... but you know what this means?"

"What mum?"

"We're having a party!"

CHAPTER FIVE

CHARMAINE

I woke out of my sleep at six in the morning. I could hear Marcia talking loudly on the phone to one of her relatives in Jamaica. She only paused to take her first few drags from her cigarette and coughed. I can't make out her words, but I could tell she was angry by her aggressive tone. It takes quite a bit to upset Marcia. She is normally cool, calm, and collected; but when she loses her temper, you just can't reason with her. She was having her first cigarette of the day. I know this because not that long ago I would have been on the doorstep with her having a crafty drag and a natter before the twins got up, egging her on by adding my two pence worth to the conversation.

Marcia often falls out with her family in Jamaica. Over money mainly. They were constantly requesting funds to be sent by Western Union and with Christmas approaching, their demands were more frequent. But she kept reminding them that, "De streets are not paved wid gol, Sister Mammy, I will send what mi 'ave!" I miss smoking, especially when I am stressed like today. Junior is laying next to me because I have asked him to take the children to nursery so I could go to my job interview. To be fair, he said yes but I know he would rather have stayed with Mandy as her baby was due any day now so he rarely spent the night here

I quickly got dressed into my tracksuit and trainers and exited the house. I was disappointed that Marcia had already gone back inside or gone to her early morning cleaning job. Either way, we have not had a good catch up since I came back from Jamaica. I had a fridge magnet and a bottle of Wray and Nephew rum for her.

Outside was still dark, damp, and cold. So different from running on the beaches in Negril. But running first thing in the mornings is so ingrained now and I am seeing the results. My legs are toning up and I continue to lose weight. I sped across the road to the park and started to run in an anti-clockwise route around the park, looking out for dog walkers who had let their dogs off their leads and also looking out for Dave. Although he ran fitness classes in the park, he told me he also ran in the park most mornings.

Running has given me the opportunity to clear my head and focus on the tasks I need to complete that day. The first task today was the dreaded assessment centre and job interview in Romford. Then, I have to be back in time to attend, what did Antoinette call it? Stratford Shopping Day? No, that isn't right. Westfield Wednesday! I was looking forward to catching up with the ladies again. I also wanted to get to the bottom of where I knew Antoinette's face from. I know I have met her before, but I just couldn't place her......

"Oh Shit!" I shout as it hits me and at the same time I almost run into another jogger. "I'm so sorry."

"You need to watch where you're going!" The bearded black man said, angrily stopping and wiping gravel off his black tracksuit bottoms.

"Man's needs to stop blacking up like he's on his way to commit a burglary," I shout back at him.

I take him in briefly, all I can see is his dark complexion and a beard. I quickly sprint off.

"Oi oi you got jokes this early in the morning," he yelled after me.

I continued to run until the cold sun shone through the trees and rested on the park benches, swings, and other playground equipment. When I got back indoors, Junior is up making the children's breakfast. He offered to make me a bowl of porridge, but I declined. Other than communicating about the children, we had nothing to say to each other. I just wanted him to leave my bed, my house, and leave me alone.

The shower was nice and hot, I rushed to get myself ready. Today I was dripping in Primani from my head to my toes and wearing it like it is Prada. A crisp white shirt, black pencil skirt, size 14, with black opaque tights and ankle boots. When I kissed the children and grabbed my new coat, I caught Junior studying me, but he doesn't say a word, not even good luck.

"Kids, Nanny is picking you up this evening."

Then I turned to Junior, and I remind him that I'm going to Westfield this evening, but he doesn't answer.

"Can you collect them from my mum's after they have eaten? And put the Christmas tree up with them?"

"Yes!" the children shout. They had Christmas fever for sure.

I rush to the bus stop and wait with a world of people for the next bus. Everybody looked vex, hiding behind winter hats, thick coats, and gloves, blowing warm air out of their mouths, huffing and puffing. Some school children are still thinking it's Summer by only wearing their school uniform, but they are huddled together trying to stay warm like a pack of wild animals.

I was not able to get on the first bus, but I got on the second. Everybody was scrambling to get on. It wasn't that long ago when you formed a queue for the bus or you let the elderly get on first, those days were long gone. When I found a seat, it was on the upper deck, I'm sitting on an aisle seat with this woman who has decided that now was the right time to finish applying her make-up, Fenty foundation and everything, my word. But now she's taking a wig out of a Tesco carrier bag and putting it on her head back to front. I almost fell off my seat with laughter, having to pretend I was watching something on my phone.

At Stratford Station, I made my way through to the platform for trains heading to Shenfield, Essex. This was packed with commuters too. I had ample time to get to the interview at 10am but I'd rather be early and go for a coffee in Romford than run late. I checked my phone. I've received a text message from Rose wishing me all the best and I smiled. She remembered, I am looking forward to seeing her again this evening, if she can get out of the house.

When the train arrived, it was bedlam. People were trying to get off the train whilst others are trying to get on. Tempers and cuss words were flying. I had to run along the platform to find space in a carriage and I even found a seat close to the door. I climbed into my seat by stepping over an older gentleman to sit by the window. I sunk into the seat, put my handbag on my lap, and stared out the window. I tried to empty my mind of Junior rarely coming home, Mandy being pregnant, and what might happen at Westfield Wednesday this evening.

Soon enough, we reached a very dreary Maryland station and more people piled onto the train. I reached into my bag for my water bottle and take a few sips. I was trying to swallow back my nerves, but my anxiety was rising about the assessment centre. From what I read up on last night, I was expected to sit a written and math test. Only those who pass are invited to individual interviews. The last time I sat a test was my GCSE exams. I didn't study so my results were so poor, I didn't even bother going to school to collect my certificates. Shame guy. My brainy peers who I taunted and bullied at school probably earned good money now, driving nice cars, or going on fancy city breaks and holidays.

The train stopped at Forest Gate station and the commuters piled in like canned sardines. I reached for my folder which had my documents in it, and my application form. I wanted to read over my statement where I demonstrated how I met the personal specifications required for the job. My friend, Shamilla at the Westfield branch, helped me to fill it in. I thought I had no skills whatsoever, but she was able to link all of the criteria to my role of managing a household, and her efforts got me shortlisted. It was over to me now.

Boy, I wanted a cigarette to take the edge off things. I imagined pulling a long drag, breathing the smoke into my lungs and out my nostrils. I closed my eyes and sighed. The train was held at Manor Park station for ages. The driver announced signalling problems. Passengers started to mumble, and I got the impression that this was a regular occurrence. If I get the job, I will have to learn another route to work just in case? 'Ark at me talking about going to work...my first job having money of my own. I would work all the hours allocated to me and save money to get as far away from Junior as possible. I would sell the house, give him half and buy a house on the coast.

Well, that's the dream anyway. The train jolts forward, out of the station with no announcement. I looked at my watch, and it's only 9am, I still had an hour to get to Romford, but I can tell by the people tutting around me, they are already late for work. The old man next to me starts to get himself together as the train pulled into Ilford. I guess at least three quarters of the passengers alighted here; mums pushing buggies, children rushing to get to school. The heavy rainfall is drenching the platform and the people alike.

The rain continued to pour as I exited the station at Romford and walked on the slippery cobble stones towards Primark. What a contrast from coming up here to window shop with mum last Summer in our Summer dresses, sunglasses, and sandals.

We had lunch alfresco at Weatherspoon's pub; mum pushed Geraldine and I pushed Garrison in their buggies. It was such a lovely day just people watching while the children enjoyed their ice creams.

I manage to avoid the puddles, but I was shivering with cold. I couldn't wait to get into the store for shelter. As I walked in, I caught my reflection in the window. My afro puff had shrunk to two thirds of its original size. Moisture was a bitch!

The security guard escorted me through a maze of corridors and stairs to a brightly lit training room. A few people are already waiting there, and they turned to look at me. I was overdressed and probably the oldest person in the room. I felt ancient. If one of these youngsters get up to give me a seat or call me Auntie I'm chipping and going back home!

A woman in a suit appeared at the entrance to explain there had been a mix up, we have all be given the same interview slot. She had the revised times, and my slot isn't until 3pm. After the written and maths tests, which thankfully I passed, I could go back home and come back later but I decide to get some breakfast and stay local.

Thankfully, it had stopped raining, so I walked up to the market, figuring I'd find a greasy spoon and treat myself to a full English breakfast. I was not disappointed, if there is one thing Romford was full of, it's cafés, bars, and restaurants. I ducked into a small café off the market which looked empty from outside. It was warm and inviting.

"Eating in or taking away?" the waitress asks.

"Eating in please," I replied.

"Sit anywhere you like, love," she said as she busied herself clearing a nearby table.

I tucked myself into a corner booth, looking out at the market stalls. The barrow boys are stringing up fairy lights, getting their fruit and veg stalls ready for Christmas.

"Shit," I said to myself.

Christmas preparations were starting earlier and earlier. I was normally so ahead of the game. This time last year I had already bought and hidden the children's Christmas presents. With the sudden death of Pops Morgan, and the expense of going to his funeral in Jamaica, I was starting to fret.

Is this our last Christmas together as a complete family? Surprise, surprise Junior did not celebrate Christmas. To be fair, he doesn't celebrate anything, tight bastard. He says Valentine's Day is a rip off and so was Mother's Day. Funnily enough he always sends his mother a greeting card even though they don't celebrate Mother's Day until May.

As far as Junior is concerned, Babylon is out to rob him of his hard-earned cash, so for Christmas day I buy the children their gifts and we spend the day with mum. By the end of the day, he would get caught up in the 'Christmas spirit' fuelled by Wray and his nephew and sing carols while strumming his acoustic guitar. There would be a face time call with his parents, when he thought they were back from church, then his mates would come round to play dominoes before they went out raving.

"What you havin', darlin'?"

I snapped out of my daydream and focused on the menu. It's the kind of menu that was laminated and had photos depicting examples of the food all over it.

"A full English brekkie please, no toast, and a cup of tea, thanks," I say, folding the menu and handing it back to her.

"No problem, the tea is coming now."

The café was getting busy now, with a long queue of people who looked like they are getting a late breakfast or early lunch break from work. I wonder what their lives were like, I imagine they are filled with liquid lunches and fine dining. Do they all live in big houses in Essex? Or riverside apartments on Canary Wharf? Do all the women have designer bags?

I caught my reflection in the window and for the first time in a very long time I'm not ashamed of what I see. My double chin was gone and so were the sad, dark circles from under my eyes. My hairstyle is still recovering from the earlier downpour, but I liked myself.

As if by magic, my tea was placed on the table so quickly that I don't get the chance to say thank you, as the waitress hustles to serve another customer. I stirred two sachets of sugar into my tea, I figure I will need the energy for my interview later. When my breakfast finally arrived, consisting of two rashers of bacon, a sausage, mushrooms, tomatoes, a sunny-side egg and a generous portion of baked beans I gobbled the food down quickly. I haven't eaten since last night, so I have to force myself to slow down and stop eating like a pig. I jumped when a text message came through on my phone.

It reads "All the best Charms. Love Patti." A text message from my lovely sister-in-law, I thought to myself.

I reached out to her when I got my phone fixed and she sent me a text message once a day to check in with me. I was looking forward to seeing her, Rose, and Patti's friend Antoinette later. I was nervous about meeting Antoinette again as I finally put two and two together when I was out jogging this morning. She was the flashy barrister that represented Junior at court, how frigging embarrassing. I just hope she didn't tell Patti my business. Aren't they bound by some oath some confidentiality thingy? I panicked wondering if Marcus had told his wife anyway.

"Anything else for you, darlin'?"

"Yes, please that was munch! Thank you," I said as she reached for my empty plate. "Can I have another cuppa please?" I say, exaggerating my Cockney accent.

"No problem, darlin'!"

Several cups of tea later, I re-joined the teaming market outside. It's just after 12 o'clock and the market was busy. I bought some pear drops from a stall that sold sweeties by the ounce. I pop one into my mouth, savouring the coarse granulated sugar on my tongue, I promised myself I'll give the rest to my mum. I walked over to The Brewery shopping centre.

My friends and I came down here when the centre first opened back in 2001. It is a corner shop compared to the likes of Westfield shopping centre, but it was easier to get to than Lakeside and Bluewater. I walked into one of the clothing shops expecting to be followed around the store like in my younger days, but the security guard doesn't even bat an eyelid in my direction. I lose time like this for a couple of hours before I decide to go back to Primark.

I figure maybe they are able to interview me earlier. It was now 2 o'clock. I thought about ringing Junior to remind him to pick up the twins, but he won't want me to remind him. He had that one job to do for the day. I walked swiftly and I entered the store before another downpour of rain. I found my way back to the training room and I played with the tills for a little while, imagining myself on the shop floor.

"Ah great, you're back early. We're running ahead of ourselves would you like to come in now Mrs Morgan?"

"Yeah sure," I said, suddenly feeling highly anxious.

When I entered the room, there is a long table with three people sitting at it. The lady from HR introduced herself as Sally, she had an open, friendly face and she gave me a smile. Muhammad was the manager at Romford, and he looked serious as a heart attack and in the centre was Jamal, the manager from Stratford branch, he took the lead.

The first thing I notice about him was his beard. What was it with young black men these days? All these hipster beards, well-groomed with oil and shit. Looking like a black lumberjack. Underneath all that hair I bet he was cute looking too. *Concentrate, Charms.*

"So, tell us, why did you apply for a position with us today, Ms. Morgan?"

I cleared my throat.

"Please call me Charmaine. My father-in-law died..."

"My sincere condolences, Charmaine," Jamal interrupts.

"Thanks, but that came out wrong. When my father-in-law died, we needed to travel urgently. Because of your store, I was able to shop for everything I needed from towels and travel size toiletries to flip flops and even an outfit to wear to the funeral. Primark became my one stop shop. I want to be part of serving my community at a time when customers need them the most, especially when people are on a budget."

Jamal stared back at me; his smile broadened with every answer I gave.

"And finally, Charmaine, are you interested in a career in retail fashion?"

"I most certainly am! As you can see, I'm dressed in Primani from head to toe today..."

I trail off as Muhammed and Sally look mortified.

"Oh, you got jokes?" Jamal said, chuckling.

Now that is the second time I've heard that phrase today. First from the fella I bumped into in the park. He had a beard, too. I dismiss the thought.

After my interview, I raced straight to the loo. The whole thing was a blur. I remember Muhammed asking about my first aid qualifications and he appeared to be impressed. Sally explained how a zero hour contracts worked, what areas I was expected to work in and when I would start training. Jamal was skinning his teeth throughout the whole thing, putting me off my 'A' game.

When I checked my shirt in the mirror, I had two visible wet patches under my arms from perspiring so much. I hope the panel didn't see it. On exiting the store, I headed towards the station. It is now 4.30pm, somebody was calling my name, it's Jamal. Thinking I left something behind, I wait for him to catch up to me.

"Girl, you walk fast. Almost jogging!" he said, out of breath.

I looked at him, confused.

"You almost knocked me over in the park this morning!"

I stood still.

"I thought it was you!" I responded, "What a small world."

"Yeah.... You did a really fab interview just now, Charmaine. Whatever the outcome, be proud of that."

"Thanks, Jamal. My first interview in a very long time," I confessed.

"Listen, if you want to get on the fast train, we have to run for it. Shall we?"

And just like that, I made a friend.

CHAPTER SIX

ROSE

I t was Monday night and Manley insisted that I attend choir practice, even though I was exhausted. Although I cooked corned beef, rice, and plantain, I was not permitted to eat with the family, another one of Manley's punishments, so I was hungry too.

When I arrived at the church, the lights in the building were already on. Thank the Lord for men in the church like Brother Moses. He always arrived half an hour early to switch the heating on, especially in the vestry.

Tonight, we were having auditions for the lead singers to sing on Christmas Day and to sing at the jamboree on old year's night. When I entered the building, a few of our young people are already there sorting out the drum kit and warming up by singing choruses. I said hello and quickly made my way to the back office. Brother Moses sees me and greets me with a hug.

"Welcome home, Sister Rose! Good to see you"

"Thank you, Brother Moses," I replied.

"Tea or coffee?"

"I'll have a tea please, with one sugar."

"Coming right up," he said, as he fills the kettle with water. "How did it go? How's Pastor bearing up?"

"Everything went well, thank you and Pastor will be fine. It was good to see Mother Morgan and my aunt and uncle."

"Glad to hear that. I bought a packet of chocolate biscuits to go with our teas, you fancy one?"

I nodded. Did I fancy one? I could eat the whole packet. I took two out of the packet and join Moses at the table. I figured a good strong cup of tea would fill my empty tummy and hold me until the morning, when hopefully I will be able to eat.

After our drinks, we joined the young people in the church. We had three young people here to try out for the solo, Take Me to The King by Tamela Mann. A beautiful contemporary ballad. The two teenage girls who auditioned, did the song justice, but when the young brother Jefferson sang, I was so moved by his voice, I wanted to cry. Brother Moses and I agreed, brother Jefferson would sing the lead solo on Christmas day, the announcement will be made on Sunday. After choir practice, I waited for Brother Moses to lock up the building. I intended to walk home but he volunteered to drop me off on his way home.

"I don't know about you, but I fancy a patty, you want one?" he asked.

Thank the Lord for this man, I think to myself.

"That's just what I fancy too," I replied.

Moses drove the car around the corner and came to a halt outside a Caribbean takeaway called Jerky's. He jumped out the car and ran inside. I could see him in the queue waiting to be served. Ten minutes later, he was at the passenger door holding brown paper bags and drinks. I opened the car window to assist him.

"I didn't ask you what you wanted Sister Rose, so I got you two patties, one saltfish and the other is lamb. If you don't like them, you can swap with one of my beef ones. This drink is for you, Guinness punch!'

When he got back in the car, I thanked him, and he drove off towards my house. I couldn't bring outside food into the house; Manley would go ballistic! I will have to stall Moses in some way. I started in on the patty, the saltfish one. It was piping hot, but I managed to blow on the filling and devour it at the same time, it tasted so good. Crumbs from the flaky pastry were littered all over me and the passenger seat.

"So sorry Brother Moses..."

"Don't worry yourself, and when we're not at church, feel free to call me Moses."

"OK Moses, please call me Rose."

I could see him smiling in the dark. Once we got near my home, Moses parked across our driveway, blocking Manley's car. He grabbed a paper bag and started eating his patty.

"I think we made the right decision with Jefferson for the lead solo, he has a blessed voice don't you think so Rose?"

"I one hundred per cent agree with you Moses, he is destined for the music ministry for sure. He'll have to find a wife soon..." I paused, "how come you never married Moses?"

Moses stopped eating.

"Sorry for asking such a personal question, you don't have to answer."

"That's OK."

He grabs his drink from the cup holder and takes a long sip.

"I'm thirty-nine years old but I haven't found 'The One' yet. When I meet her, I will know. I'm in no rush."

"Very wise words Moses."

The old people say, 'Marry in haste and repent at leisure.' The reality of that saying resonated with me, I wanted to cry. All of a sudden, there was an abrupt knock on the passenger car window, making us both jump. Before I can blink, Manley has the car door open.

"Get out of the car Rose, whatever will the neighbours say about you sitting outside my house in another man's car?"

I slowly got out of the car; my face flushed with embarrassment. I brushed the crumbs off my clothes, hiding what remains of the second patty in my coat pocket. I heard the two men's raised voices as I raced up the path to the house.

I clearly hear Manley say, "She's my wife and she's Sister Rose to you!"

I locked myself in the downstairs loo and finished eating my patty. If I was going to get another beating, it wouldn't be on an empty stomach.

~~~~~

I slept with one eye open last night, uncertain when Manley would pounce. It was Tuesday now and I found myself going through the motions. By the looks he gave me, anybody would think I got caught having sex in the car not eating a patty! Manley surprised me by coming home at lunchtime and gave me the keys to the lean to. I made us both sardines with a little tomato sauce, scallions, and sweet peppers, served with buttered crackers. Afterwards, I joined him at the table, and he let me eat.

"Just imagine how I felt seeing you and him in the car like that."

I dared not answer.

"Your reputation and my standing in the church is important Rose. "Shun every appearance of evil," he quoted. "You ever see me dropping sisters in the church anywhere?"

He looked at me sternly, so I shook my head.

"One more move like that and I will come down on you like a ton load of bricks. Do you understand me, woman?"

I nodded again.

"Take out the things you need to feed my children and what you need for prayer meeting this evening and give me back my keys."

~~~~~

Every Tuesday evening, I hosted a prayer meeting at home. In my prayer cell, there are eight other women. They are the mothers of the church with more than forty years of church life and experience. I get on with all of them except for Sister Adanna, Deacon Maurice's wife.

The church gossip is that she was after Manley for years, but when he announced his engagement to me, she then switched and pursued Maurice. Since then, she has put herself in competition with me. Who could have the best wedding, who had the first baby, who could sing soprano or wear the most elaborate hats?

I did ask Manley to swap her out of my prayer cell, but his stance is "the church is like a hospital, with people at different stages of their Christian walk."

He also says I could learn a lot from Sister Adanna how she carries herself and hiw she manages her home. When Sister Adanna and her noisy brood of boys turned up, they rushed past me to play with my girls.

We are cordial with each other, but not close. I ask her how her pregnancy was going, and she said she was blessed to be having another boy. I showed her to the front room whilst I prepared the refreshments in the kitchen. I was jealous of her having yet another boy, but I wouldn't exchange any of my beautiful daughters for a son, period.

Adanna made herself useful by answering the door until my little front room was filled by my group. Once everybody had their fill of tea and sandwiches, we began to sing and follow with testimonies. Of course, Sister Adanna goes first. God was so good to her. Her due date was coming up and she was ready to give birth the natural way. All it took was a little faith, like with her other babies and she gave birth without pain relief. One or two of the other women looked at me and then back to her. I wanted to say, "Award yourself a gold star Mother of the Year 2015!" but I kept my own counsel. After a few amens, Sister Reynolds spoke.

"Good evening, Sisters. God is good?"

"All the time!" we piped back.

"So good to have Sister Rose back safely. I really missed praying with the prayer warriors! I just wanted to thank you for your prayers, my son Aaron, got a conditional offer from Cambridge University to study Philosophy! He is on target to attain three A stars next year."

"Hallelujah!" everybody shouts.

We give her a round of applause. Sister Carole goes next.

"Goodnight, Sisters, just want to let you know that God has been good to me and his mercies endureth forever. Hallelujah! Wesley got the role in the Lion King, and he starts rehearsals in the New Year." Another round of applause erupted.

"God is not sleeping; not at all." Sister Doretta joined in. "Cecelia gave her heart to the Lord at the convention, and she is enjoying her walk with the Lord!" Amens sounded all around the room.

"Sorry to report that Sister Macky's husband, Ralph, was admitted into Chelsea and Westminster hospital with a suspected stroke. Can we remember them both in prayer?" Sister Doretta continued. "Not sure who's around tomorrow but I would like to go and see him." One or two volunteered but they still look at me, I was quick to respond.

"I cannot go tomorrow but I will go on Thursday or Friday." Changing the subject, I said, "I am grateful for my bundle of joy. By God's grace we made it through and both of us are alive and well. Mother Morgan sends her kind regards to you and hopes you are able to lift her up in prayer in the coming weeks and months. So, let us pray!"

I loved being in that zone where I forgot about other people, and I just cried out to God. Tears were a language that only God understood so I cried out to him. The older women surround me, laid hands on my shoulders and prayed with me. We prayed for Sister Adanna and each woman in the room. After the meeting, I felt so light that I could genuinely embrace Sister Adanna and wish her all the best for the remainder of her pregnancy as Deacon Maurice dropped Manley home and collected his wife. Manley was upbeat and chirpy as usual after his "Men in Ministry" meeting.

Deacon puts his head to his wife's huge belly affectionately saying, "Come on little man Palace needs a new wing attack!"

We all laugh as Sister Adanna playfully pushed him away. Manley tried to be affectionate towards me as he always does in company, normally I play along but I flinched at his touch and left the front room to wake up their children who were asleep on the sofa.

~~~~~

It was Wednesday, the only thing on my agenda today was to open a bank account to deposit Uncle Samuel's cheque and to attend Westfield Wednesday. I was looking forward to going and being one of the girls. None of them had any expectations of me. I was walking along the road, pushing baby Esther in her pram when I remember to text Charmaine to wish her all the best with her job interview. Hopefully she'll get my message before her interview. "All will be well," I said. I crossed the road at the lights and walked through the automatic doors at the bank.

I was praying for a sympathetic advisor. I needed to open an account with a cash card that I can collect at the bank without letters coming to my home address. I had an appointment at 11am but they were running behind. I quickly called my mum to pick up Ruth and Rebecca from the nursery. For retired people my parents were busier now than when they were working. I sighed with relief when she said they can help me out. Eventually, I was called into a booth. It was so tiny I had to leave the frame to baby Esther's pram in the corridor and keep her strapped in the car seat. I left the interview door open so I could see it from where I'm sitting. A black woman about my age came in. She looks very smart in her navy suit, and she introduced herself as Mrs Steph Gayle. We exchanged pleasantries and she cooed over at my baby.

"Your first baby, Mrs Morgan?"

"Oh, no,'" I said smiling. "She is my fifth daughter and last child, if I can help it."

Mrs Gayle observed me and then dropped her gaze to shuffle the paperwork on her desk.

"You sound very sure," she finally replied, looking awkward.

"Mrs Gayle, I need your help."

"Well, that's what I am here to do, Mrs Morgan."

She was giving me eye contact again.

"I don't know where to start?" I confessed.

"Start at the beginning, Mrs Morgan"

When I started crying, Mrs Gayle got up to close the door behind me. By the end of our conversation, I managed to walk out with an online bank account which I could access from my phone and my cash card would arrive at the bank for collection. Not only could I transfer funds to the children's accounts, but I also had Mrs Gayle open a savings account for Esther. She told me her story of how she too suffered at the hands of her now ex-husband, and she reassured me that this was all survivable. As I was leaving, she asks me a question.

"Are you a woman of faith?"

"Yes, I am, why?"

"Well, I was reading The Daily Bread today and it was about the good Samaritan. The action for me, was to help a stranger in need. It was a pleasure meeting you today, Mrs Morgan. Here is my business card if you need help with anything else."

I swallowed the urge to cry again, and I thanked Mrs Gayle several times from the bottom of my heart.

~~~~~

I timed things so my folks could meet me outside my home with the children. Once indoors, I fried some fish fingers and chips for the girls. As soon as that cheque cleared, I could start making an exit plan. I researched this on the home computer. I was hoping to discuss this in depth with Patti and her friend Antoinette later this evening. While the girls were eating their lunch, I changed and fed baby Esther and put her down for a nap.

I turned my thoughts to dinner; Manley hasn't left out much for me to cook at all. Fried dumplings and baked beans will do for the girls. But Manley would quarrel with me if I didn't cook something substantial for him to eat, and I needed to leave the house by at least 5pm if I stood any chance of getting to East London by six o'clock.

I spotted a small cabbage and veg that had seen better days in the vegetable rack, maybe I could salvage that. I got to work preparing dinner and sent Ruth and Rebecca off to lie down on their mats with their blankets for a nap. It was 1:30pm now; I needed to keep an eye on the time.

It took fifteen minutes to cook the veg, after which, I drained it in a sieve over the sink, then transfer the cabbage and carrots to the frying pan. I used all of the seasoning I could find in the cupboard, namely, thyme, all-purpose seasoning, black pepper, salt and a little finely chopped Scotch bonnet pepper. Lastly, I added a dollop of cooking butter and stir.

I left that to simmer while I washed my hands to make a batch of fried dumplings. I would make enough so that Manley could get some as well.

When 2:30pm came around, I stopped what I was doing and got the children ready to pick up Mary and Martha from school. It was a good walk away and Rebecca was reluctant to come along, but I have no choice. I couldn't drive, and even if I could, I didn't have access to a car. I thought of calling my folks again, but I knew they are at adult choir practice this afternoon so they couldn't help. I saw Brother Moses' car pass us on the way back from school and I waved, but he kept on driving, appearing not to see me. I listened to the girls talk about their day and I spoke to them about going out this evening.

"Who's in charge Mummy?" asked Mary.

The girls surround the pram shouting, "Me! Me! Me! Me! Me!"

"OK, today I'm leaving, Baby Esther in charge!"

We all laughed together, making jokes all the way home. The girls enjoyed their dinner which I topped up with yoghurts and blueberries.

I had a quick shower, in cold water as I was not permitted to switch the emersion heater on and rushed to get ready. I was embarrassed to say that I didn't have any casual clothes, it was either church clothes or formal attire. So, I put my jeans back on and I found a black jumper. Now what to do with my hair? While I rushed to get ready, Mary came upstairs to my room. She helped with my hair and brushed it into a ponytail. It still looks better than the battered old wig. I heard the front door slam, and my heart skipped a beat, Mary picked up on my fear.

"It's alright mummy, it's daddy."

We walked downstairs and greeted him. Manley gave the girls a hug. He looked in the pot, screwing up his face.

"Is that all there is?" I nodded. "Where's the meat?"

"You didn't leave anything out for me to cook Manley," I said, trying not to sound accusatory.

"And you couldn't remind me?"

So, it was my fault, I think to myself.

"Well, there's enough for you, I'm off in a minute..." my voice was shaky.

"Off to where?" he asked, putting Rebecca down.

"It's Westfield Wednesday"

"But you're not going. I forbid it." He was coming towards me as I backed up against the door.

"Manley, my feet haven't hit the ground since coming back from Jamaica. I have been to church, choir practice, and prayer meetings. And I'm visiting the sick tomorrow. I need time off!"

"Time off from God's work Sister Rose? To hang out with unbelievers?" Manley snorted.

"Those unbelievers are my sister in laws! They are married to your brothers! I want to go; I'm not turning into a reprobate overnight." I grabbed my coat off the newel post at the bottom of the stairs and turned the lock on the door. Manley grabbed my ponytail and I fell backwards to the floor.

"Mummy!" Mary ran past Manley as he tried to compose himself. "Are you alright?"

I got up and tried to comfort Mary.

"Silly Mummy, I just fell over!"

"Mummy, if you don't leave now, you're going to be late. We don't do lateness, do we Daddy?"

"That's right, baby. Are you OK, Rose?"

"Yes, I'm fine Manley. I won't be late."

I grabbed my purse, ran out of the house, and didn't stop running until I reached the bus stop.

CHAPTER SEVEN

PATTI

I arrived at the office at 7:15am. I had to complete the last of the mid-year appraisals and upload them all on SAP, which was the HR application used by the organisation to manage the workforce. It didn't matter how early I got here, there is always somebody in the building before me. I swear people slept in the office sometimes.

Today somebody from the NPS was on the ground floor and we greeted each other as I walked through the lobby. My mind crossed on Beverley, as I saw her cardigan hanging over her chair in reception. I have not seen or heard from her since we returned. I made a mental note to call her again this evening. She was probably embarrassed about the whole Junior saga. And Antoinette told me, Charmaine threw a glass of red wine all over her dress at our wedding reception.

~~~~~

Once I completed and uploaded the appraisals, I exited my office to put the kettle on. With my second ginger tea of the morning, I planned to announce my promotion and pending departure under AOB right after we had set a date for the office Christmas party. I would do what I had done every year since becoming a manager; I'd have my meal, soup for starter, turkey with all the trimmings, and Christmas pudding for dessert. Then I'd put money behind the bar, keep my eye on the door and make an early dignified exit. My team deserved to get drunk as farts, snog each other and dance on the tables without thinking I am there monitoring them. Furthermore, I didn't want my image circulating on social media, or worst still, The Daily Mail, with the headline "Senior Manager drunk at Office Party".

I made my way to the meeting room, and I was surprised to see everybody there waiting to begin. I laid down the law a few meetings back about what my expectations were going forward, we needed to be more business-like. I went through the standard agenda items and discussed the impending home office thematic inspection. Everybody groaned as we have inspections coming out of our ears, even Ofsted had been in to inspect our educational provisions for our young offenders between 18-21 years old. I knew my team was resilient and would support each other after I had left.

The subcommittee decided that we would have our Christmas party at the Westfield Holiday Inn on Friday 18th December, that date suited my diary. I followed up with my relocation announcement. My team didn't take it too well. Although they were happy for me, some were understandably sad to learn I was moving on. Of course, they also wanted to know who would manage them when I left, and I promised to let them know. After the meeting, I told my fellow managers, who had probably heard through the grapevine; they expressed how happy they were and said it is long overdue.

~~~~~

At the end of the workday, I decided to go straight to Stratford Station. Some retail therapy with Antoinette would sort me out before meeting with Rose and Charmaine, my new sisters in law. Antoinette congratulated me on my promotion, and we went for champagne cocktails at the Sky Bar after purchasing Christmas presents for the children and two mobile phones for Rose and Charmaine. Antoinette and I had made significant progress with the domestic abuse worker, collecting information that we would eventually share with them.

As Antoinette was practically banned from most of the restaurants in Westfield, we decided on eating at Levi Roots Smokehouse. We got there early, and we were seated at a corner booth.

I asked Antoinette if she's heard from Beverley, to which she said, "Why would I hear from the home wrecker?" I didn't bother pushing Antoinette, Beverley was officially off her Christmas card list this year.

~~~~~

We are joined by a very smart Charmaine. I asked her how the interview went, and she said she would know the outcome this evening. Antoinette made a fuss of her by ordering Champagne to celebrate and we toasted both of our successes.

I was getting hungry now, so we ordered two plates of fishcakes while we wait for Rose. Charmaine assured us that she was on her way. During our conversation, Charmaine got a text informing her that she got the job in retail, and she was due to start at the Romford branch next week.

I was delighted for her, and she looked as pleased as punch. Hell, it was the first time I had seen her smile. The high we are on soon faded when Rose arrives, she looked dreadful. She had clearly lost more weight since Jamaica, and she looked like she hasn't slept since then either. I sensed Rose was reluctant to order anything until I said tonight's meal was on me, since I got a promotion at work and Charmaine got a job. She is so pleased for us. We ordered our food and got busy. Antoinette took the lead.

"Ladies we picked up the Children's Christmas presents. These aren't any ordinary backpacks, they are filled to the brim with pens, colouring pencils, felt tip pens and colouring books. Everything a child might need when moving somewhere new."

Antoinette paused for effect.

"'Ladies expect a call from our girl Kerry any day now, she will call you on these phones."

Antoinette hands over the Samsung bags with brand new phones.

"The guy in the shop has already hooked the phones up and entered our numbers in them. I strongly recommend that you keep them hidden and check them at least once a day."

Charmaine took hers out of the box straight away and started to tinker with it. Rose cried.

"Nah Nah none of that, girlie!" Antoinette reaches over to her. "You prayed for help and help has arrived. There is a note in there somewhere, Charmaine will show you how to prepare your INCH bag."

The women looked puzzled, I clarified it for them.

"INCH is an acronym for 'I'm Never Coming Home'"

"Oh," said Rose.

"Yep, I found it in 'one notes,' let me show you Rose." Charmaine held her hand out for Rose's phone.

Poor Rose looked lost, or 'monkey handling gun' as Veronica would say, when trying something new.

She will soon get used to it, I reasoned with myself. Our mains arrive, I tried not to notice how Rose devoured the meal before her. It was clear she hadn't eaten properly for a while.

It was a classic domestic abuse tactic to deny the woman a regular meal, not giving her money for shopping or padlocks on cupboard doors. I had seen it all on home visits, which is why I stressed that visiting our service users at home was so important.

Years ago, we had a child who had lost a significant amount of weight and the health visitor was convinced the mother, who was my client, was not feeding her daughter. It was puzzling because her son was thriving and healthy. I stopped by her home for an unannounced home visit, only to find out that, not only was she cooking, she had leafy vegetables alongside chicken with rice n peas. Her fruit bowl looked better than mine. It turned out her daughter had an undiagnosed health condition to do with her digestive system. I still think it was a good call to do the home visit as part of my assessment. I wouldn't have been able to manage the risk she posed to her child if I hadn't.

I made a snap decision.

"Don't worry about how you're getting home Rose, Marcus and I will take you."

"And I'll drop you off Charmaine. Order yourself something else to drink, working girl!" Antoinette added.

"Damn right!" said Charmaine, trying to catch the attention of the waiter.

"I'll join you in a glass of something sparkling please," Rose said, "I'm no longer breastfeeding," she hastened to add.

"Alright den, Well let's celebrate. Where's that young man?" Antoinette hollers.

"Let me call him", I said, I don't want to get us kicked out of here too.

~~~~~

"Where are you babes? Car Park B level 2? OK we're coming now."

We said our goodbyes to Antoinette and Charmaine. I reminded them both about my party at Veronica's on the first Saturday in December. We dumped the Samsung bags in the bin and went to meet Marcus. He was standing by the ticket machine, and he immediately helped Rose with her bags. When we were in the car, he leaned over to give me a kiss.

"Goodnight, Empress," he said.

"Goodnight, King," I replied.

"What are you two newly-weds like!" Rose says in mock embarrassment.

We drove in relative quiet. Rose was on her phone, as I listened to Marcus talk about his day rigging at the O2. He asked if we could stop by the flat on the way back because he needed to pick up more stuff for his trip. We drove over Tower Bridge, and I could see Battersea Power station in the distance. I tried to engage Rose in the conversation, but she just kept giving one-word answers.

About ten minutes later, we are pulling up outside the terrace Victorian house on a quiet road. I committed the address to memory since I was going to ask a member of the IOM to check whether there have been any call outs to the address.

Surprisingly, Manley opens the door all smiles. He was either watching out for Rose from the window, or Rose had forewarned him of our arrival. I suspected the latter. Vibes cannot lie, despite Manley's friendliness, you could cut the mood or is it fear, with a knife.

Their daughter was still up, and she looked relieved to see her mother. Marcus introduced her to me, and Mary gave me a friendly hug. She took the presents from Rose to hide behind the sofa until the Christmas tree was up next week. She warmed my heart when she said, "Night, night, Uncle Marcus and Auntie Patti" before disappearing upstairs.

"Are you stopping for a cup of tea?" Manley asked. "Come on, I haven't seen you since the wedding!"

Marcus looked at me. He was probably concerned about keeping me out too late since I had another early start in the morning and a group to run in the evening.

"Of course, that's fine I'll help you, Rose," I said brightly. Rose looked at Manley, and when he nodded, we left the brothers to catch up. Rose made small talk loud enough for Manley to hear, while opening the cupboard doors for me to see how empty they were. She switched the kettle on and took out four mugs. I peered outside to see the piles of tin food and a large chest freezer in the far corner of the lean to. Rose looked surprised when she saw a pint of milk in the fridge. Manley joined us at the kitchen table where I was showing Rose photos from the wedding, just candid poses taken by Antoinette's husband Malakai.

I'm sure Manley was hoping to catch Rose and I out doing something wrong. We took our teas back into the front room and made small talk, like how long have you lived here? What are your neighbours like? What do you think of gentrification of the area? What are the local schools like? How well are the girls doing at school? Manley answers my questions, Rose sat there mute. Marcus invited the whole family to my party and said he would text them Veronica's address.

Realizing the time, we had to hit the road. We thanked Rose for her hospitality and Manley closed the door behind us. Something told me the night was just beginning for Rose and my blood ran cold. In the car, I text her on her new phone, **call 999 if you need to.**

CHAPTER EIGHT

CHARMAINE

We missed the train! We took the slow train, which was less crowded, and we are able to talk. When I say 'we,' I meant Jamal Green, the retail manager from Westfield, and when I say, 'We are able to talk,' I meant he was the one doing all of the talking. He can run up his mouth! I must confess, I couldn't take my eyes off his bottom lip, it needs a Chapstick. It was sooooo dry. Every now and then, he fires a question at me, like "What school did you go to?" I answered, "St Angela's" and he's off talking about himself again. He went to St Bonaventure's, the boys' Catholic school, he was head boy.

"Do you have children?" I replied twins but before I could mention that they are fraternal twins, he is off again talking about his daughter, Malia. Apparently when he was at college studying for his A levels, he was in a relationship with a girl who went to my old school, across the road. Long story short, his words not mine, she was pregnant and expected him to give up going to university so he could go out to work and look after them. His parents insisted that he continued with his education, and they would look after the baby. By the time the baby was b they had broken up, but he has found a way to co parent his daughter with her mother for ten years.

"I know you're married." I nodded as he spoke, "But I'm not on that for now. I'd like to travel a bit more. Did you get the chance to travel?"

"Yes, I just came back from Jamaica."

He continues without pausing for breath.

"Yes, you said that in your interview, I'm well Jel. Jamaica is so on my list of places to go to. I've been to Lanzarote and Ibiza."

Beam me up, Scotty! Does he run his mouth by his brain? I went to a funeral, not on a jolly, and Spain is hardly world travel. Between Seven Kings and Goodmayes stations, I managed to tune him out. I was proud of myself today; the old Charmaine would not have applied for a job at Primark. The old Charmaine would have kicked off at the thought of waiting around practically all day for a poxy job interview and the old Charmaine would have boxed him in the mouth and shut it for him. Fortunately for him, he is dealing with the new Charmaine.

I reasoned with myself that if I got the job, I would need an ally, someone who is in a position to offer me shifts, especially with Christmas just around the corner and I had no intention of fucking that up! Is this man still talking? KMT. As my mum would say, his "mout run like sick negro batty". I chuckled to myself. I wanted to speak to her now and tell her how my interview went, but black lumberjack kept talking and talking.

As I prepared to alight at Stratford station, my new BFF says he's meeting up with the lads at Liverpool Street which was the next stop. He wished me a good evening and told me to look out for a text from HR later this evening.

I thanked him and made my way off the train towards Westfield. The platform was heaving with people, but I managed to navigate my way through them and follow the directions to the shopping centre. It was late night shopping, but I guess it was even busier because it was the second to last payday before Christmas. People don't just come up here to shop, they come to Westfield to meet up with friends and socialise as well.

Making the hike over the bridge that crosses over the trains wore me out. I took a moment to rest and use the time to make a call and check in with my mum. I told her about the interview and how I'm on my way to meet up with the ladies at Levi Roots restaurant. I promised her that I'd get his autograph and a photo with him if he's in situ. I sighed with relief to hear that Junior did pick up the children and they are well.

I left the Christmas tree and decoration's box in the lounge with a note, asking Junior to put it up with the kids. I doubt he would do it, but it was worth a try. I knew Mandy was about to drop any minute now and I'm not sure, when it comes, who Junior will prioritise. He wasn't very good in a crisis. I thought back to the birth of the twins. He knew the date I was going into hospital to be induced, yet he had to be dragged from the recording studio, only to come into the labour room late, trying to take charge. My mum was fuming. The midwife told them both to calm down, otherwise she'd call security and get them banned from the entire hospital. The arguing immediately stopped.

Yet when the twins were born, Junior was warm, affectionate, and tender towards me, our children and my mum. He promised to be a better man and a good dad. I wonder what promises he was going to make to Mandy. Would they be promises that he couldn't keep?

~~~~~

I lost my bearings a bit, but I wasn't far away from the restaurant. I might, however, be a few minutes late. I checked my phone; it was just after 6pm. There was a text message from Rose saying she was running late but we should go ahead and order without her. My belly was grumbling loudly, reminding me that my full English breakfast was a long time ago. There was a queue outside the restaurant, but I couldn't see Patti, so I stepped inside to scan the room. Patti waves me over to join them. I indicated this to the manager, and I went over to the corner booth. They looked like they've been Christmas shopping.

"Hey, Charmaine!" Patti said, giving me a hug. "You look great!"

"Well, if it isn't Miss Jamaica 2015!" Antoinette said, making a fuss and hugging me too.

They made room for me to sit down, and I filled them in on my day. I know I've got a lot of mouth, but I felt tongue-tied around these women, like I lacked conversational skills. It's like when I was doing the parenting course, I was frightened of saying the wrong things.

Antoinette ordered champagne to celebrate. Patti had got a promotion, and Antoinette was bigging me up for the having a job interview. We talked about my children, Patti's new job and the wedding, of course. I needn't have worried; these women are very inclusive, and I felt like one of the gang. We ordered a couple of starters to tide us over until Rose arrived. Just then, my phone bleeped with a message, I read it aloud with eager anticipation.

'We are delighted to inform you of the successful outcome of your interview, you will be based at Romford branch.

Confirmation and more details to follow by post. This position is subject to receiving references.'

"I... I got the job!" I stuttered out in disbelief. I was genuinely in shock.

"Congratulations Charmaine. Well done, girlie," said Antoinette.

After 7pm, Rose finally arrived, looking like she had been dragged through a hedge backwards. I could tell she felt a way when she saw how smart we all looked. She kept apologising to us for her lateness, and we kept telling her not to worry about it. We ordered more food and drinks.

Antoinette and Patti gave us new phones! I was so shocked; Christmas had come early. I've never had a new phone before. Whenever Junior got an upgrade, he gave me his old one. I never complained because the phones I inherited were only a couple of years old. I ripped into the box to play with the handset while I listened to Antoinette. My heart almost flipped out of my chest and dropped on my plate when she said to expect a phone call regarding my room at a women's refuge. Even though I wanted to leave, I didn't feel like I was ready. Rose started to cry. Instinctively, Patti halted the conversation taking charge, by saying, "We'll eat first and talk more afterwards."

When the food arrived, Rose suggested that we hold hands to pray, right there, publicly in the people's restaurant. I felt so embarrassed when the other diners looked over at our table. Her faith is unshakeable! I think I have only prayed a couple of times in my entire life. I don't think praying to win the National Lottery counts.

Although I went to a Catholic school, prayer was led by the priest and I just recited and repeated, "Lord hear us" in the appropriate places. Even attending confession was a struggle for me and I stopped going when my dad died. I didn't even know if I believed in God anymore. Yet here was Rose praying for me, Patti and Antoinette and blessing our food.

Thankfully the food is still hot, plentiful, and tasty. Rose tucked into her food, and she even had a glass of bubbly. We ate in silence, and it wasn't awkward, we were just enjoying the food and each other's company. It reminded me of the book I was reading called Waiting to Exhale by Terry McMillan. All the women in the book just chilled out together with no bitchiness.

As we finished our meals, Patti picked up the conversation again. It is like she flipped into business mode. She told us that the most dangerous time for women in our situation was when they were making plans to leave their partners. This was well documented by police statistics. Under no circumstances were we to threaten to leave or even tell family members. Now the latter was hard for me to understand. I could easily conceal a mobile phone. I had loads of secret places to hide money and other bits and pieces indoors, but I was close to my mum, and of late, I updated her on everything I was doing. Reading my expression, Patti explained that once I left, the less our loved ones knew about our whereabouts, the better. Them knowing would put them at risk of harm from the perpetrator as well. I knew after Junior worked out that we escaped, he would go straight to my mum's. And that fact worried me so much, I felt sick.

"I tell you what Charmaine, send me your mum's mobile number, I'll tell her when you're safe and keep her informed," Patti said.

I pulled out my old phone and sent her mum's number.

"That's enough talking for now. If either of you changes your mind about leaving, that's fine."

Patti paused to give the waiting staff time to clear the table. They seem to sense that they have interrupted our conversation.

"Women stay in a domestic violence situation for a number of reasons," she continues. "All you need to know is that Antoinette and I are committed to keeping you and your children safe."

Patti told Rose that she and Marcus would be taking her home and Antoinette said she would drop me off. We were fine with that arrangement. Patti gave Antoinette directions to my place and where to pick up the A13 from there.

"Plan as though Christmas is happening in your homes, keep everything as normal as possible as you prepare your INCH bags." Patti said to Rose and I, "I will send further messages about finances, transportation etc. via the new phones, so don't forget to keep the phones silent and check them for messages at least once a day. These gifts are for the kids."

~~~~~

I was well impressed when I saw the whip my girl, Antoinette, was driving. A Mercedes SLC. Black of course, which suited

Antoinette down to the ground. I wished we could drive with the roof down, but it was bitch ass cold as the temperature plummeted at night. The interior was clearly customised with newly cream polished leather. As we pulled out, I noticed my bottom was getting toasty from the heated seat. The music from Antoinette's in car system was crystal clear. She was playing Agent Sasco's latest album, the track playing was Winning Right Now. I think to myself, *What does this sophisticated woman know about Assassin, the dancehall artist?* Within a few minutes, we are outside my house parked up behind Junior's old BMW. I thanked her for the lift.

"Before you go, may I have a word?"

I took my seat belt off and faced her. "Yeah sure."

"I'll come straight to the point. I was the barrister that represented your husband at court," she paused. "I recognised you when we were in Jamaica, and I think you remember me, too."

"Your face looked familiar at the wedding, but I still couldn't place you until earlier today. Does Patti know?" I asked, sighing and feeling embarrassed.

"Yes, she does, not all of the details due to client confidentiality but your husband is a client of her employers, with her new promotion, she needs to be transparent and let them know."

"Shit!" is the only word I can muster up. So, it was likely Junior's conviction may cause problems for Patti at work? I pondered, how embarrassing.

"Now, don't worry, Charmaine. She has put protocols in place, like restrictive access to his case files so don't sweat."

"OK thanks for letting me know."

She reached over and gave me a hug. "Hey, girlfriend. I got your back!"

"OK, Antoinette," I said, smiling.

I gathered my bags and exited the car. Antoinette's engine purred as she speeds off down the road. I was busy looking for my keys in my pockets when I spotted Marcia standing on her doorstep smoking a cigarette.

"Oh, you look smart. Where are you coming in from so late on a school night, young gal? And who was that in a fancy car? Your new man?" We both laughed.

"Put the kettle on and I'll fill you in," I said, stepping over the short wall that separated her property from mine. Do we drink tea doh? I tell her about the job as she reached for two glasses and a bottle of Wray and his cheeky nephew. We chased our drinks with cola, she switches on her stereo, and we had a bag of man – like John Holt, Beres Hammond and Mikey Spice – serenading us in the lounge. We had a right old natter, and we danced when a back in the day tune hit us. This scene reminded me of my dad; he loved his music.

I felt sad all of a sudden. I was really going to miss Marcia. I swallowed the urge to cry. Marcia had stepped in the middle and separated me and Junior more times than I could remember. She has looked after my children, patched me up, accompanied me to the medical centre and even drove me to A&E after one of our punch ups. She was my ride or die for sure.

She did confess that she had run from Jamaica to the UK to escape the same bullshit from her ex-husband. He sounded like a right brute, and it got worse when he had a stroke. He would seem helpless at medical appointments but always found the strength to beat her with his walking stick. Marcia said his family colluded with him, accused her of playing away from home. All while expecting her to work and look after them in a tiny house outside Mandeville.

But Marcia was good with money, and as soon as she had saved her airfare, she chipped and joined her aunt in London "until she could ketch herself" as she put it. Marcia got her British Citizenship and has been in London for 25 years. The house is all hers, she finally paid off the mortgage last year. All the bills came in her name and not one night does a man sleepover in her bed.

She's never been back to Jamaica, not even for a holiday or for the birth of her grandson. She prefers to send money to her son, who lives in the house with his young family, and when his wicked stepfather died, she even sent money to bury him.

Marcia is good people. The only regret she has was not escaping with her boy Tyrrell. She didn't know what she was running to in the UK, it could quite easily have been jumping from the frying pan into the fire. Her ex-husband's hatred was reserved for her alone, so he was quite safe where he was. Now Marcia was free and safe. She enjoyed her job as a cleaner and happily 'rub a dubbing' with her main man Beres.

~~~~~

When I finally noticed the time, it was after 11pm. I could listen to Marcia's stories all night and I suggested that she should write a book about her life. She accompanied me to her door and said goodnight to me as I fiddled with my door key, pissed as fart. I felt so happy knowing that soon I would have my own money in my purse, no longer financially dependent on Junior.

I got indoors and I put my bags on the floor so I could double lock the door. I was still smiling when I turned and caught sight of a fist coming out of the darkness of the hallway towards my face. I didn't stand a chance. He landed an uppercut with so much venom and force that I rose up from the ground and shot backwards, hitting my head against the door frame. Junior then rained punches about my body, but I couldn't feel them. The last thing I saw was the lights from the Christmas tree. He had put the tree up with the kids!

CHAPTER NINE

ROSE

T he fear of being beaten was actually worse than the beating itself. Once the beating was over, it was over. But the fear of getting a good hiding could last anywhere from a whole day to a couple of weeks but it will come. Manley was playing the long game and he has become very skilled at it, too. He bumped into me with a hot cup of coffee, spilling some of it on my arm. Not enough to scald me, but just enough to burn me and cause me pain. He almost closed the kitchen draw on my fingertips saying sorry but smiling sinisterly.

I had a ritual that I followed every time I went out; my keys in my left coat pocket, my mobile phone and purse in my right pocket. This saved me from carrying a handbag when I'm out and about with baby Esther. I couldn't manage my handbag and Esther's baby bag, too.

It was Thursday morning and Manley volunteered to take the children to nursery and school before he went to work. I wanted to run errands and visit a parishioner's husband in the hospital. I also wanted to pick up my new account card from the bank.

Patti said the most dangerous time for a woman was just before they left, so keep things as normal as possible. Baby Esther and I were practically ready to leave when I went and donned my overcoat and instinctively checked the pockets, my keys were missing. I checked my coat pockets several times, but I know Manley had taken them. I was trapped indoors. I called Manley and told him I have mislaid my keys indoors somewhere and asked if he could pick the children up from nursery at lunchtime.

I used the time to collate the documentation for my INCH bag. I found all of the girls' red books with details of their birth weights, growth charts and immunisations. I sieved through a box of paperwork and found my birth and marriage certificates. I made sure I placed the box back in its rightful place at the bottom of the wardrobe. All of our clothes were going in one suitcase, it was just going to be the necessities. I figured that if I needed anything else, I would use the money Uncle Samuel gave me.

I spent the rest of the time cleaning the inside of the windows, pulling down the net curtains, washing them and putting them back up again. With the funeral and going to Jamaica, I was so behind on my preparations for Christmas. It was my favourite time of year—an important event on the Christian calendar. By now, I would have put up my Christmas curtains and the Christmas tree for the girls. By now, I would have purchased small gifts for the girls to open on Christmas day. I felt like such a failure.

The first thing Manley said when he came home with Ruth and Rebekah is, "Mummy is such a silly billy losing her keys, she would lose her head if it wasn't screwed on!" He tried to pass it off as a joke and the girls laughed along.

I read a message from Charmaine saying she had a fight with Junior, and he had been arrested again. He was due in court in the new year. I deleted the message in case Manley is able to access it. No wonder I had been praying for her and her children. I wondered now that Junior was out of the house if she was still planning to go to the refuge?

I was looking forward to seeing her on Saturday at Patti's party. Marcus had personally invited us, the children included, and made Manley promise to attend. I will find out then if her plans have changed.

~~~~~

I was still cooped up in the house on Friday, putting the tree up. I painstakingly placed every bauble on the tree from yesteryear and switched on the lights. I let Mary balance herself on the arm of the settee to put the star of David in its place. Once the star was secured, I stood back to admire my work. The honest truth was, the tree could do with a new set of decorations, and I promised myself that next year, wherever we happened to be, me and my girls would have a real tree with beautiful decorations.

I saw some beautiful ornaments of black angels on the local news. The TV presenter was talking about black representation and how it was important that black children see themselves in all positive images at Christmastime. The woman had designed a set of black angels for her girls. When Manley caught me watching it, he turned to another channel in my face.

I was trapped in a memory of when my school put on the nativity play. It was decided that the recorder group would be angels that year. I was so excited, until the teacher said there were no black angels in the Bible! My parents were so accepting of that at the time that they didn't challenge the school. I was just happy to dress up in my mum's heavy curtain and wear a tea towel on my head as part of the crowd scenes and sing carols. Fast forward several decades, and my Mary was playing Mary mother of Jesus in this year's nativity play and my Esther was debuting as baby Jesus.

"Are you deaf as well as stupid?" Manley's booming voice made me jump out of my thoughts. "Didn't you hear me woman?" He didn't wait for an answer. "We have fellowship over at Deacon Maurice's home tomorrow and the head pastor and his wife are coming on Sunday after church. Bake a Christmas cake for Friday and kill the fatted calf on Sunday. Do you hear me woman?" I nodded dutifully. "Good."

Manley took his wallet out and threw a few notes on the coffee table. "By the way, I don't know what game you're playing at, but I found your keys...they were in your pocket all this time. I swear you're losing it!" he said harshly. "If you are going to the shops now, wake up the baby and take her with you, she could do with the fresh air." He strolled out the front door, banging it so loudly behind him that it woke Baby Esther up.

~~~~~

After I bought food for Sunday, I washed my hair while two Christmas cakes were being baked in the oven. I used all of the minced raisin, currants and prunes which I had set to ferment in rum last Christmas. The aroma coming from the oven quickly consumed the small kitchen and travelled around the house. I planned to ice one cake with fondant icing for the fellowship's end of year get together and have one on display just in case we had unexpected visitors during Christmas week. As Patti said, keep things normal.

I was up early this morning, pressed my hair and set it in rollers in preparation for tonight. I came upstairs just now and saw my dreadful wig on its stand, mocking me, as though the natural hair growing out of my head wasn't good enough.

"I'm wearing green," Manley stated.

I went to the wardrobe and took out an emerald dress to wear with gold platform heels. I had not worn either of them in a while. I waited for Manley's approval, but he didn't comment. I styled my hair into an up-do style, and I was quite impressed with myself for having a go at it. I heard my mum knocking on the bedroom door.

"Are you two decent?" She came in anyway without waiting. "Good evening, Pastor. Hello, Rose. Mary let me in."

"Hello, Mum," we said in unison.

"I'll be downstairs with the girls," she said, leaving the room.

Manley waited until we were in the car before he started on me again, telling me how mawga I looked and my dress was dated, making me look like an old woman and my nappy head resembled an old dry crocus bag. According to him, I looked dreadful. I wanted to tell him to stop the car so I could get out and make my own way home. I welcomed the darkness of the car so he couldn't see my tears falling.

As we arrived in Clapham, I wiped my eyes and blew my nose on a bit of tissue. Before I got out of the car, I took a deep breath. The cold instantly bit at my bare legs as we stand on the doorstep waiting for the host to answer.

"I hope for your sake you don't embarrass me up in here Rose, you will regret it."

"Welcome, welcome, come in. Don't stand on parade! How are you both doing?" Adanna, Maurice's wife, greeted us in her sing song Trinidadian accent. Without letting us answer, she continued, "One of your delicious cakes Rose? Let me take that for you. Hubby take Rose's coat will you?" I smiled and passed my coat to Maurice.

"Oh, my goodness. Would you look at you in that dress. You look A-maz-ing. Your waist is just snatched," Adanna remarks all animated, balancing my cake in one hand and gesturing up and down my body with the other. "Manley is such a blessed man."

She continued chatting as she pulled me towards the back of her beautiful home.

"I hope I get my figure back after this one, I feel like a beached whale! And don't get me started on your style! Classic, sophisticated, and very much en vogue. You started a revolution in church last Sunday. Were you aware?"

Again, I didn't get the chance to reply, and I was somewhat taken aback by her barrage of compliments. "Let me introduce you to our friends."

I was shocked by the number of guests in the room as Manley and I were introduced at the party. We shook hands and greeted everybody. Not all the couples were from our church, but we are all part of the same church family. Quite a few folks recognised me from my sermonette and dancing video in Jamaica, which had gone viral. I quickly shuffled on to greet the next person, hoping Manley didn't get upset.

I have to say, Adanna had put on a lovely spread of Trinidadian and Jamaican fusion food, all presented so exquisitely on her dining room table in chafing dishes.

"So, on these platters, we have Pholpurie, aloo pies, and accra," she looked at my confused face.

"Accra is like the Jamaican fritters, only better!" she laughed. "Under the dishes we have..." she lifted each dish to check. "...yes, we have prawn curry, baked chicken, veggie pelau and channa." I followed her down to the end of the table. "And the pièce de résistance.... roti and buss up shot."

My tummy groaned, craving the aromatic food.

"But when did you get the time to do all this?" I was so impressed.

"Fancy a cocktail?" she asked, crossing her kitchen to the cupboards, reaching for two martini glasses. "It's a Trini cocktail Rose, non-alcoholic, of course."

"Yeah, why not, it's nearly Christmas."

Adanna grabbed some crushed ice from the dispenser of her huge American style fridge freezer. She opened a can of cream soda and poured the drink into our glasses. Next, the woman opened a tin of carnation milk, poured it in as she stirred with a cocktail stick.

"Look at God, Sister Rose. This is like drinking nectar and just as sweet, hence I made it in a martini glass and not a tumbler." I wasn't keen but I took the glass from her and took a sip. "Ah, what a way dat drink nice!" she groaned, and we both laughed.

Maurice and Manley joined us in the kitchen. "Oh, you've introduced Rose to our favourite drink?"

Adanna passed her husband her glass as he tenderly held her around her bulging waist. The tenderness between them was heart-warming and a tad embarrassing too. Manley tried to do the same to me, but I flinched at his touch and moved away from him.

"Go back inside and let me fix you a plate Manley," I said. He and Maurice did so as I dutifully prepared his plate.

Adanna filled the silence, "My family are caterers, they have restaurants in North West London. I placed an order for tonight and they turned up and set everything up!"

I turned and looked at her.

"Good for you honey. No judgement here."

"Yes," she said, flicking her long jet-black hair over her shoulder. "I take all the help I can with four boys. I don't even have time to tidy the house. The boys' schedules are busier than mine. Take earlier today for example. The boys had swimming lessons, Kumon maths and piano lessons. It's like that most Fridays. I'm so glad it is Christmas next week so I can get a break. I have a woman originally, from Grenada, who comes in once a week and does my cleaning for me. She even changes the beds once every two weeks."

"That is amazing, Adanna!"

"Happy wife, happy life, that's what I say." She raised her glass towards me, and then drains the contents.

Manley never misses a chance to compare me with this woman, when she has a cleaner and outside help. I've been hating on Adanna for no reason at all.

As we joined our husbands, they were debating a well-known passage of the Bible. I hand Manley his plate, a fork and napkin. Then ate with my fingers, using pieces of the buss up shot roti to scoop up the juicy king prawns and hot curry sauce.

I still hadn't eaten properly since Westfield Wednesday. Mary and Rebekah had taken to leaving me food on their plates so I could eat once Manley has left the dining table. With the constant put downs and name calling, I know they were worried about me. They had also asked their father why I hadn't taken them to school lately. This was why it was imperative that I get me and my girls out. It was a stressful environment, and I was scared that he would turn on my children and start hitting them.

Over the years, I have heard this debate over and over, should women obey or submit to their husbands. It was a derisive argument set to divide opinions between the men and women in the room. It was working and things quickly escalate. Of course, Manly implied that females should submit to their husbands in every way, but I kept my own counsel.

"Rose, you're very quiet, what do you think?" someone asked.

I felt as if I was put on the spot, so I took a sip of my cocktail and answered as best as I could. "Well, I'm no scholar...I didn't go to Bible school, but the Apostle Paul wrote several letters to the Ephesians at a time when the early church needed instructions for the period they were in. For example, Paul talks about children obeying their parents and none of us would disagree with that?" The group nodded. "But further on in the same chapter, he writes about slaves obeying their masters. Surely none of you are advocating we return to slavery?" Everybody agreed and started chattering at the same time.

"What I'm saying is, every courting couple should have a discussion about what submission is and do what works for them."

"What about women taking high profile positions in the church?" One of the brothers piped up.

I waited for Manley to answer but Adanna looked at me for a reply.

"I don't agree with women becoming pastors or deacons. Their job is to support their husbands and look after the family," Manley said, looking smug.

"What do you think, Rose?" asked Adanna. "If the woman has worked hard in the church, why not recognise her contribution in the same way you would a man?"

"When I grew up in my uncle's church in Jamaica, the sisters often took up leadership roles because there were no men! A lot of churches in Jamaica would have closed if the women in the congregation didn't step up."

Manley was about to interrupt me, so I said, "I quite like the scripture Galatians 3 verse 28 that talks about the church as being neither Jewish nor Greek, slave or free, male or female. Paul was talking about equality, way before phrases like diversity and unconscious bias were coined.

Everybody laughed except for Manley.

"But you threw off your wig in frustration. Was that a defiant move by you to protest against how women are expected to act in church?" a young sister asked me. I had the room and I thought about my answer.

"I'm sorry sis, remind me of your name?" She looked a little wary of me.

"My name is Nicole and this is my husband, Daniel."

"Ahhh lovely...Nicole, I do not use the pulpit to make political statements. In that moment, while I was asking the church to get closer to God, I was reminded that I was created in His image and the last time I checked, no offence to anybody here, I wasn't born with 21-inch Remi hair! That realisation and desire to be my authentic self, made me take my wig off. Little did I know that my sisters followed my lead and did the same. They probably went looking for their wigs in the lost and found box after the service."

There was laughter in the room again.

"That service went viral on social media, too," Nicole said.

"Can we watch it?" another woman asked.

"That would be so cool! Maurice, set it up on the big TV. Rose, have you got a minute?" I prised my hand away from Manley's grip and I followed her out of the room. We went up to her bedroom.

"What a beautiful space!" I said in astonishment.

"Thank you, Rose. Take a seat." I did so at her dressing table chair, noticing she has every lotion that Avon had in stock and seven polystyrene heads, six with wigs still attached to them.

"Ahhhh you've noticed my girls. They have names too," she said, flopping on her king size bed and pointing at each wig in turn. "Monday, Tuesday, Wednesday, Thursday, Saturday and Sunday. As you can see, I'm wearing Friday at the moment."

I was flabbergasted. All this time I thought the jet black wavy hair was her natural hair inherited from her father's side of the family. She constantly referred to her family originating from India and travelling to Trinidad in the mid 1940's.

"I would have loved to cast my wig to the floor like you did, but I couldn't. My children would have been so embarrassed and here's why."

She removes her wig to show me her bald head. I gasp and get up to hug her when she spoke.

"Rose, I do not need you to pity me." I sat back down.

"I had a full head of hair when you visited our church and Manley introduced you to me as his fiancé. I was really hoping that you and I would become friends. After all, Maurice and Manley were childhood friends. I imagine someone got to you first and mentioned I was after Manley, and it was true."

Adanna covered her mouth smiling shyly.

"I have always had time for a dark skin brother, to my mother's dismay. When I introduced Maurice to the family, they were not impressed at all. Firstly, he was Jamaican, and that was a big no-no. My mother said, 'With the whole of the men in Trinidad, you had to go to England to find a Jamaican man?'" Adanna exaggerated her Trini accent. "Then she said, she was concerned about how black he was. Can you believe that? Little did mummy know that any man that approached me had to be at least ten minutes to midnight before I would even give him a chance."

She laughed, reminiscing.

"Most concerning was Maurice being a born-again Christian. Our family were Sikhs. They weren't practising or anything since they jumped up in Carnival like everybody else, but they wanted me to tow the party line and I was stubborn. I guess the stress of planning my wedding without their support really got to me. Every day I woke up to clumps of my good hair on my pillowcase. Even with the specialist, the dietitian and herbalist, I saw during that time, my condition still got worse. I was diagnosed with alopecia shortly after my wedding.

"I knew Maurice was the man for me when I showed him my head and he still wanted to marry me. He pays for all my wigs to be custom made by a beautiful sister named Juliet." We were both quiet for a while, each woman in her own thoughts.

"I am sorry if I made you feel any type of way, Adanna. That was not my intention."

"Definitely not, Rose. I haven't shared this with anybody outside my family and I wanted you to know... you're special, Rose. Chosen."

"What do you mean chosen?" I asked, feeling nervous.

"Matthew 22 verse 14 For many are called but few are chosen."
I was familiar with the verse.

"I didn't go to Bible school," she said, mocking me, "and I'm
only a woman..." We smiled at each other. "...but I interpret that
scripture so differently from everybody else." I must have looked
confused. "Let me explain."

She reached for a pillow and made herself more comfortable.

"Manley is called. He's a minister, his father was a minister, his
grandfather was a minister and so forth, not so?" Adanna was right,
the Morgan's can trace their lineage back to the plantations.

"Hopefully Mary will become a minister too...if you don't have
a boy." I felt slighted but I didn't want to stop Adanna's flow.

"But you are chosen, Rose. Every time you speak, you have
an impact in the church and beyond. God has chosen you to do
so much more than being Manley's wife and the mother of his
children. When the scripture talks about a chosen generation, it
was talking about men and women like you. Do not let anyone
come between you and your mission." She lets that sink in.

"Here endeth the sermon for today. Help me off the bed and put
Friday back on my head."

I looked at our reflections in the mirror. Adanna was beautiful
with and without her wig. All this time Manley and a couple of
horrid women have led me to believe she is my rival when she
has been an ally from the beginning.

After re-joining the group, we played several games of charades
and listened to tracks by Freddie Hammond and Kirk Franklin.
Manley announced that we were leaving, and Adanna loaded me
up with roti, giving me instructions on how to freeze it. She also
gave me a large container of chicken curry. After dreading coming
out, it had turned out to be a lovely evening. I was on a natural
high that I had found a friend in Adanna.

"What were you two upstairs talking about?" Manley demanded
accusingly.

"Just girlie talk," I said, trying to keep my voice even.

"You see how she keeps that house so clean? You could eat your
dinner off that floor!'

"Yes, she has a cleaner, the woman comes in once a week."
Manley took his eyes off the road to look at me. I could tell he
is surprised.

"Well, the spread was scrumptious. You cannot argue with that, Adanna can cook."

"She probably can, but tonight's festive buffet was made by caterers." Manley took his eyes off the road in disbelief for a second time.

"What?" He was getting annoyed, to the point where he started driving aggressively, changing gear and speeding up.

"Yes, she gave me their business card, it's in my purse. You need to stop comparing us, Manley. It has always upset me, but no more."

If looks could kill, I would be dead. He sped up, doing more than 40 mph through the streets. I felt anxious.

"Slow down, Manley!" I cautioned him. "You're driving too fast!"

He scoffed.

"If you don't like it, get out of my car."

"Yes, let me out!"

He looked at me to see if I was serious and he screeches the car to a halt by the side of the road. I got out of the car, bringing my food containers with me. The cold air hits me like a brick wall. There was nobody around and I could hear my heels as they clink along the pavement. Manley drove off around the block as I headed towards the high road. I guess I was about two hundred metres away from home. Not far at all, a five-minute drive in the car, but a fifteen-minute walk in high heels in Winter.

I was sure Manley would come back for me because he could not go home without me. The first thing my mum will ask was where I am. As I predicted, Manley sped around the corner, he slowed down beside me, rolled down the passenger car window and yelled at me.

"Get back in the car, Rose!" I kept walking and didn't answer. "Stop being stupid!"

I continued, ignoring him. I knew I was going to be in for a kicking when I got back indoors but I was beyond caring. Manley suddenly drove off at full speed, imitating Louis Hamilton racing in Monaco. *One of these days he is going to end up wrapping that car around a lamp post*, I think to myself as his car light faded out of sight.

I looked into all the houses lit up with Christmas lights, thinking about the people who may live there, looking forward to Christmas. All of a sudden, one of the dustbins spilt over and crashed with a bang on the pavement. My heart jumped into my mouth. I saw a skulk of foxes escape from behind the bins to cross the road. Urban foxes were quite a common sight in London. The vixen looked heavily pregnant as she stood in the middle of the desolate road, like a lollipop woman escorting her cubs across the road. Look at that, where is the male fox? Even in nature, the female is doing it all on her own.

As I reached the top of my street, I saw an ambulance parked up about halfway down my road. I quickened my steps, warm air forming fog every time I exhaled. To my horror, our Ford Focus had collided with the lamp post opposite our drive. As I approached, I saw the front passenger side has caved in, it was unrecognisable. Fifteen minutes ago, I was sitting there arguing with Manley. Now he was lying bent over the steering wheel with the airbag deployed. Members of the fire brigade from Battersea fire station were trying to get him out. I dropped my food containers and ran towards them.

CHAPTER TEN

PATTI

T hursday morning started off well. Waking to enjoy an interlude with my husband. Marcus dropped me off at the office nice and early. I picked up my messages and I was upset to learn that Charmaine had been to the hospital after an altercation with Junior. She had a split lip and concussion, then discharged. That man really was a nasty piece of work. At least he was bailed to another address pending investigation, hopefully he'll be arrested and charged.

I went online to make an appointment with my GP, and to my surprise, there was an available slot today, a miracle! I send an email to Beverley, inviting her to have dinner with me on Friday night. For obvious reasons, she had declined the invitation to my party, and I understood that she didn't want to bump into Junior's wife again. Who knows what Charmaine might have thrown at her next time; hot cooking oil? Petrol? No, Bev and I will meet up privately and have our own celebration.

It took me a while to get back into my groove, but I managed to countersign several assessments and rolled one back to a new officer for improvement. I had a phone call from reception to say a police officer was there to see me. It was Detective Constable Wilson from Camden Police Station. We both previously sat on The Multi-Agency Safeguarding Hub. The MASH brought together key professionals to facilitate better quality information sharing on vulnerable children and young people more effectively.

She explained one of our service users, a Mr. Cross, was in custody for a sexual offence. He claimed he was here at probation, at the time of the offence. The detective requested to speak to his supervising officer. I immediately check the suspect's name on the computer, he is known to one of my probation service officers, Rihanna. I pick up the phone to call reception. I am surprised to hear Beverley's voice. "Hey, Bev. I have a police officer with me at the moment. Can you do me a favour please?"

"Sure, go ahead." I give her the name and date of birth of the suspect.

"He said he had an appointment with Rihanna Smith at 2 yesterday, but can you check the diary for the whole day in case he saw another colleague please?"

"Yep, I'm on it."

Turning to the detective, I told her, I would fetch Rihanna. Rihanna was able to quickly confirm that Mr Cross did have an appointment with her, but he failed to attend. Beverley then called to confirm Mr Cross did not attend Camden office the day before.

After escorting the officer out of the building, I worked on disposing old confidential paperwork and sorting through staff case files for my successor. I was in a reflective mood. When the dream team; Jerome, Steve and I arrived after the last restructure, Camden was one of the poor performing offices. In two short years, we had turned things around, picking up awards along the way. I was going to miss everybody here.

~~~~~

I needed to leave the office at 2pm to get to my doctor on time for my appointment. As I was leaving the office, a woman came into reception with a young man, I assumed was her son. She asks to see a manager. We lock eyes through the reception glass and I tell Beverley, that I have 5 minutes before I need to leave. I escort them to an empty interview room, taking the seat nearest the door.

"Thank you for seeing my nephew and I," the woman says. She was a mature black woman, plump with hair greying at the temples of her forehead. "You looked like you were on your way out?" She inquired. Before I can respond, the young man pipes in saying

"More like skiving off for the rest of the day." He was so rude. Both me and his aunt look at him. I take him in before answering. He was the stereotype of a typical young Londoner. Wearing a baggy dark tracksuit pulled down low exposing his underpants, with matching hoodie.

"I wish. I'm working from another office this afternoon, finishing at 9 tonight." I watch his face fall apart in disbelief and the woman looks so embarrassed. "What can I help you with?"

The poor woman had her nephew living with her since his release from Thameside Young Offenders Institution. He received a letter informing him a warrant was issued for his arrest, for failing to appear at court. He can prove he was in prison at the time. They were uncertain about what to do next. I suggested that he surrender himself at his nearest police station today. He would probably be detained overnight to appear in court the following morning. He was reluctant to do that.

Alternatively, I suggested he appear at court in the morning, with a copy of his licence. Again, he would be detained but his case would be dealt with that day. What he didn't want to do is do nothing and risk the police showing up in their numbers at his aunt's house, threatening to break her front door down. His aunt promised to escort him to court the following morning and I promised her that I would notify probation at court to look out for him.

~~~~~

Thankfully, when I arrive at the doctor's surgery the doctor, I was due to see, was running late. Doctor Singh wasn't my usual doctor, but I was grateful to be seen. He advised me to undress behind the curtain from the waist up while he called for a health assistant to act as a chaperone during my examination.

"Ms Scotland, I am going to refer you to a consultant at the hospital. I can feel one lump, but a scan will tell us more. Pick up a choose and book form from reception and try not to worry."

I dressed quickly and went to the bus stop to wait for a bus into Ilford. I drew my wrap coat around me, feeling cold. The weather had dropped a few degrees since this morning. I was born and bred in the UK, but I still couldn't get used to the Winter months. I could quite easily hibernate until next Spring. Where was a hot flush when I really need one? I sucked my back teeth.

I took off one of my gloves to Google my private healthcare provider on my phone. I figured I was paying the premiums every month, so why not use it. I dialled the number, and I was surprised when the receptionist offered me an appointment at Roding Hospital on Monday morning. Most people were trying to fend everybody off until the new year. I took the appointment, which he said he would confirm by text message and send me directions. I had a rough idea of where it was since it is only walking distance away from my home.

I didn't have to wait very long for the bus, and I sat at the back so I could check the emails on the work's mobile phone. I alighted at Ilford which was packed with the hustle and bustle of shoppers. One mother with a trailer load of children getting on her nerves let me know that the kids were already off school for the festive period. She snapped at them in her mother tongue, which given the demographics of the borough could be Urdu, Bengali, Gujarati or Punjabi. The children quickly stopped what they were doing, only to start misbehaving as soon as her back was turned. I stopped to buy a copy of the Big Issue, the magazine sold by homeless people. The young woman was grateful when I told her to keep the change and she wished me a Merry Christmas.

I entered Mark's to buy a Christmas present for Gemma and her family. Inside the shop was packed but I persevered. I paid for a luxury tin of Scottish shortcake biscuits and exited the shop via the self-service tills. I made my way through the Christmas market and my tummy rumbled with the aroma of hot dogs, burgers, and curries. I hoped Gemma's mum knew I was co-facilitating the group with her daughter and has sent me a plate of food.

~~~~~

The Ilford office is situated at the end of the high street near the council offices, opposite Ilford police station. It was one of the newer purpose built probation buildings which HRH Princess Anne opened.

After checking in at reception, I was given a fob and I made my way to the first floor, scanning the office for a hot desk. It was like the Mary Celeste, absent of staff and managers too. I suspected the facilitators were either running groups, or in meetings planning groups. I chose a desk and stripped off my coat and gloves. Retrieving a manual from the cabinet, I familiarised myself with the session. I was happy to help Pippa cover the sessions and I sympathise with her acute staffing problems, but I know with my promotion, I won't be delivering groups anymore.

As promised, I fired up my laptop and sent an email to my colleagues at Highbury Corner Magistrate's Court. I hoped the young man surrendered himself at court in the morning. When I was caught up with everything, I rang Mr Man, he picked up straight away.

"Yesssss, Empress and how art thou this evening?"

"I'm OK, darling," I said in warm tones. "I'm at Ilford office...where are you?"

"Mi deya, still at O2," he replied. He seemed distracted, I could hear Christmas music in the background.

"I'm up a cherry picker at the moment rigging some lights. You know how it goes."

I have a flash of Marcus off the ground at a dangerous height and I felt sick.

"Marcus, you know you shouldn't be answering the phone!"

"Mi alright, girl. I have to answer the phone to my wife." His comment warmed my heart.

"Well, please be careful. I'll see you later?"

"Yeah man. I'll be parked up on the side road at 9pm. Love you!"

"I love you, too, Hun."

I waited for him to hang up then I sent texts to Yolanda, Rose, and Charmaine. The latter two were expecting a call from the women's refuge any day now. Yolanda got back to me straight away. She was with her nan, preoccupied with whatever Veronica had her doing. Probably cleaning. I chuckled to myself.

Gemma walked in about half an hour later, dressed in her winter coat and hat, dragging a laptop trolley bag containing what I hoped was our dinner. We greeted each other like lovers. Gemma gave the best hugs.

"Season's Greetings, Patti!" she screamed, still hugging me.

"Yeah, girlfriend. Merry Christmas, Gemstone."

We caught up on each other's lives. Gemma was dating and I couldn't be happier for her. Well, Gemma's mum did not disappoint me at all. We had stew chicken, rice n peas, fried plantain, coleslaw and salad. The food was room temperature, so we warm it up in the microwave. We watched it spin around in silence as the appliance hummed away.

"What is it with black people and microwaves?" asked Gemma, "We don't feel good unless there's an actual flame glowing in the middle of the plate,"

We both laughed.

"Girlllll! I don't know," I replied, thinking of Veronica. She thought the microwave was the best invention in the world, since the Dutch pot and pressure cooker. I was sure that the latter two were older than me. Veronica always said "Ya cyan rush good food!" Meaning, good food took a long time to prepare and cook, but she loved warming up leftovers in the microwave.

I could imagine right about now, Veronica was in her element, at home, preparing to cook up a storm for my party on Saturday. I mentioned getting caterers in and suggested the same caterers who were doing the food for my leaving party at the office, but she was not having it. I knew mum had her circle of friends who will help her out. Her sister, Aunt Cynti, made the best fried fish in the world.

I added salad and coleslaw to my plate and waited for Gemma's food to warm up. "You are coming on Saturday, right?" I asked, panicking. I can't remember if Gemma and her family had replied to my invitation.

"Patti, we wouldn't miss it for the world. And you know your mum has got my mum doing the curry goat!"

We sat down to eat. I scoffed the food down, enjoying the hot spicy flavours on my tongue. The plantain in particular is very sweet. I was acutely aware of the fact that I haven't eaten anything since breakfast.

We had one hour before the session, so we moved quickly. We set up two rooms, one for the group and the smaller room with the monitoring equipment. All sessions were recorded to ensure that we, the facilitators, were sticking to the integrity of the programme. Our performances were scored at a later date by the treatment manager.

By 6:15pm we were ready to rock-n-roll. Gemma had an advantage over me because she had been working with this group for quite some time. But it was a rolling programme, meaning participants were able to join the programme at any point. The only closed session was the session about sexual abuse.

Gemma took responsibility for the register. She told me we were expecting two more men this evening for our session. I made us hot drinks while, Gemma went downstairs to get the participants. I tried to be as upbeat as possible when the men came in, allowing them to make themselves hot drinks. Some of the men had come to group straight from work, so they appreciated a hot drink and a biscuit.

At 6:30pm, I introduced myself to the group and we started the session. Late-comers had ten minutes to join the session before the cut-off point. Every session of the group started with a check in. The facilitator went around the group asking the men to check in by answering questions written up on the flip chart. The man furthest to my right started to talk, obviously a long-standing member of the group.

"My name is Clyde, my ex is Natalie, we have four children...............there have been no incidents or offending since the last time I was here, and I have not drunk alcohol or taken drugs in the last 24 hours," he smiled triumphantly.

Gemma returned the smile and asked about his daughter's school play. "It was really good, you know..." he turned to address his peers. "My daughter was the narrator in the school nativity play," he beams with pride. "I have a video clip on my phone, I'll show you at the break."

"Wonderful," Gemma said. She was obviously delighted for him. I guess he may have recently renewed contact with his daughter. In my experience, fathers not having contact with their children was a big issue in domestic abuse cases. Gemma moves on to the next person as I made a few notes on my pad, his name and how he presents.

"My name is Mustafa. My wife's name is Miriam. We have a baby son together. No incidences. No arrests. I do not imbibe alcohol or take drugs." His voice was stern, Gemma smiled but he doesn't return her smile.

Gemma told me all about him when we were planning the session. He told his story last week, his wife was a local solicitor, commanding a lot of respect in her profession and in their community. They got into an argument about money. He told the group that she pressed his buttons, and he only gave her a few slaps for answering him back.

The facilitators knew he broke her cheekbone and social services were involved because of concerns for their unborn child following their presentation at A&E. By the time he appeared in court for sentencing, her family had persuaded her to go back to him and not bring shame to the family name. Miraculously, he escaped a custodial sentence. We were going to unpick his fixed beliefs, minimisation and blame during this session.

We are approximately eight minutes into the group, when there was a knock at the door, all eyes watched as the late comer entered the room. He was clearly enjoying the attention. He looked up and our eyes locked, it was pissing Junior Morgan.

CHAPTER ELEVEN

CHARMAINE

*T*here is no light at the end of a tunnel and no one to greet me. I am in a dark place, but I'm not scared. There is something strangely familiar about where I am. The room is warm and what's that smell? It's a scent that I used to wear......when I was back at school. I sniff the air again. It's white musk. The alarm clock going off startles me, and as I reach to switch it off, a hand beats me to it, annoyed. A door swings open and a voice says,

"Good morning Charmz, the bathroom is free."

I am confused. This cannot be right. The hand reaches out to switch on a bedside lamp and the room is flooded with light. I am standing in my childhood bedroom at my mum's house. I scan the room, taking in the single bed, the small dresser and matching wardrobe. Magazines are stacked in one corner over by the window. Above my bed is a poster of the Heartless crew; Mighty Mo, DJ Fonti and my crush Bushkin. While my school friends spent their breaks learning the steps to the Pussycats Dolls routine, I stayed loyal to my garage crew.

My younger self rises from the bed, dutifully kisses Bushkin on his full lips, then grabs her towel and heads for the bathroom. All of this feels so real. My dressing table is crammed with lotions and perfumes my mum got me, samples from running her Avon catalogue. All probably discontinued now. My wardrobe is packed with clothes I did not want to wear. I wanted crop tops like the girls on the Heartless Crew videos, but my dad put his foot down, saying those outfits made me look too womanish.

After he died, I traded clothes and make-up with my new mates and switched from garage to dancehall music. I hope my dad isn't spinning in his grave.

The next moment, my younger self is sitting at the breakfast table. My mum is at the stove with her back to me. Even from this angle, in the hall, I can see she is slimmer than I ever remembered. My younger self is eating a bowl of cereal in silence, listening intently to the radio. Britney Spears is belting out 'Hit Me Baby One More Time'. When my dad walks into the room, I want to rush to him and hold him, so much so I think my heart will break, but I cannot move. My younger self barely looks up to say "Good Morning."

"You going back to work again?" Mum asks.

"Yes love, mi 'ave no choice, the project has to be completed by next week."

"Anybody can see how tired you are...Len," mum says, placing a plate of hard food and mackerel in front of him.

"I know. When this job pays up, I'll drop the night work," he sighs.

My younger self wrinkles her nose at the heavily scented food.

"Oh, my days, who eats fish, yam, green banana and dasheen for breakfast? That's dinner, not breakfast!" I protest.

"You think a bowl of Sugar Puffs can keep me fill 'hole day, Charmaine?" he asks, patting his belly.

We all laugh. I am scratching my head to remember the conversation. Dad eats quickly and he kisses mum, then my younger self before reaching for his flask and heading out of the door. I am willing myself to follow him, to look at his handsome face and tell him not to leave, as I now realise today is the last day I will see my dad before he dies. To this day, I think of my dad when mum makes dad's favourite breakfast for our dinner.

In the blink of an eye, I am at St Angela's, my secondary school. The school uniform was a dark brown pleated skirt, a yellow polo shirt and a brown matching blazer with yellow piping around the edges. The uniform was awful.

Whilst my classmates pimped up their uniforms to look trendy, I looked like a hot mess. Mum would not let me relax my hair, so I made my skirt shorter en route to school by doubling the waistband over until the hem was resting on my thigh. I wore white over the knee socks and far too much perfume. My favourite at the time was White Musk from the Body Shop.

I am seated at a desk at the front of the class in Sister Calder's maths lesson. On the eve of starting year 7 at secondary school, my dad had warned me to sit at the front of the class so I would not be distracted by those who did not want to learn, take notes, ask questions—there was no such thing as a stupid question, and lastly to start my homework on the day it was given. After my dad died, I did not care anymore and the further back I sat in class, the worse my grades became. My younger self was completing my work without a care in the world. Little does she know, her life is going to change forever.

I stand in the corner of the classroom, observing her like an Ofsted inspector. On cue, Monique comes into the classroom with a note and my younger self is instructed to go to the head of year's office. Younger me reluctantly grabs her books and stationery, puts everything into my old Adidas satchel, and follow Monique down the halls.

I sit on one of the chairs next to my younger self. Moments later, I watch as my younger self runs down the hall, straight for the exit. She is quick as I run after her. Fortunately, I know exactly where she is going. She is heading for the park. I sit next to her on the park bench while she is bawling her eyes out. I cannot console her, I feel useless. I am joined on the bench by a man.

"Charmaine!" It's my dad. "I'm talking to you."

"Daddy, can you see me?" I ask, reaching for him.

"Of course, I can love," he says, cradling my body and resting his chin on my head. I inhale his cologne, Old Spice.

"They said you were dead! I don't understand."

I pull my head back to look into his warm brown eyes.

"Listen, child. I am dead."

"Am I dead, too, dad? Have you come to take me with you?"

"No child, you are very much alive, but that's what I have come to warn you about. You let that man hit you one more time and he will kill you! You have children to save and children to raise. What do you think will become of my gran kids without their mother? You get back home and take the opportunity to get my grans and get out of there, ya hear me?"

I nod.

"I love you, daddy!"

"Mi know. Mi love you, too."

~~~~~

I couldn't move but I could hear everything.

"You fucking gone and done it now!" I hear Stepper saying. "I'm tired of telling you to stop putting your hands on her."

"But she's taking the piss out of me, got some next geezer in some posh car dropping her off. Kissing him and everything. I just gave her a slap and she hit her head against the door, I swear I didn't mean it."

"That doesn't sound like Charmaine at all, but even if she has a man, I wouldn't blame her, you treat her like shit. Fortunately for you, she's still breathing but we're going to have to call an ambulance mate, that wound to her head looks like it might need stitches."

"Nah, Stepper. No ambulance. That would bring Babylon right to mi yard and I'm already on probation!"

"You called me because you thought you killed her, I'm not a medical professional but this looks serious." Stepper opened his phone. I could hear Junior pacing the floor and cussing.

"I can't do time, bruv. I can't do time."

I heard Stepper tell the dispatcher my address. I pried open my eyes. I had a splitting headache, and I was seeing double.

"It's OK, Charmz. It's Stepper. An ambulance is on its way." I closed my eyes again.

When the police arrived, Junior was sitting slumped in an armchair nursing a rum. He was arrested as the paramedics checked me out. As they lead him away, I heard Marcia cussing him off. She told the officers that he beats me all the time.

"Shut your bloodclaart mouth," Junior yelled.

"Or what you piece of shit? You think you can beat me like you beat her? You couldn't let the girl have one nice day? I hope this time they lock your rass up! You pussyhole!"

Junior tried to retaliate but he was overpowered by the officers as he shouted his parting message.

"The next time I see you, Charmaine, I'm going to fucking kill you!"

The paramedics were concerned about a neck injury. They had put me in a neck brace, and I was so shocked they put me on a gurney and took me outside. The whole street was up and out in their nightclothes.

Three police vans, four police cars and loads of officers littered the street. Anybody would think they are responding to a terrorist attack. This was a clear example of why some black women did not call the police to intervene. Their response was always over the top and heavy handed.

I was conveyed to Newham General Hospital A&E department. Marcia stayed with my children and Stepper never left my side. Twelve stitches and a CAT scan later, I discharged myself from hospital. I just wanted to be at home with the kids and come hell or high water, I was going to start that job Monday morning.

Stepper told me that Junior had spent the night at Plaistow police station, but he would be released on police bail. He was going to be staying at Stepper's in Chingford. His missus wasn't pleased with Junior coming to stay, but he can't come anywhere near me. The plan was that Stepper would collect his clothes and the police were coming to take my statement in the next few days.

My mum was livid when she found out. I think if Junior was in front of her, she would take the nearest knife and sink it into his chest. Imagine that outcome, taking my children to the cemetery to see their dad and passing by Holloway prison to see my mum!

With the support of my mum and Marcia, I took my painkillers and slept for as long as possible, knowing my children were safe. I was supposed to go to Patti's party on Saturday, but I wasn't up for it. I felt like shit. I'd come on my period as well and the stomach cramps were killing me. Patti was very understanding, giving me the option to stay put if I wanted and to call off leaving Junior, but I still want to leave him, get me and the kids as far away from him as possible.

Rose was crying down the phone when we eventually got to talk. Patti said that Manley was pretending to be a saint when he was talking to Marcus about it, saying he was going to have words with Junior. Like he can talk.

~~~~~

With my ears still ringing, I presented myself at Romford Primark. Happy to see Monday morning. After more form filling, I helped a colleague in the men's department. We are tearing off barcodes and marking down all of the Christmas Jumpers. The store had led a successful Christmas jumper campaign and the few remaining jumpers were for people looking for a last minute deal to wear on Christmas day. The store heaved with customers all day, and the Christmas songs were driving me around the bend. If I hear Merry Christmas Everyone by Slade one more time... I'm sure it's making my headache worse. It's 4pm when I get to the tills. I help my colleagues with bag packing as I am yet to be trained to use the tills.

I work consecutively for the next three days. Yesterday evening, Muhammad asked for volunteers to work at Westfield Stratford and I eagerly put my hand up. I figured I would attend the kid's nativity play in the morning, then work a late shift. Given the festive period, most shops didn't close until 10pm. It's 1pm on Thursday, I presented to the manager's office, and I was delighted to see Jamal. He was very professional, not letting everybody know that he knows me, and I am cool with that.

He's put me to work with two others in the women's department. Most of the clothes were thrown across the floor and items were dumped in the wrong places. Jamal also made me aware that I was the only first aider until later that day. I worked solidly for four hours in the department, taking one break. It is a good distraction from recent events, keeping myself busy.

By now, the police had taken my statement. I found the policewoman worse than the male officer. Her eyes kept darting around the yard like I'd stolen something. I suspected that my home was nicer than her gaff and I was waiting to cuss her off, if she'd dared to ask me where I got my stuff from or how I could afford it. I was the victim of a vicious assault, how dare she treat me like a criminal! Nope, I wasn't going to have any of it. The male officer did let me know that Junior was charged with GBH and due to appear at Stratford Magistrates Court in the New Year.

~~~~~

I liked my job, it's only been a few days, but I was already counting the money in my pocket and spending it too. I was going to take driving lessons and put aside some for my driving test as soon as possible. It's about time I got my licence and I'll get myself a little run around vehicle, like a Corsa, Cleo or Fiesta.

"Can we have a first aider to the third floor please!" The call over the tannoy was more of a command than a request. I let my co-workers know that I was leaving the department and I made my way to the third floor. There were a few yellow cones warning customers to avoid a slippage which I nearly step into myself. Someone had spilled a clear fluid on the floor.

As I walked into the baby & nursery department, I saw a man crouched down, rubbing the back of a heavily pregnant woman who is sitting on a chair outside the staff room. It is obvious her water had broken. I took her in, not being funny but pregnancy did not suit her. She was wearing a pink Adidas tracksuit with a black puffer jacket and fake Ugg boots. Her hair was a brassy blond colour, it needs a good treatment and trim. Her whole body is swollen, her face, hands and stomach. I suspected her feet were swollen too. She looked hot and bothered. She was a woman that had reached the final stage of her pregnancy where enough is enough.

Well knock me down with a feather! The man was cussing the poor shop assistant, saying his wife needed urgent medical assistance and where exactly was the ambulance and where is it coming from, Jamaica? He sensed me walking towards him and shifted his gaze in my direction, we made eye contact, it was Junior.

"Nah, nah, nah man, not her!" Junior yelled at the shop assistant.

"She's the only first aider we have on duty I'm afraid."

"I want to see the manager right now!" Junior demanded.

The woman moaned, stealing everybody's attention.

"I am happy to leave you all to it, trust me..." I said starting to turn around.

"Please don't go." the woman pleaded. "Junior don't make a fuss. I need help!" She is talking to Junior but looking at me. She looked way younger than me, with a pasty white complexion and dark freckles spotted around her puffy nose and cheeks.

"That's Charmaine...my wife..." Junior trailed off. I watched the woman's face pale in recognition.

So, this is the infamous Mandy, who visited my mum's house when I was in Jamaica supporting Junior. The old me, wanted to drop kick Junior, Mandy, and the shop assistant, who took the stance of security on *The Jeremy Kyle Show*. He was expecting a brawl at the revelation. He had a smirk on his face as I put the first aid kit on the ground and start to wring my hands.

The "not so bad" Charmaine was reasoning with me, saying, "Be professional, you need this job, remember your goals, you're leaving him any day now."

I finally speak. "Mandy, is it? I will stay with you until the ambulance arrives, but it's up to you."

"But what do you know about delivering a baby?" Junior spits angrily at me.

"I have delivered two at the same time, I think that qualifies me, remember them? Garrison and Geraldine?"

Junior stood up, approaching me with his fists clenched.

"Should I remind you of your bail conditions, no contact with me directly or indirectly?"

Junior stopped still in his tracks. Mandy moaned again.

"For God's sake, pack it in you two and help me!" She looked so uncomfortable.

"Right!" I said, taking charge and I turned to look at my colleague.

"What's your name?"

"Ahmed," he replied, looking like he wished he had called in sick and stayed indoors playing his PlayStation.

"Ahmed!" I repeated, snapping my fingers. "I need you to focus."

By now, a small crowd was gathering around us.

"Run to the homewares department and grab towels, a couple of pillows, a shower curtain and a king size duvet. You got that?"

He mumbled something and barges through the crowd.

"Junior, can you help me lift her into the lady's changing room?"

He was about to protest but seeing shoppers, some with their phones recording, he readily agreed with me. With our help, Mandy eased herself off the chair. She was clearly in a lot of pain, but she managed to walk the few steps into the changing room.

"I don't want to have my baby in here!' Mandy began to wail.

"And you probably won't. We're doing all of this as a precaution. Now, let me help you out of these wet trousers."

Junior and I took off her boots. I was right, her ankles were swollen.

"When is your baby due?" I was trying to make small talk.

"The second week in January. I don't think I can get me trousers off."

"Well lucky for you, I saw 'Call the Midwife' on the telly the other day," I said, trying to sound light hearted. I took the first aid scissors and cut through the elastic band of her trousers. Ahmed rushed in and saw Mandy's exposed belly. He dropped what he was carrying and started to retreat.

"Ahmed?" He turned back around, keeping his eyes low. "Go to the cashier's desk and use the tannoy to ask for a doctor or nurse to make their way to the third floor changing room, capeesh?"

Ahmed trotted off and I praised myself for not adding "or a vet" to that list. The spiteful words got trapped in my throat. Junior and I worked together to prepare a makeshift bed on the floor. When we were done, Mandy got onto the floor. She appeared to be feeling a bit more comfortable than before. Junior wedged two cushions behind her back. We all paused to listen as a highly anxious Ahmed cleared his throat to deliver the following request.

"Can a doctor or nurse please make their way to the third floor immediately? Thank you."

"There you go," I said reassuringly. "Help is on its way." I smiled at her, but I catch myself. She is supposed to be my enemy. My worst enemy, yet when it came down to it, I was hoping that everything was going to be alright.

"Ahhhhhh!" Mandy screamed out in pain. I glanced at my watch, it's 17:14.

"Junior, I think we need to start timing these. This doesn't look like Braxton Hicks contractions to me." If Junior wasn't so black, he would have turned pale. "If the next contraction is under ten minutes, we need to call 999 again and get the operator to stay on the phone."

Junior nodded in agreement. He helped Mandy take off her coat and jumper. Ahmed came back in the room composed, despite the scene in front of him, a ghetto nativity scene. He looked at me for his next instruction.

"I take it no one came forward?" I asked. He shook his head. "Can you get me two Paracetamol and a few bottles of water?"

Ahmed scuttled off.

"Paracetamol?" Junior asked, looking confused.

"Yeah, I've been suffering from really bad headaches since..."

"I'm sorry," Mandy interjected.

"Sorry for what?" I asked.

"For the affair... I didn't know he was a married man."

I cut her off. "Love, he knew he was married, but as far as I am concerned, you two are welcome to each other. Let's just concentrate on the matter at hand, shall we?"

Mandy's face flushed red as she cried out. "I feel like pushing!"

I looked at my watch, it's 17:22. *Oh, shit! Oh shit! Oh shit!* I think to myself, not wishing to alarm Mandy. I gave Junior the look and he left the room to dial the emergency services. He came back in and handed me his phone.

"Hello?" I said.

"Hello, Charmaine," said a man with a deep Caribbean accent that I couldn't place.

"My name is Patrece, dispatcher for the London ambulance service. Your husband explained everything to us..."

Explained what? I thought. *That I'm here cutting off his girlfriend's panties?* I sucked my back teeth.

"Are you with the patient now?"

"Yes, I am. How far away is that ambulance?" I demanded.

"The crew is on its way and should be arriving in Stratford shortly. What's happening with Mandy right now?"

"Her water broke about half an hour ago and her contractions are approximately eight minutes apart," I said with an attitude. "Look geezer, I haven't delivered a baby before." There was more fear in my voice than I wanted to portray.

"And it sounds as though you are managing really well..."

I cut him off. "Exactly where is this ambulance now!?" I shouted into the receiver.

"Hold on, let me speak directly to the driver."

There were muffled voices in the background. Ahmed was back with the Paracetamol and bottled water. I handed him the phone in exchange for a strip of medication. I slipped the tablets onto the back of my tongue and gulped down the water.

"Charmaine? Charmaine?"

"Go ahead, the phone is on loudspeaker."

"Charmaine, they were coming from Whipps Cross hospital. They were stuck in traffic, but they are at Bow Flyover now, expected to be with you shortly. I will stay with you until they arrive."

I massaged my temples, wishing the headache away. We are on our own. I grabbed some sanitiser from Ahmed then reached for the medical kit to find a pair of latex gloves. Mandy was panting away.

"Charmaine, I really need to push and I'm so scared!"

"Let's do this then."

I kneeled between her legs. My first observation was that Mandy is not a natural blond. The second was, she had blood between her legs, which was not a good sign. Ahmed held the phone out for me at the business end while Junior tried his best to support her by holding her hand and saying comforting words. Very similar to the words he had said to me when I was in labour with the twins. Mandy screamed out again. I steal a look at my watch, the time was 17:31, Mandy was in full blown labour.

"Check her cervix, Charmaine," said Patrece.

"I would if I knew what I was looking for," I replied.

"OK describe what you see."

"A lot of dark red blood at the opening and I think I can see hair, black hair!" I reported.

"Okaaay, Mandy don't fight it. When the next contraction comes, I want you to push as hard as you can. You hear me?"

Mandy manages a weak "OK". My heartbeat was so loud, I was sure everybody could hear it. We do not have to wait too long before another contraction came. Mandy leans forward, pushing against my hands which are gripping her legs.

"Well done. Keep going, keep going, keep going!" I supported her.

The poor girl was screaming so loudly, I thought she was breaking in half. I silenced the spiteful Charmaine who surfaced in that moment. She was saying, "Shut the fuck up! Were you screaming like that when you were in bed making a baby with my husband?" But instead, I encouraged her to save her breath and get ready to push with the next contraction.

"This is nothing like my textbooks," Ahmed said.

"Textbooks?" I looked at Ahmed in surprise.

"Yeah, I'm studying medicine at Imperial College," he replied sheepishly.

"Get your backside down here immediately and grab a leg."

Mandy was really exhausted, huffing and puffing for what felt like ages, but it was really only a few minutes.

"The crew is approaching Westfield," Patrece announced. But the next contraction comes. Mandy dug into her reserves and pushed against me and Ahmed, who looked awe struck. We could see the head emerging.

All of a sudden, the baby slipped out and plopped into my waiting hands at 17:52. A girl, all pink, covered in a layer of blood. She was a screamer, and it was the best noise I had heard all day. Her newborn screams echoed around the small changing room. I tied the cord using dressing ties before I cut it, and I wrapped her in a towel. She looked exactly like Geraldine when she was born. When I handed her to Junior, he was crying and so was Mandy. It was an intimate moment that I should not have to witness. I had just helped to deliver my husband's baby. I was fighting the urge to break down and cry.

"Well done, Charmaine, the crew is pulling up now. Can somebody meet them at the back entrance?"

"I am on my way," Ahmed said, stealing a look at the newborn before leaving.

Mandy yelped in pain again. I suspected the placenta was coming out and I did not want to see it. When I was giving birth to the twins, I requested to see it. The placenta looked like a joint of pork and it had put me off eating pork for a hot minute, much to Junior's delight. Mandy was pushing like an expert now, a real life Amazonian princess.

"Stop pushing!" I shouted. Between Mandy's legs, there is another baby's head struggling to get out. The baby has it's umbilical cord wrapped around its neck. Instinctively, I used my fingers to grip the slippery cord and pull it over the baby's head. "You're having another baby, Mandy, but it needs to come out now. Give it some welly, girl!'

I screwed up my face, then held my breath as Mandy defecated and pushed the baby out. The baby slipped into my shaking hands, it's a boy. He was significantly smaller than his sibling, cool to the touch and not making a sound. His lips were blue, and I couldn't find a pulse, he was not breathing.

"What's going on, Charmaine?" asked Patrece.

I looked up at Junior through Mandy's open legs and shook my head. Then all hell broke loose.

CHAPTER TWELVE

ROSE

T hank God for Jesus, Manley was going to be OK. His hand got stuck under the steering wheel and he had a small hairline fracture, but nothing more. His right arm was set in a cast at the hospital, and he had been discharged. He had an outpatient appointment at the fracture clinic after Christmas. Deacon Maurice has brought us home. It was the early hours of Saturday morning. My mum had fallen asleep on the sofa, and I didn't have the heart to wake her.

As I entered the kitchen, I was pleasantly surprised to see that she cooked two whole chickens and made two trays of macaroni cheese. All of the vegetables were soaking in a bowl of water. In another bowl, she had soaked red peas, which will be added to the rice later. With the car accident and all, I had forgotten the head pastor and his wife were due to come over for dinner on Sunday afternoon after church, Manley did not want me to cancel. Thanks to my mum, all I needed to do was switch on the stove to make the curry and make a salad.

~~~~~

My mum was a godsend. I wish I could tell her what has really been going on. How I willed Manley into having that car accident and that tomorrow was potentially my last Sunday at church. She mistakes me holding on to her before she left as shock, when I was really saying goodbye.

After she left, I helped Manley to change out of his clothes and put him to bed. He slept blissfully for the entire day. Manley was due to preach on Sunday, but I would put Deacon Maurice on notice just in case Manley was not up to it. Sister Adanna called the house phone to ask if we are alright. She was thankful to God that I escaped unhurt. I did not have the energy to explain that I was not in the car, so I said very little.

~~~~~

At church on the next day, everybody made a fuss of us. Applause sounded all around as we came through the door. Manley had a noticeable bruise around his forehead where the airbag impacted his face. As we are escorted to our seats, I noticed quite a few new faces in the congregation, who appeared to know me, so it was important that I acknowledged them by smiling back and shaking their open hands.

Manley took his seat on the rostrum with his peers. The praise and worship session had a festive tone. Christmas was on a Friday this year, so today's service was also the last Sunday service before Christmas day.

I heard my name being called to sing, but with everything going on, I was not prepared. I placed baby Esther into her car seat and asked Mary to look after her. What shall I sing? *Oh, Come All Ye Faithful?* No, this is my last service too, and I wanted to make it memorable. I needed to send the church a message. I whisper to Brother Gareth, our pianist, as I passed him, and I took the two steps up to the platform. I could feel the excitement building as I instruct the choir to stand.

"Greetings Church!" The congregation greeted me back. "I don't know who needs to hear this, but I'm going to sing what is on my heart, Amen."

The church affirmed saying, Amen back to me. Brother Gareth played the first few chords of the introduction. Tears are threatening to tumble down my face, so much so and I missed my cue to start singing. I nodded at Gareth to start over, and I heard somebody shout.

"That's alright, now. Take your time."

That was just the encouragement I needed to hear. I was about to sing quite a complicated song by esteemed gospel singer Tramaine Hawkins. The last time I sang one of her ballads was at Overseer Morgan's funeral.

"What shall I do?
What step shall I take?
What move shall I make?
Oh Lord, what shall I do?"

There is a little applause, so I carried on singing the second part of the chorus.

"I'm going to wait
For the answer from you
I have nothing to lose
Oh, Lord I'm going to wait."

The tears were sitting just behind my eyelids, so I held my head back to stop them from bursting the dam and rushing down my face.

"I know you'll come through
With a blessing for me
Please Lord, set my soul free
Oh Lord, I know you'll come through."

More applause came and people in the congregation were starting to stand and raise their hands in worship. This song was really a prayer, requesting strength, answers, and above all, eternal peace. Whoever wrote this song, certainly went through some difficult times and every word resonated with me.

I had two options, to stay in my marriage and take it or run for my life. I was so torn as I looked around at my beloved church family. Would they ever forgive me for leaving them? Would they ever know the truth?

The choir joined me in the chorus. The blend of soprano, alto, baritone, tenor and bass was heavenly, filling every inch of the building. During the second verse, I surrendered to the tears and by the bridge of the song, people were escorting some of the newcomers to the altar and praying with them.

"Oh there's no one like Jesus,
Who can heal broken hearts
And put them back together again!"

This was it, I don't know where I was, but I was not on an earthly plane. I felt my spirit rising as I belted out the last notes, singing better than I had ever sung before. By the time I finished, the choir members were jumping behind me. I wept with so many emotions running through me. Sister Adanna had somehow made it to the stage to hold me up.

"See what I mean, Rose. You're chosen!" she exclaimed.

Even Manley was standing, although he was not applauding. He was too busy looking at the mass of worshippers who have gathered below. God was in the building, moving amongst his people. I tried to give the microphone to Elder Jones, who told me to preach and minister on. I did, but not for very long. Ending with telling those at the front that they were going to embark on a very special journey. I loved them, but Christ loved them more.

Manley must have been gutted. He hadn't had the opportunity to preach. He had long stopped practising his sermons in front of me, preferring to run his sermons by Deacon Maurice. I heard them talking on the phone earlier in the week, but he stopped talking whenever I entered the room. He spoke to Maurice most days.

After the benediction, signalling the end of Sunday service, it felt like every church member has sought me out to wish me a Merry Christmas. I wanted to say goodbye to members of my prayer cell, too. I so wish I could confide in them. Adanna told me that Maurice had dropped Manley home with the children, and he would be coming back for us. We sat at the back of the church.

"How does it feel Sister Rose?" I look at her confused. "When God uses you like that?"

I smiled and paused to think. "It is tiring and exhilarating at the same time. You get me?" It was Adanna's turn to look confused. "A bit like being in labour, then the rush of love when the hormones kick in." I chuckled. "It's all worth it in the end."

"I understand, now." She checked her phone which beeped. "It's Maurice, let's go."

~~~~~

Back at home, I spun around like a madwoman. I gave the children their dinner and I feed baby Esther. I knew I was snappier with the girls than usual. I wanted them to quit talking and eat up. I was exhausted after being at the hospital with Manley, then cleaning the house on Saturday. Not to mention, singing and preaching at church today. I was really praying for a good night's sleep, but I was not confident that would happen. I put Mary in charge of the girls as they filed upstairs to play. Manley came downstairs dressed in slacks and a shirt. He lifted the lids on the saucepans to check on today's menu.

"Today has to go well, Rose. I suspect Overseer Harry and his wife are coming to announce that I will be preaching at headquarters on Christmas day."

I said nothing, fearful I may say something to agitate him. These days, it is safer to stay silent than risk saying something out of turn. He was openly pushing me in front of the girls now.

"Do not say anything controversial, like 'Eve was framed' and all that feminist crap you were spouting on Friday night. Only speak when you are spoken to, keep the food coming and for heaven's sake, do something with that nappy head of yours! I was so embarrassed when everybody was staring at you in church this morning."

My hair got wet when I was walking home in the rain on Friday night. It was the kind of rain that was not enough to warrant using an umbrella. Not that I had one, but that rain was enough to soak you to the bone if you walk in it long enough. I had run out of time to do anything with it this morning and now Manley was making me feel all self-conscious about it. With just a few short words, Manley could suck the joy out of everything. Twenty souls gave their hearts to the Lord and all he could do was insult me about my hair. It is like he is fixated on my hair! We both jumped when the doorbell rang.

Overseer Harry Taylor and his wife, Mother Loretta, had travelled all the way from Hemel Hampstead to have fellowship with us and they have arrived earlier than expected. I took off my tatty apron, studied the table to ensure everything was in place and followed Manley to the door. He turned suddenly, knocking me with his plaster cast into my breastplate.

"Spoil this for me and I will spoil it for you," he menaced.

He was all pleasantries and smiles when he opened the door, like Dr Jekyll and Mr Hyde. It took me a few seconds to gather myself. My chest really hurt.

"Come in out of the cold Overseer Taylor and Mother Taylor," Manley said, taking charge.

I smiled and took our guests' coats. There is something different about Mother Taylor, but I couldn't put my finger on it, until Manley compliments her.

"You look so young Mother Taylor."

"No need for formalities, please Manley. Call us Loretta and Harry. And thank you, dear Brother Manley. I've taken a leaf out of your beautiful wife's book and taken out my weave for good."

"Well, it suits you," Manley replied.

I pick up on the slight dig at me. Her wearing her God-given hair suits her, but not me.

"Let's come through to the dining room," I said, eager not to let him upset me.

"Oh, this room is so pretty, Rose. Isn't it, Harry?"

"It most certainly is. I love your Christmas tree."

"Thank you, Loretta," Manley said, taking the credit.

"Shall I put these under the tree Rose?" Loretta asked as she looked for space under the tree to place the wrapped parcels she is holding.

"Oh, thank you, you didn't have to do that," I said.

"Of course, we had to buy the girls something. We only have the one daughter and she's away studying for her PhD at Princeton University in New Jersey...no marriage or grans for us anytime soon."

"How about a cup of tea to warm you up after your journey?" Manley asked.

"Or we could go straight to dinner, everything's ready," I said, cutting Manley off.

"Well, I'm famished. Could we eat now?" Harry replied, smiling and patting his large stomach.

His wife shot him an embarrassed look.

"Then come on through," I said, leading the way.

"Oh, the table looks lovely, Rose," Loretta remarked.

"I have a request please." said Harry. "I'd rather not sit at the head of the table, may I sit next to my wife?"

"But of course, how lovely?" I responded. "Yes, I have spent years watching my wife from the pulpit while she sat in the front row, nowadays every chance I get I want to sit next to her."

I immediately shifted the plates and cutlery around to fulfil his request. Then Manley piped up saying, "I want to sit with my wife, too."

It was on the tip of my tongue to say, "But do I want you sitting next to me, doh?" When he saw that I didn't move, he shifted his plate and cutlery before placing the mat next to mine.

The girls came downstairs on cue, to say hello to our guests.

"Oh, my. They look like little angels," Loretta said. "Manley and Rose, you must be so proud."

"We are. Even more so, when we finally have a boy. Anyway, girls back upstairs please, and let the grown folk talk."

The girls obeyed their father and filed back upstairs noisily.

"Boys or girls, it doesn't matter. Children are a blessing. I so wished we were blessed to have more," Loretta said, reaching to place her hand on top of her husband's.

He gave her hand a squeeze. Manley looked embarrassed and rightly so. As usual, I came running to the rescue.

"Harry, will you pray?"

"Of course. The food looks amazing, Rose" I was beaming with pride.

"Well let's eat, then."

I passed the bowls of food to our guests first, then Manley. I poured the tumblers with sorrel and ginger punch from a large pitcher, then I served myself. We were silent for a while, concentrating on our plates, then Loretta said, "I heard your singing this morning Rose, you blessed our souls."

"Aww, thank you, but how? Surely you would have been on the motorway at that time?"

She placed her knife and fork down. "Our nephew records the Sunday services each week. You must know him, his name is Moses."

My heart skipped a beat. Moses was at church this morning? I thought to myself. I did not see him, and I did not get the chance to say goodbye to him either.

"Yes, our dear brother helps out at the church on choir night. Doesn't he, Rose?" Manley said snidely.

"I don't know how we would manage without him," I replied.

"Well, you all will have to. He felt he had to leave," Loretta said sadly.

"Oh, how so? He didn't say anything to me?" Manley said innocently.

"Well, between us, strictly confidential, Moses told us he was warned off by one of the brothers at Battersea branch. He accused Moses of making a pass at his wife," Loretta said in hushed tones.

"Now, now, Darling. Let's not spread gossip!" Harry chided, covering his wife's hand with his.

"I'm not gossiping," she said, grasping his hand, she was turning red now.

"I won't say anything more other than Moses saying, the man was a right demon...Imagine that?"

I bit down on my lip to stifle a laugh. I stole a look at Manley, and it looked like steam was about to escape from his ears.

"Loretta, the church is like a doctor's surgery, people are there with all types of injuries, illnesses and diseases. Let's hope the man receives deliverance in due course. Amen?"

"Amen!" We all say in unison.

"That brings me nicely to the other reason why we came to see you," Harry said, clearing his throat. "Pastor Manley and Sister Rose, your work at Battersea branch has not gone unnoticed."

Manley was holding my baby finger under the table. If I moved it, he could easily break my finger.

"You are at liberty to say no, because it is such short notice, but we would love you to come to HQ on Friday to preach on Christmas day!" The couple was beaming at us. Manley released my hand to shake Harry's.

"I accept, thank you."

"Don't you need to discuss this with your wife first?" Loretta asked.

For a moment, Manley looked ashamed. "My wife knows that church business comes first."

"In our home, home drums beat first," Loretta responded.

Reluctantly Manley asked, "Honey, what do you think?" He tried to grab my hand again, but I put my elbows on the table, resting my chin on my hands.

"Well, you know, Manley had a car accident on Friday night and thank God he's OK, but our car's written off. If Deacon Maurice can take you, I don't mind getting a taxi to church on Christmas Day. What do you think Manley?"

I turned my head to look at him.

"I will ask later, I'm sure that will be OK," Manley responded.

"That's great!" said Harry. "Oh, Rose, is that a burn on your arm? That looks sore and blistered." Loretta said, reaching out to touch my hand.

I quickly adjust my sleeve and put my hands back under the table.

"That was my fault I'm afraid," Manley confessed. "I was making a hot drink, we both reached for a cup at the same time, spilling

the hot water from the kettle. I love my wife but she's so careless."
They laughed, pacified by Manley's answer. I was the only person
not laughing. I rose to start clearing the table.

"Rose, please take a seat, I have another announcement."

As I sat back down, I felt my phone vibrate with a text. It was
the phone Patti and Antoinette gave me, so I was dying to excuse
myself from the table.

"Rose? Rose? Harry is talking to you!" Manley said, trying to hide
his annoyance.

"I do apologise. I thought I heard my baby crying, I'm all ears."

"As I was saying, your work has not gone unnoticed either, Sister
Rose," he paused. "It is clear you have a calling on your life as well.
We would therefore like to offer you a bursary at Bible school for
four years and ordain you as a Pastor in the woman's and youth
ministries. What do you say, Rose?"

CHAPTER THIRTEEN

PATTI

I honestly do not know how I got through that session. When Junior boasted to the other participants that he had been arrested for hitting his wife, my head almost came off its axis. He was laughing like it was something minor, saying that he was not guilty, believing his wife would not testify against him.

At break time, I could not wait to disclose how I knew Junior. Gemma mentioned an email she had received to say his wife needed twelve stitches to the back of her head. She strongly recommended that I let Pippa know what had happened in case there were any repercussions from tonight's session. She and I agreed that we would not put it past Junior Morgan to take out a formal complaint.

I was so wound up by the end of the group that I had a difficult time trying to calm down. And when I entered the car it didn't help that Marcus was wound up as well. He had seen Junior and the conversation did not go too well.

"I swear down, Patti, I almost got out of the car and gave him a good slapping myself. I'm fed up hearing about him putting his hands on Charmaine like that. He was eating humble pie when I told him your best mate Antoinette had given Charmz a lift home, and we took Rose home. Look, if you're not feeling 'Date night' now, we could go straight home."

I'm not feeling it either, but if we don't go out tonight, we won't get to spend any proper time together until well after Christmas.

"Let's go, I've got the tickets and maybe a good laugh is what we both need now." Marcus started the engine and headed towards the Theatre Royal Stratford East.

~~~~~

The show had already begun but we would be on time for the second half at least. We arrived a few minutes before the show recommenced. The only free table was right in front of the makeshift stage opposite the bar. I believed it was left empty for a reason. Some comedians tend to single out patrons sitting in front of them. I did not want to sit there, but Marcus insisted.

Quincy takes to the stage, dressed in a pair of jeans and his tight slim fit t-shirt. His locs were tied back into a ponytail like Marcus', but Quincy was wearing a "bring back the funny" baseball cap. He was talking about his last holiday in Barbados and getting so lost, he had to stop and ask a local for directions. His Bajan accent was hilarious and had me in stitches.

Just what the doctor ordered. My upcoming hospital appointment, the refuge stuff with the girls, and the horrendous group session with Junior were slowly becoming a distant memory. I would send an email to Pippa in the morning and formally resign from running the groups.

Quincy introduced a rising star in the comedic world, he describes her as one of Angie Le Mar's protégé's Nicola Mc. Everybody clapped and hollered, she clearly had family and friends supporting her tonight. When I looked around, I noticed Juliet Gee and her crew at a table nursing their drinks. Juliet and I used to work for Probation way, way back in the day. She was now a radio presenter on Supreme Radio. We blew each other kisses.

Nicola was into her routine, talking about growing up in London in a Jamaican household and what our English friends could get away with that we couldn't. Marcus was laughing, showing off his gold tooth.

"Let me see who's in tonight? What a way black people look good, eh?"

She scanned the crowd, holding the microphone with one hand and shielding her eyes with the other.

"Oi, oi Mr and Mrs Allen are in tonight." Everybody turned to look at them.

"Happy Wedding Anniversary Suzie Wong and Mello Al!"

Everybody clapped, congratulating them. Nicola continued to scan the room. "Who else's in?... Let me see...oi! Juliet, we see you looking as gorgeous as ever. Big up yourself, darling," Although it's dark, I can tell Juliet was smiling, happy to be acknowledged.

"And who do we have down here?" she said, looking at me and Marcus. "You do realise you shouldn't have sat at the front of the stage at a comedy jam? What's your name, handsome?" She was referring to Marcus.

"Marcus," he replied.

"...And what's your mum's name?" Well, I wanted to die. Everybody was laughing and Nicola was laughing at her own joke.

"Ain't it nice when a mum brings her son out on a school night!"

Everybody burst out laughing again as Nicola pranced up and down the small stage. All I could do was squirm in my chair. Marcus whispered to me. "It's just jokes, Patti."

I tried to smile.

"We're newlyweds!" Marcus heckles back.

"Newlyweds?"

Nico stopped in her tracks, looking deadly serious and said, "Congratulations... and good luck with your spousal visa application form. The lengths some people will go to, to stay in the country!"

Well, the place was exploding with laughter and applause. Even I laughed at that one and Marcus was banging the table, gleefully.

"Nah, nah, nah look at our girl Stella. She looks like she's getting her groove back for sure, if you know what I mean ladies!"

I held my drink up at that to salute Nicola, she was very funny indeed.

~~~~~

Back at home, I asked Marcus if he is bothered about our age difference and him not having children of his own.

"All I see is a beautiful woman before me that I am happy to call my wife. As for having children, I would like to try for a baby with you right now!" He pulled me into him and kissed me in my favourite spot, between my neck and shoulder. My eyes rolled back in my head as I greedily pulled his shirt off and he pulled my knickers off. It was just the kind of sex I liked. The kind that quelled my fears and put me to sleep.

Unfortunately for me, Marcus liked early morning sex. Luckily, there was no rush to go to work at the crack of dawn, so we spent the whole morning in bed. I was much less cranky to be around now that I was getting sex on a regular basis. Antoinette had surely commented on it the other day when we went shopping for Rose and Charmaine's new phones. I was blushing when she said how less uptight I was.

"Just mind you don't get pregnant, hear?" We both laughed, believing it is impossible for a menopausal woman to get pregnant.

"Antoinette, it's funny you said that because Veronica has been dreaming about fish!"

"Well, she's never wrong, but it's not me. Perhaps it's Rose or Charmaine." We had left the conversation there.

~~~~~

Today was my last day in the office. Marcus dropped me off to collect my food order from the Caribbean takeaway near the office. Our bring and share lunch went really well. Being in a diverse office meant we could get samples of food and drinks from all over the world. Jerome gave a moving speech, and I was presented with flowers and a parting gift from my team.

"Get off now, Patti, and take back some flexi leave. Jerome and I can hold the fort here," Steve informs me. "We'll see you tomorrow night at your mum's. The missus and I are really looking forward to it."

"Okaaay you twisted my arm. There's not much I can do here now they have taken my laptop and printer."

I swept the floor, wishing my team a Merry Christmas and receiving good wishes. Poor Femi cried. I slipped her my personal number and leave things open if she wanted to stay in touch.

~~~~~

Marcus was going away on Monday, and I wanted to make sure all of his clothes were clean, so I went ahead and washed two machine loads. When it came to household chores, Marcus had taken responsibility for all of the food shopping and cooking, he did the ironing, too. I admired how Mother Morgan did a good job with my husband, but I was struggling to know where she went wrong with Manley and Junior.

I composed an email to Pippa using the work mobile phone, courtesy copying in my new line manager. And as I got ready to meet Beverley for dinner, I received a reply from my manager saying that following a discussion with the head of programmes, the decision had been made to remove Carlos Morgan from the group in Ilford. After Christmas, he would recommence with a group in Hackney at Reed House. I was relieved, I pulled my boots over my knee, and I gave Veronica a call.

"Hey, mum! How are you? How are things going?"

"I'm not doing too bad, sweetheart." she appeared to be in a good mood. "Everton and his workmates just put up the marquee in the back garden. It looks so nice, Patti. I'm here having a cuppa with Everton, now. So, I've got to go. I'm going shopping with Yolanda tonight."

"OK we'll speak later."

~~~~~

I jumped in my car and headed towards the Portuguese Restaurant on Fencepiece Road in Barkingside. Today was the last Friday before Christmas and it appeared as though everybody was out at work at Christmas dos and parties. I was wearing my knee leather boots with a black dress that had a Christmas cracker print all over it. I pulled my Winter coat from the back seat of my car and strolled from the car park into the restaurant.

Capriccio's was heaving with customers, but the front of house manager recognised me as a regular diner and asked if I had booked a table. I was soon seated and offered some bread and olives with oil and balsamic vinegar. I checked out the menu while I waited for Beverley. She arrived not long after, looking flustered, her boobs spilling out of her dress.

"So sorry I'm late. The bus from Debden took forever!" She rubbed her hands, trying to get them warm before kissing me on both cheeks.

"I just got here, how was training today?"

"Nothing new to be honest but it was good to be out of the office. Only sorry I missed your leaving lunch."

Beverley was invited to my party but when she heard I had invited Charmaine and Junior she naturally declined. Hence us meeting to celebrate my promotion tonight. I didn't have the heart to tell her they are no longer coming. As much as I love Beverley, there is no accounting as to how she would behave at my party. I did not know whose husband she is going to cop off with next, so it was best she didn't come at all.

We ordered our food and we both decided not to drink alcohol. Beverley polished the bread and olives off, and as the waiter passed by our table she asks for more. He was most obliging, and

Beverley then scoffs all of the bread without offering me a slice. To be fair I did eat quite well at lunch, but still. I ordered the traditional Christmas dinner with a Portuguese twist and Beverley ordered the full rack of lamb with sweet potato mash and seasonal vegetables.

We pulled our Christmas crackers, wore our Christmas hats and took selfies, pulling silly faces. When the meal arrived, we took photos of our food. The food tasted good, and the portions were huge. I couldn't imagine Beverley eating a full rack of ribs, I expected her to request a takeaway box at some stage. But the more my girl tucked into her food, the more I begun to join the dots together. When she asked for one of my pigs in blankets, I blurted it out.

"Beverley, have you got worms?"

"No!" she laughs. "Why?"

"Because you're eating everything in sight."

I was measured in my reply. I really wanted to say, "Because you're eating like a pig!"

"I was off my food for a while with that virus that's been going around. But now that I'm over it, I'm making up for lost time, I suppose."

"Did the doctor say you had a virus?"

"What's with the twenty questions, Patti? Spit it out."

I took a sip of my apple juice before facing her. "Beverley, are you pregnant?"

Beverley started laughing. "Nooooo! What's made you ask me that?"

I felt embarrassed, knowing Beverley had fertility problems. She had fibroids littered throughout her womb. She was supposed to have a hysterectomy, but decided at 35 years old, she is too young, preferring to adopt a vegan diet. She has had some success with some of the growths disappearing or not increasing in size. She had surgery about two years ago to remove some of the more considerable growths, the largest one was the size of an egg, and here she is yamming lamb!

"I don't know, perhaps the way you waxed off the bread and your meal. You were never a big eater. Now you're ready to chomp down on the bones."

Beverley stopped eating, noticing for the first time that she has cleared her plate at record speed.

"Beverley," I asked in a friendly tone, "when was your last period?"

She was about to answer but then she closed her mouth. She looked confused. Our desserts arrived and Beverley ate mine, along with the sticky toffee pudding with custard!

"Okay, we're going to pay for our meal and then we're going to Tesco to buy a pregnancy test."

Beverley stopped licking her spoon.

We raced to my car and drove up Barkingside High Street towards Tesco. I could feel Beverley shaking but I'm not sure if it was because of the cold weather or fear. We walked around the supermarket looking completely out of place compared with the other shoppers. The pregnancy kits were in the pharmacy department but locked away behind a glass cabinet. We had to find a member of staff to open it. Beverley was clearly embarrassed. I selected the most expensive one, it had 99% accuracy, a 'pregnant' 'not pregnant' reading and also told you how many weeks you are as well.

"£12!" Beverley complains. "I'm not paying £12 to tell me something I already know."

"Oh, yes, we are. We need to sort this shit out! Come on." Beverley dragged her heels to the till, and I drove her home to Debden.

Beverley lived in a beautiful, semi-detached house on the outskirts of London. Not many people at work knew that she originally inherited a lot of money and she bought the house in her twenties. She got a job in Probation as a receptionist, but didn't need to work for the money. When the owner of the paddocks behind her property put the land up for sale, she bought that too. The people who owned the horses had to pay her a fee for keeping their horses on her land.

A very shrewd business woman, but when it came to men, she is two steps away from heartache. I put the kettle on whilst Beverley slipped into the downstairs loo. I suspected whatever the outcome, she was going to need a cup of herbal tea.

I was trying to start the coal fire when Beverley came back into the room. Unbeknownst to me, she had gone upstairs and

143

changed into a pink velour lounge suit. Even though she had removed her make up, she was still beautiful. She took the matches from me, and I sat nearby, cross legged on a large cushion, having taken off my boots in the hall. Beverley lights the kindling and added firewood to the open fire. She studied the flames, and I studied her face, now lit up by the fire. She leaned back on her haunches and looked at me. Her puffed up eyes confirmed my suspicions, she has been crying.

"I'm three weeks pregnant and the baby's daddy is Carlos Morgan."

CHAPTER FOURTEEN

CHARMAINE

E verybody was screaming, the baby girl, Mandy, Junior and even Ahmed. I sat back on my haunches, trying to recall specifics from my first aid course. The baby was definitely not breathing. The acronym ABC sprung to mind, which stood for Airway Breathing and Circulation. I opened his mouth to check if there were any obstructions. I pinched his nose and breathed into his mouth. I was encouraged to see his little chest rise. I used my index and middle fingers to press down on his chest and counted fifteen compressions in my head, then I tilt his head back to administer two more breaths of air. He is still blue and cold to the touch, but I refused to give up. I don't know how long I repeated the cycle for, but in the middle of a set of compressions, he coughed, and he started to cry. I covered him in a blanket as the paramedics came in.

"This baby wasn't breathing when he was born, please help him!" I cried. I was absolutely exhausted.

"All fun and games in 'ere. I'm Mike, let me 'ave a butchers at him then?"

He swiftly took the baby from me to examine him.

"Well, he may have had problems to begin with, but he sounds fine to me. I'll pop an oxygen mask on as a precaution, but well done. Where are you doing your midwifery course?" He asked as he works.

"I'm not at college," I said as I pulled off my gloves and made way for the other paramedic.

"Oh, you're a doula?" the other paramedic asked. I didn't know what a doula was, so I didn't answer. He was tending to the other twin.

"Mum, did you know you were having twins?" Mike asked Mandy.

"No, I missed quite a few scan appointments," she said, not taking her eyes off her baby boy.

"It looks like this little fella was hiding behind his sister, it's more common than we know. I'm going to leave you with my colleague Damien for a few minutes and get the gurney brought up here. Today is your lucky day, we're taking you to London Hospital."

I stepped outside and sat on the very chair where Mandy had been sitting not that long ago. My head was throbbing. I popped two more tablets and swallowed them without water. I pulled the hairband out of my hair, convinced it was the cause of my headache and I massage my temples. Jamal came over and kneeled down, so he was at eye level with me.

"Ahmed said you helped deliver not one, but two babies and you successfully resuscitated one of them. I am so proud of you. Well done, Charmaine."

"It was nothing," I said, lifting my head to face him.

"Please don't underestimate what you did, Charmaine. That baby wasn't breathing, and you saved his life. You saved the pair of them. You wait until head office hears about this."

I started to worry. "Jamal, I'd rather head office not know I helped deliver my husband's babies.... but if you must share, please say I helped a customer deliver her babies, and I have an additional favour to ask you."

Just then, the paramedics left the changing room with Mandy on a trolley. Junior was carrying his shopping bags and his daughter. The paramedic, Mike, was still using an oxygen mask on the baby boy.

"Are you coming with us?" Mike asked me.

"No, I said I would stay until the cavalry arrived and you're here."

"I think we may still need your help. Damien is driving the ambulance. I'm tending to this baby, and we need you to stay with mum and the other baby, you are her doula after all."

That word again.

"No offence mate," he said, turning to Junior, "but if it comes on top in the ambulance, I'd rather her than you any day of the week."

Junior looked put out, but he finds his voice.

"I would like you there, too, Charmaine. I saw you keep a level head when we were all losing it."

I looked at Jamal.

"All up to you, Charmaine." He turned to Junior. "Mr Morgan, I am Charmaine's manager, Jamal Green. Congratulations, on the birth of your babies. Charmaine, give me your locker key and I'll meet you at the hospital."

I reluctantly took the baby girl from Junior, she looks so much like my Geraldine and the sight of her made my heart soften.

"Mr Morgan if you follow me, I'll give you a lift to the hospital." Junior had no fight left in him. He dutifully followed Jamal, still clutching his shopping bags.

~~~~~

Fortunately, the trip to the hospital was uneventful. I asked Mandy if she had any names for her babies.

"I already had the name Marlee, M.A.R.L.E.Y for a boy and M.A.R.L.E.E for a girl." She spelled the names out.

"Oh, that's a pretty name" I said.

"Bob Marley would be proud," Mike said.

"Who's Bob Marley?" Mandy asked.

Mike and I looked at each other, disappointed but not surprised.

More staff were available to assist with the family when we arrive. Marlee stayed with her mother, and her son, baby boy of Mandy O'Reilly D.O.B **17 December 2015,** was transferred to the Special Care Baby Unit next door to the maternity ward. Mandy asked me to stay with him for her. I watched as the nurse looked after him. They are concerned that his lungs are not as developed as they should be. He looks so tiny, so vulnerable.

"Can we have some details for our records?" the nurse on duty asked.

"Yes, I will try."

She is very impressed with what I was able to recall. Junior arrived and the first question he asked me was not about his new babies.

"So, are you fucking him then?"

I could not believe what he was asking me.

"You should have heard him in the car. 'Charmaine's this and Charmaine's that.' He thinks you're the dog's gonards."

"Junior mind your pickneys! Your son is in there fighting for his life but you're out here questioning me." I did not give Junior the chance to respond. "Furthermore, your bail conditions are for you to stay away from me. I'm only giving you a bly because of the circumstances, do you think I've forgotten what you did to me?"

Jamal walked around the corner.

"Ah! There you both are. Here's your handbag. Sorry if I interrupted something. Shall I go?"

Junior said yes and I said no at the same time.

"I'm ready to go now," I said to Jamal. Finally, I was the one walking away from Junior and it felt so powerful. Jamal followed, running after me, stepping inside the lift before the doors close.

"Can I give you a lift home?"

"Thank you, Jamal. I need to get a packet of cigarettes on the way home first."

Jamal didn't judge me, but I wanted to give him an explanation.

"I gave up a while ago, but today has been mad!"

~~~~~

After he paid for parking, I followed him to his car. It was a bottle green Land Rover. I climbed in and inhaled the new car smell. The traffic was heavy, travelling back into Stratford. We were both silent, listening to Maxi Priest's album. Jamal stopped at the corner shop where I bought ten Bensons.

"Fancy going for a drink in The Lamb?" Jamal suggested as we passed the pub.

I paused to think. "Yeah. One drink though, but I'd like to go indoors and change first. Is that alright?"

"Yeah sure," he replied.

"Good, I'll meet you in there. Get us a table and I'll see you in about 20 minutes."

I rushed into my house, not intending to leave until I found out what the hell a doula is. I get on the internet and Google search what a doula is. I find out that it is a companion that helps with the complete birthing process. After I finish the search, I change my clothes and head to The Lamb

I enter the pub half an hour later and scan the room to see if there was anybody here Junior had slept with, or he owed money to. When I was sure the coast was clear, I exhaled and found Jamal who had secured a small table in the corner by the jukebox which was playing reggae Christmas carols. He stood up as I approach him.

"You look nice," he said.

"It's leggings and a t-shirt, Jamal."

He winced. I wish I'd just accepted the compliment rather than acting like a bitch.

"Sorry, Jamal. Thank you."

"What can I get you to drink?"

"Can I have a blackcurrant and lemonade please?"

"Yeah sure."

I checked out his backside as he walked to the bar. *What do you think you're doing?* I asked myself, looking away. *You are not available. You are not on the market. You are still a married woman.* I shift my gaze as Jamal returned to the table.

"I decided to join you and have a soft drink too," he said, handing me a glass. "Cheers, Charmaine. And Merry Christmas."

"Merry Christmas. What are your plans for the big day?" I asked.

"I'm going to spend the day with my family. My parents live in Stratford, off Manor Road. Everybody's bringing a dish. I'm making the dessert this year."

"Oh, what are you making?"

"Christmas pudding and two cheesecakes, not sure what flavour yet."

"Oh, I'm impressed. I didn't have you down for the domesticated type," I joked, and he laughed.

"I'm a proper Mary Berry fan, but don't tell anybody at work that." He paused to take a long sip of his drink. "What are you doing for Christmas, Charmaine?"

"I'm leaving my husband..." I blurt out.

I know Patti warned us not to tell anyone of our plans, but I needed to trust someone, so why can't that person be Jamal? He almost choked on his drink.

"Earlier, I was asking for a favour. If you're going to inform HQ about what I did today, please ask for a transfer out of the area. Only I don't know where."

"Consider it done, Charmaine. Take my number, and when you know where you're going to be based, we'll get you transferred to the nearest shop. How does that sound?"

"Sounds like a plan to me Jamal. Thank you."

We finished our drinks and I walked Jamal to his car, then I walked to my mum's, enjoying another fag. She was not going to believe this next episode of my life. The phone rang in my handbag. I answered it just before messaging service kicks in. I didn't recognise the number.

"Hello?" I said in trepidation.

"Hello, is this Charmaine?"

I stopped walking.

"Yes, it is. Who is this?"

My heart began to beat faster and louder. I pulled a long drag on my cigarette.

"My name is Samantha Wilson. I am the Independent Domestic Violence Advisor from Essex. Are you safe to talk?"

"Yes," I replied.

"Great, a room is available for you and your children on Friday, Christmas Day."

Chapter Fifteen

ROSE

I am prepared for the assault that was about to follow. There is no point in hiding in the bathroom. The last time I did so, he simply took the door off its hinges. There is nowhere else to hide indoors. He had frightened the children to no end today. I had never seen Manley so angry. He could barely contain himself as he closed the front door behind our guests. I was surprised he did not catch their heels in the door as he slammed it shut.

Anybody would think I had invited them here and begged them to ask me to become a Pastor. I was flattered for a millisecond, but I declined, citing I was too busy being a Pastor's wife to become an actual Pastor myself. I could tell both Loretta and Harry were very disappointed, telling me to discuss their proposal with Manley and come back to them after Christmas.

Apparently, I did not decline hard enough, I left the door open, and I did not shut down the proposal. Manley was pacing up and down the kitchen, ranting and raving. Who do I think I am even thinking about it? I could not go to bible school. I did not have what it takes to study at that level. I may have a degree, but I did not finish my teaching qualification. Now that was true, but the decision was made when we got engaged that I would give up studying and support him through bible college. And that was my problem right there in a nutshell.

Manley saw things through a distorted lens. I held my own counsel, but nobody knew that Manley was failing his assignments until I stepped in. I wrote the majority of Manley's essays. I researched and edited his dissertation. Sometimes Mary, a babe in arms, would be reaching for the keyboard, too. Until recently, I was the sounding board for his sermons. And now, he was treating me like a dunce.

I so wanted to cut my eye at him, but it was safer to keep my eyes fixed on the discarded rice grains on the tablecloth. Any look of disrespect and Manley would shoot me a box before I can say Jack Robinson. Apparently, he gave me permission to complete the online classes, but I could not use his computer. I wanted to say, "You mean my computer. The one you use for online gambling?" The money my uncle gave him had probably disappeared by now, with nothing to show for it. I swallowed down the comebacks.

I almost laugh when he said I could go to Bristol and take the weekend classes, but I would have to take all the children with me, because he "ain't minding no girl pickney". Anybody would think I'd sat here and made all of these children by myself.

My eyes followed him, pacing the floor. He was raging. Apparently, there was only room for one minister in this house, his grandfather was a preacher, his father was a preacher, it was in his DNA and his son, when I could produce him one, would be a preacher too. I want to say 'which son?' because no more children are coming out of my womb and calling me mama, god forbid. Was Manley so ignorant that he didn't know it was his genes that determined the sex of the developing foetus? Yet I am the ignorant backward one. I really want to suck my back teeth at that one.

My phone vibrated in my pocket for the second time, I dare not even touch it. Manley heard it and kicked off! He wanted to know which man was calling his house at this time of night. I glanced at the clock on the gas cooker, it is only just after seven in the evening. He wanted my phone, but I didn't want to give it up.

Apparently, I was on my final warning with him and by the time he counted to three, I had better hand it over. If it was Brother Moses, he would kill me like Cain slew Abel. I gave the phone to Manley, I was eager to avoid another beating before Christmas. He almost broke my little finger at the table earlier, so I handed him my phone. I can tell he was disappointed with what he read. He scrolls through my messages, looking for any minor infraction. Seeing nothing of interest, he puts my phone in his back pocket.

For the next few moments, he diverted his venom by cussing out my new friends. He claimed Patti is nothing but an old dried up Obeah woman who bewitched Marcus into marrying her and stealing his mother's engagement ring. Charmaine was nothing but a mampy Jezebel who was with Junior for his money, and the small island woman with the loud mouth had better know her place and keep her big trap out of his business. He had his back to me when his anger turned against his mother. It's her fault his brothers were so weak.

"She forced me to 'man up' and tow the party line. I went along with it to keep the peace. But I hated all of it, being in Sunday school while Marcus got to play football. I wanted to stay in Jamaica with my grandparents. But oh no, they could not leave the 'Chosen One' behind! They meant the world to me, and I never got to see them again.

"The abuse I received at school was horrendous, from the teachers and children alike. All because of the colour of my skin. It was not easy growing up in the 70s you know. Did you know I wanted to be a solicitor? Nope, you probably didn't. But the great Overseer Morgan said, 'Become a carpenter like Jesus'. I do a trade that can barely feed my family, because I am not good at it. I have more luck at the races and look how that is working out for me." He laughed wryly.

I tried to conjure up some compassion, to be the supportive wife, when he continues his monologue.

"I did not want to get married, not to you, not to anybody." He glanced over his shoulder. "I was quite happy being a single man. It was 'she' that noticed the sisters in the church noticing me. I was not interested at all. She wanted to see me 'married off' before they retired back home to Jamaica. They would not leave me alone and let me find my own bride.

"Nope, they had to be involved in that too. She and Overseer Morgan planned everything, and they selected you. The virgin Sunday school teacher, pretty but not showy, black but not too black, simple and compliant."

His words cut me to the core, but I felt compelled to continue listening.

"I really tried hard to love you, Rose, but I never have, and I never will. I just go through the motions with you because it is expected of me. You do not please me sexually either. I do it as a means to an end. As soon as we have a boy, I will never be intimate with you again."

He turned around slowly, looking surprised to see that I was crying.

"The only thing I have ever been good at is preaching. Granted, I am not as good as my father and I'm not the next Morris Cerullo, but for the first time in my LIFE, I was good at something. I knew how to work up a crowd, until someone gave you the microphone."

He raised his hands and I flinched because I think he was going to lash out at me, but he was stretching.

"I coped quite well with the odd solo here and there and the odd testimony. I saw how the congregation reacted to you and I saw the board giving you more responsibilities too. Can Sister Rose do this? Can Sister Rose do that? Whatever they asked you to do, you willingly took it on and did it well."

Manley clapped three times, his face couldn't mask his pain.

"Your behaviour got worse in Jamaica. Lord knows I wanted to go home on my own, with my brothers but oh no, she said 'Bring mi gran pickney baby, let me see her, shame it wasn't a boy'."

That part...that part stung.

"You won everybody over, and they all ended up loving you instead of me. I knew that Medina was guarding your door every night so I couldn't see you? Do you have any idea how humiliated I felt?"

He banged the table. I sat down on the chair, afraid. I saw Manley winced in pain, he must have forgotten his hand was still in a cast, I thought.

"Now you're throwing off your wig and upsetting the apple cart. And what does headquarters do? Offer you a pastorship and a full scholarship to Bible school. Well done, Rose. Well newsflash, Rosie. Every time you get up to preach, I will beat the black off of you until its white."

CHAPTER SIXTEEN

PATTI

I was exhausted by the time I made my way to Marcus' apartment and my head was reeling with Beverley's revelation. I have to admit, I was tempted to call Antoinette on the drive back but decided against it. Antoinette was not a fan of Beverley's lifestyle, and she wanted nothing more than to have a child of her own. Nope, telling her would be like adding fuel to the fire.

It then occurred to me that Veronica was right! Somebody in my crowd is pregnant! I had ruled myself and Yolanda out of that one. I had hoped it was Antoinette, I prayed it was her. But what was going to happen when Charmaine found out about yet another pregnancy? She would kill Junior for sure. The WhatsApp group was hot the other night when Charmaine dropped the birth of Junior's new babies into the group chat!

I crept into Marcus' queen size bed, hoping not to wake him. He was sleeping on his side, facing away from me. But sensing my presence in the bed, he turned to face me.

"Did you have a nice time, Empress?" he mumbled.

"Yes, I did thanks."

"Want to have an even better time?" He smothers me with kisses on my lips, neck, and shoulders.

~~~~~

When I eventually woke up, I was wrecked and needed a well-deserved lie in. I wanted to pull the covers up over my head and sleep until it was time to get ready for my party.

Marcus had already risen and was out for the day. He set the machine to wash the clothes he wanted to take away on his trip and asked that I put them in the dryer for him. It was a simple request, which he made before telling me to "keep tings tight till

I get back". Mr Man certainly knows how to make an old woman smile.

I made myself a hot cup of herbal tea and sipped it out on the balcony. The view from his apartment was a hive of activity out on the river Thames, with small boats travelling up and down. I was so peaceful here until I glanced at the clock and realised, I need to make haste before I was late for my hair appointment. My usual girl was not available, so I had an appointment at the Purely Natural hair salon.

Marcus told me that Manley said they weren't coming either as he was involved in a car accident, and he had broken his wrist. It was a shame because it was going to be our last meeting before D-day. The ladies would get their slots to leave any day now if they hadn't already.

I arrived at the salon a few minutes to ten, delighted with my time keeping and impressed with how easily I found a space in Morrison's car park. At precisely 10 o'clock, the shutters came up and I ascended the steps into the salon.

Anastasia, the owner, greeted me with a smile and we make small talk before my stylist Natalie came to take my coat. Two hours later, after washing my hair and giving me a rosemary and eucalyptus steam, Natalie interlocked my re-growth and hooked me up with a petal Mohican hairstyle. I loved it and I was looking forward to being a rock chick later that evening. I decided I was going to wear my leather outfit with my high heels later.

I swerved going into the supermarket since it was packed with Christmas shoppers. My next stop was D'Secrets in Gants Hill to get a pedicure and manicure with Dina.

By the time I got back to my home, Marcus was in the kitchen, making corned beef and rice, I guessed by the aroma coming from the galley kitchen.

"You know Veronica is cooking tonight, Hun?"

I took my bowl from him and sat at the dining room table.

"I know babes, it's just a lil someting someting to tide us over until later. I bet you missed breakfast and lunch!" He was right.

~~~~~

We stepped into the Uber like we are going to the Met Gala. Marcus was wearing designer black leather trousers with a tight black tee shirt, matched with a black blazer, showing off his post workout physique. I was wearing a leather knee length dress with tassels at the bust line and at the hem. We are soon on the A12, heading to my childhood home in Romford.

I know it's snobbish, but I could not help comparing Veronica's home to the others on her road. Everybody had increased the value of their homes by either going up and creating a loft conversion or down, creating a cinema room or indoor swimming pool in the basement. Next door had an extension and an office space at the end of their garden. The only thing Veronica had done was to have double glazing fitted, and that was over twenty years ago. As we pull up outside, I could see her Christmas tree lights blinking on and off in the front room.

I gave up trying to ring the bell after two attempts. Nobody answered so I used my key. I was surprised to see a plastic runner across the entrance hall to the kitchen which was designed to protect the carpet. Where the hell did Veronica get that from? Talk about old school. We turned right into the front room, this was Veronica's best room, it was off limits to her foster children, except when she had meetings with social workers.

Back in the day, Veronica would have made visitors take their shoes off, but not today. The room has not changed in decades. Hanging on the wall opposite where I stood, was the inscription *"Christ is the head of this house, the unseen guest at every meal, the silent listener to every conversation."*

Below on the mantelpiece, there was a very unflattering graduation photo of me and another framed photo of me holding a three-month-old Yolanda at her christening. Sharing the mantelpiece were the knick knacks Veronica had bought from all over the coast. There are ornaments from Brighton, Margate and Little Hampton. Basically, anywhere Veronica's friend Laura visited. We went on these excursions with them at least twice during the summer holidays.

The first people I introduced Marcus to were Veronica's friends, Mr and Mrs Clarke, they are sitting on the settee. We insisted that they didn't get up, preferring to squat on the side of the couch. Mrs Clarke was elegantly dressed in a floral tea dress, complimented with matching pearl earrings and a necklace. Her make-up was flawless and when I gave her a compliment, she blushed.

"Where is your family from Marcus?"

"St Andrews," Marcus replied.

"Ah," Mr Clarke responded, smiling up at Marcus. "Whereabouts in St Andrews?"

"We grew up in Half Way Tree," Marcus said proudly.

"Ah we know it very well."

"OK, it's a beautiful village, but my parents...I mean my mum, lives in Negril now."

The smiles left their faces.

"Veronica told us about the passing of your father, please accept our condolences." Mr Clarke said, his wife nodded in agreement.

"Thank you both very much," Marcus replied.

"Clarkey," Mrs Clarke nudges her husband gently, "give Patti and her husband de ting you 'ave for dem,"

"Yes of course," he replied, reaching inside his breast coat pocket. "Patti, we heard the two of you got married in Jamaica and now that we have met Marcus, we couldn't be happier for you. Here is a small gift from the wife and I."

He hands the envelope to Marcus. It was a cheque for one thousand pounds.

"We left it blank because we don't know if you're planning to have a joint account or not. But God bless you with many happy years together like my wife and I."

They gave each other a knowing smile. We thank them by giving them kisses before moving on to greet our other friends. Veronica's neighbours Ev and Dee were standing by the fireplace nursing their drinks. They are with their grandson Kyland. Ev and Denise moved in next door to Veronica about two years ago and she adored them. They were a sociable couple, loved their family house parties and bar-be-ques. Dee was a mean home baker and cake decorator, so I was right to suspect she made my cake.

"I hope you like it, Patti!"

"I'm sure I will" I assured her.

My reiki teacher, Diane, was smiling away at me over in the other corner. She gave me the longest hug and whispered, "Congratulations" in my ear. We introduced our husbands and the two men Marcus and Henley exchanged handshakes and bro hugs.

Marcus then introduced me to his work colleague Mr Frank, which I thought was rather formal, and his cousin. The two men laughed, obviously an inside joke. I didn't quite catch her name, as Yolanda came into the room and drags me away.

"We've been waiting for you, mum! Come on, Marcus! Let's get this party started." The music got louder and louder. The marquee looked fantastic. I said quick hi's and bye's as she drags me through the kitchen diner into the tent.

The dance floor is already crowded with our friends and family. I was not surprised to see Mr and Mrs Husbands dancing to soca music like nobody was watching them, only everybody was. Jerome, Steve, and their wives are cutting a rug, enjoying themselves. I manage to break free from Yolanda and introduce Marcus to our family friend DJ Marky Mark. He always made himself available to play a set at all of my milestone birthday parties. We had to shout to be heard over the music, but I understood he was proud of me getting a promotion and us getting married.

The gift table was crammed with gift boxes and the cake looked fabulous. It was rectangular in shape and resembled a business card. Even the purple probation logo was in the top right corner and across the centre of the cake, it read, Patti Scotland-Morgan DipSW DipHE BA MA (Hons) Assistant Chief Officer. I wanted to cry.

I walked back through to the kitchen to say hello to Veronica before she had a fit. Veronica was at the stove frying some fishcakes. I remembered being upset at my 18th birthday party, because I claimed the smell of the potent salted fish was stinking up the house. Birthday party or no birthday party, Veronica let me know, in front of all of my college mates, that when she goes to an English party, she expected to eat sausage rolls, when she goes to an Indian party, she expected to eat samosas, when she goes to a Trini party, she expected to eat roti, and God bless Moses when a Bajan has a party, you must eat fishcakes. My English friends gorged themselves on fishcakes that night. Veronica could not make them fast enough.

"Hey, mum," I said, kissing her on the cheek.

"Hey, Mrs Scotland," Marcus said giving her a big kiss as well.

"Thanks for doing all of this, mum."

"No problem at all, sweetheart. Look your Auntie Cynti over there... and she's vex with you!"

If Veronica was the Queen, then her younger sister was Princess Margaret. She sat at the dining room table with a curly wig and a full-length fur coat. It was easily a billion degrees with the chafing dishes burning away, but Auntie Cynti was not bussing sweat, unlike me. I had a feeling she was upset about me getting married without her being there. As Veronica's younger sister, she insisted that I call her Auntie and not mind what Veronica had to say. I hold Marcus' hand as we walked over to greet her.

"Good evening, Auntie Cynti" I kissed her on the cheek, "I would like you to meet my husband, Marcus."

Marcus came in for a kiss and Auntie Cynti grabbed his hand, working her left hand up his arm to his bicep.

"Hello, Marcus," she gushed. "My name is Cynthia, but you can call me Cyn, spelled S.I.N." She cackled mischievously, while poor Marcus tried to pull away from her grasp. "Please use those strong arms of yours to pour me a drink, I'm on the hard wine tonight."

Marcus couldn't get away quickly enough and I caught my aunt checking out his backside.

"Auntie Cynti, ya too bad," I said, mockingly slapping her hand and taking a seat next to her. "And your husband's sitting right there."

Auntie's face goes from smiling to frowning, screwing up her lips in his direction. "You mean the man that lives in my house?"

I looked across the table. Uncle Jim was tucking into not one but two bowls of souse with a spoon; Another Bajan delicacy. Souse was essentially pickled pork, and the "pudding" was steamed sweet potato. Traditionally, souse was made using the pig's trotters, ears, and snout, but Veronica made hers with pork belly. Uncle Jim was guarding his like he was expecting somebody to swoop down and take it from him.

"Ya uncultured swine!" she hollered at him.

He waved his hand at her, paying her no mind.

"Patti, I beg ya a lil food please, you know I'm a diabetic and my blood sugar is down to zero!" The comment was more directed at her husband than me. I doubt her blood sugar is low, but I rushed to fix her a plate.

"Your aunt is scary!" laughed Marcus.

"Is that why you haven't come back with her drink yet?"

"Yep, I am not going back over there. Did you see her checking me out?"

We both laughed, knowing she was harmless. Auntie Cynti checked out her plate and nods, satisfied with the mountain of curried goat, rice, coleslaw and salad on the side.

"Grab a couple of those fishcakes please. I have something I need to talk to you about."

When I returned, her napkin was lying on her chest. I watched her take a bite of the fishcake.

"We would have come to your wedding with a little bit more notice, you know," she said seriously.

"I know Auntie Cynti, things happened quite quickly ..." I trailed off. I really did not have an excuse. "But you're here celebrating with us now."

"True, we're ever so proud of you, Patti."

"Thank you, Auntie."

"Now tell me, Patti," Auntie Cynti said all jovial again.

"I'm all ears."

"How does it feel when a man like Marcus grabs a full bust like yours?"

Without missing a beat, I replied with a wink. "Auntie, the next time I have them felt up, I'll let you know!"

"Ya too bad, Patti! Ya too bad!" she cracked up laughing.

~~~~~

I got up to greet Antoinette, Malakai and Elijah. It was so good to see them.

"Happy Birthday, Aunt Patti," Elijah greeted me so nicely, I don't have the heart to tell him it's not my birthday.

"Ladies and Gentlemen, boys and girls, can everybody come through to the marquee, please?"

We all filed through as requested. I hugged and kissed a few more guests who I did not see earlier, like Gemma, Leah and their mother.

"I have had a special request from Mr Clarke."

DJ Mark was scanning the crowd as the guests parted for Mr and Mrs Clarke to get to the dance floor.

"Wonderful, wonderful," Mark said. "This tune is for you by special request."

DJ Mark drops the first bars of the classic, "Too Late to Turn Back Now", by Alton Ellis. I would recognise that track anywhere. The bass line was heavy and made the marquee shake. Mr Clarke bowed to his wife, and they schooled us in ballroom dancing. The sight of them dancing together was breath-taking. By the second verse, Mr and Mrs Husbands are dancing together too. Even Aunt Cynti and Uncle Jim were dirty dancing all loved up, like she didn't just have a quarrel with him earlier. But I was transfixed, watching the Clarke's dance.

"May I have this dance?" I heard Marcus ask.

I turned to join him, but he was addressing Veronica and she graciously accepted. I was overwhelmed by the love in the room. Yolanda came and placed her arms around my waist. I was fighting the urge to cry.

"Are you having a moment, Mum?"

"Yes," I replied.

Everybody here has touched my life in some way and whilst I am grateful to be blessed with such a wonderful husband, family, friends, even absent family like Rose and Charmaine, and absent friends like Beverley, there were two important people missing from this scene, my biological parents; my mum and dad. When I've reached a milestone birthday, passed my driving test, got married, and now a big promotion, the absence of my folks twisted like a knife in my heart. Once the saga with Charmaine and Rose was over, I was going to make a concerted effort to find them. I needed answers. I needed to know why they left me 45 years ago.

DJ Mark dropped the next track from the vault. Another classic, "Margaret" by Dennis Walks. In a previous life, I swear I was a DJ! I liked my music and once I fell in love with a track, I played it over and over again.

I was getting my groove on when Antoinette asked if Elijah could sleep upstairs. Poor mite wore himself out ramping with Kyland and he had fallen asleep in the front room. Malakai carried him upstairs to my old bedroom and I looked for a blanket to cover him. He was a little unsettled, so Malakai stayed with him.

"See you back downstairs," I said, leaving him to it.

"There you are, Mum. Nan's making a speech," Yolanda told me as I arrived back in the marquee.

"I am a woman of few words..." everybody laughed, "I want to thank you all for coming to celebrate Patti's promotion. She has worked hard, and we are very proud of her. To Patti."

There were applauses and the microphone was passed to Marcus.

"On behalf of my wife and I..." there was uproar, "I would like to thank you all for coming out tonight. Please eat, drink and be merry! Happy Christmas, everybody!"

More applause followed and yells of "Speech! Speech!"

Marcus passed the mic to me, and I said, "Welcome, my family and friends. Thank you for your love and support. It took several people to get me here and I hope I continue to make you all proud of me." I burst into tears, and Marcus and Yolanda rushed in to give me a hug.

"Alrighty," announced DJ Mark, "we have another special request from our host Miss Veronica. Make room folks as she shakes her tail feather! Let's go!"

There was no party without Lady Marmalade. Veronica, Yolanda, Auntie Cynti, and I belt this track out like we wrote it and Auntie Cynti even manages a high kick. I was on the floor with laughter.

~~~~~

The party finally started to wind down at about five in the morning. Veronica insisted that we leave the tidying up to her and Yolanda. We placed all of my presents into a large bin liner and Marcus' friend, Mr Frank gave us a lift home. Once indoors, we packed the left-over party food away in the fridge, agreeing we did not need to cook later, when I noticed a letter on the shelf by the front door.

"I forgot to tell you, a letter came for you this morning," Marcus said.

I took the letter upstairs with me and opened it while I sat on the loo. Ms Scotland, hospital number RHO 4929777 *We are writing to inform you that your operation has been scheduled on Thursday, 24 December 2015 at 9am...* I felt sick.

CHAPTER SEVENTEEN

CHARMAINE

M y head was banging. I knew letting the twins sleep in my bed on Christmas Eve was a huge mistake, but they were so excited. I sat perched on the edge of the bed, nursing another migraine. I wish I had not discharged myself from the hospital since I may have hit my head harder than I first thought. I decided to get up and start my day. It was my last day in this house, but there were things I was really noticing for the first time.

One of our bedside table lamps was missing. We bought them when we first decorated our room. Junior got mad one day and threw one of them at me, it shattered against the wall and shards of glass pierced my shin. Apparently, it was my own fault because I did not move out of the way quickly enough. The crack in the bathroom mirror was where Junior hit my head against it when we had a fight two years ago. I accused him of cheating and how dare I call him out on it.

I opened the kitchen cupboards to make myself a drink, it's no surprise that I do not have any matching cups. My dinner set was a wedding present from my mum. It has long been destroyed, smashed because his record label had let him go. Somehow, that was my fault, too, and I had to be punished.

We had door panels smashed through by him and doors hanging off in disrepair. There were holes in the walls, where out of sheer frustration, Junior had got drunk and punched them in. On nights like that, the only place I could hide was in the bathroom with the twins, praying he would leave, die, or fall asleep in a drug fuelled stupor. Smoking weed or the stuff Junior smoked does not calm people down. It made them worse.

Sadly this "home" was an unsafe, toxic place to be, and I was looking forward to leaving it all behind me later today. The only fly in the ointment was that Junior wanted to see his children today on blasted Christmas Day. All of a sudden, it was important for him to come to see his children today of all days.

The twins have four Christmases before this one, and Junior had not been present at any of them. He said he didn't believe in celebrating Christmas. Well, fuck me. Junior didn't celebrate anything, full stop. In his learned opinion, everything was manufactured as a money-making business, and he wasn't "inna dat". So, he didn't celebrate Valentine's Day, my birthday, Mothering Sunday or Easter. But would hold out his hand for a gift on Father's Day and his birthday. Tight bastard. I done told him, "However you treat me on my birthday, I will treat you on yours". I bet ya he didn't even get his children presents this Christmas either.

Stepper had acted as a go between when I ignored Junior's text messages and phone calls, which have become increasingly more aggressive this week. So, I ceased communication altogether. I was convinced he only wanted to see his children so that he could get to me on Christmas Day, even though he knows he isn't allowed anywhere near me. Men like Junior don't think the rules apply to them, so I was going to try and leave London at 3pm.

In the meantime, I had other fish to fry. I needed to go and see my dad. I quickly got ready, got my gardening tools together and grabbed the two Poinsettia plants, which are wrapped up in newspaper and waiting by the front door. My one piece of luggage was also nearby. I was ready to go to wherever they placed me, anywhere was better than here. Marcia had agreed to sit with the twins until I got back. I was going to seriously miss Marcia, she had been my rock.

I borrowed her car to go pick up my mum and I drove to the cemetery about ten minutes away. I would have preferred to walk but mum couldn't manage the icy roads and it was bitterly cold outside.

Mum was sombre, she always is at this time of year. From the time the clocks go back an hour, signalling dark mornings and colder evenings, you can clock the changes in her mood. She would go through the motions and getting nice treats in from

Marks and Spencer, cooking up a storm in the kitchen. She was even delighted to see the excitement on her grandchildren's faces.

Now, I was taking them away from her too. Oh, she understood why I needed to get away and go into hiding, but she felt it is so unfair that I had to be the one to leave. I could see her physically swallowing down the tears when I told her my plans. If it was down to her, she would have stabbed Junior with her JML kitchen knife, dismembered his body to make sure he was really dead, call the police, sit down with a cup of tea and wait for them to arrive. I convinced her otherwise.

~~~~~

It was surprisingly busy in the cemetery at eight in the morning. Some people looked like they are going to spend the whole day there, wrapped up in blankets with deck chairs and a thermos of tea, hot chocolate or better still, a drop of brandy to keep out the cold. Walking up to the graveside reminded me of dad's funeral.

People said the most horrible things. Of course, they meant well, but if you cannot say anything helpful, shut the fuck up! "Don't cry Charmz, he's gone to a better place..." I wanted to scream when I heard that one. "A better place?! In a coffin at 49 years old? Where is this better place? How is it better than being with me and my mum? Please shut up!" They did not know my dad like me and my mum.

That was a bright sunny day in June when the grass was green and lush. Today, it was bleak with a cold wind rushing through and around us, stinging our hands and faces. Dad was situated in a nice spot away from the main road. It had been a whole year since I visited. After his funeral, mum and I came over here religiously every Saturday. It was hard watching my mum cry fresh tears like she just lost him. One time she threw herself across his grave, sobbing her heart out. I thought she would never stop crying.

Before I knew it, the first anniversary of his death had arrived, and I point blank refused to go with her anymore. She did not stop to think how his death had affected me at ten years old.

Mum was sitting on the bench, caught up in her own memories. I used a damp cloth to wipe away the cobwebs from his gravestone. It was satisfying to see the original colour on the marble returning with every swipe.

"Hey Daddy..." I waited for a reply, silly I know.

"It was wonderful seeing you last week." I waited again. "I'm leaving today like you said I should. I also realised when you said to save the children, you were actually talking about Junior's other children, too. I did it daddy, I saved both of them. When I get myself sorted out, I am going to train to become a doula and save other babies, too. I may even become a midwife. It took me a minute to work out what I want to do with my life, and I have not got it all worked out, but I'm happy with my decisions."

I focused on pulling out the old weeds and replanting the poinsettias. Dad would have appreciated the colours since red was his favourite colour. When I was done, I stood back with my mum, linked her arm in mine, and admired my handiwork. The wind picked up speed again, encircling us with leaves and dust, so much so we have to close our eyes. I caught a whiff off Old Spice cologne, and I knew my dad was pleased to see that we were as close as ever and that we haven't forgotten him. I broke away from mum, packed my tools away and made my way back to the car. Mum needed space to talk to her husband alone.

~~~~~

We got back home to find that the children had already had breakfast and Marcia had them dressed and ready. Marcia also left mackerel and hard food in a pot for us, and we ate while the children opened their presents under the tree. Junior face timed the children from my phone, which started off well but ended up being the Spanish Inquisition. "Is your mum there? Who else is there? Is there a man there?" I kissed my teeth and ended the call. When he rang again, I did not answer. He then sent me a text saying he wanted to see the children at two pm. I was not going to let him dictate a time to me, so I text back, "*Whatever!*"

Saying goodbye to Marcia was the hardest thing I have ever had to do. How do you say goodbye to somebody who meant the world to you? How do you say goodbye to somebody who did not know you were leaving? I just about managed it. If I was emotional like this over leaving Marcia, how was I going to manage when saying goodbye to my mum?

We spend a lazy day over at mum's, opening more presents, clothes mainly. We repacked my suitcase with the new bits, watched foolishness on the TV and enjoyed the best Christmas dinner ever. As if on cue, Junior sends a text to say he was outside the house. My heart bounced up into my throat.

"Soon come" I typed back, *"The children are eating"*

"Kl," he replied.

"It's time to go mum," I said, and the tears started.

We held each other for ages until there is a knock at the door.

"Shit! Please tell me that's not Junior Morgan at my door?" mum said, moving quickly to open the door. I braced myself.

"Merry Christmas Mrs! Taxi for Charmaine?" said a tall, fair skinned man. Mum looked around him to see a brand-new black taxi with its engine running. "I'm Chris, Miss Patti sent me."

Another text message arrived. *"If you're not 'ere in the next 5 minutes with my children, I'm going to fuck you up."*

I did not need to be told twice. I grabbed the children's coats and mum helped Chris with my luggage.

"OK mum, I don't want to go, but I can't stay. I love you."

The children started crying, only because I was crying, and their nan was bawling her eyes out.

"Mum, call Miss Patti and let her know we've gone."

"I love you, Charmaine."

"I love you more, mum."

The taxi pulled away and I kept looking at her out of the rear window until she disappeared. I was so caught up in my feelings I did not see when the taxi turned into my road. It was on the tip of my tongue to say chuck a right, but it was too late. Worst still Geraldine and Garrison started banging the glass and screaming.

"Daddy, daddy, daddy!"

At the very last second, Junior looked up from his phone, me and his eyes made four. He was holding a large bouquet of flowers. His cigarette left out of his mouth as he raced towards his car.

"Mate! Mate! Chris?"

"Yes, love?" Chris replied, switching on the internal intercom.

"I think we've got trouble."

I watched Chris double check his rear-view mirror.

"That black BMW pulling out now, that's my husband, the man I'm trying to get away from." I tried to stay calm. "Can you outrun a BMW?"

I could sense my panic rising. I remembered how he threatened me the last time I refused to come home after a few days at my mum's following a fight. "You can leave me at any time, but you leave my yout dem y'ere. Tek my pickney away from their father, to put them around a next man and I'll kill you and him. Mark my words." The taxi sped up.

"Don't worry yourself darling, I know these back roads like the back of my hand." I was not convinced.

ROSE

C hristmas Day 2015, and I felt so blessed to see it! It was baby
  Esther's first Christmas, and my 36th birthday is tomorrow.
Today was my Emancipation Day and I could not wait to get out of
here. I was trying my best to contain my excitement as well as my
anxieties and fears. My escape plan was in place thanks to Patti,
but I was hoping and praying I would get away safely with the girls
without having to involve the police. The timing of my escape is
crucial since we did not want one brother notifying the other. To
be honest, 3 o'clock could not have come quickly enough.

Manley was already up preening himself in the mirror. He set
aside several shirts as he could not decide which one to wear. I
was at my usual station, on the landing at the ironing board. I was
zipping through his shirts with ease. I thought Manley should wear
his black clergy collar shirt with either his black or navy-blue suit.
But I will not be giving unsolicited advice. He was in an excellent
mood, and I did not want to upset him and face his wrath. I doubt
he will hit me, but sometimes the verbal abuse was worse than the
physical abuse, and the physical abuse was terrible.

I was still trying to work out what I could have done to deserve
such wicked treatment at the hands of my husband. I was beaten
for the simplest of mistakes or what he perceives as slights. He
tried his best to turn the children against me, putting me down
in front of them. It was only a matter of time before he started
beating me in front of the girls or hitting them, too. They are
good girls, witty and cheeky like other children, but they are not
allowed to put a foot out of place without being on the receiving
end of "the look" Manley shot their way.

When I thought about it, my Mary and Martha were petrified of him. No wonder Mary chewed her nails down to the quick. She had developed a little stutter that got worse after her father told her off for not behaving like a Pastor's kid. He was closer to Ruth and Rebecca because they are compliant, too young to defy him. They had a ritual of running in between Manley's legs after church whilst he spoke to parishioners. To everybody on the outside it looks endearing, especially when he holds baby Esther too. It was just the image Manley wanted to project, Pastor Manley Morgan, perfect family man.

The only thing was, I was tired of putting in the required effort to play my part; I was done with the role playing. I was a fraud, giving young women a very false narrative and I was not willing to do that anymore. I needed to get through this day, hour by hour without breaking.

Manley went with his black clergy collar with his black suit. I helped him to get his hand through the sleeve since he still had difficulty with the cast. I got hold of the lint roll to brush him down from his shoulders to his ankles. He looked very smart as he checked himself out in the wardrobe mirror. I was glad to be seeing the back of that wardrobe too. Many a night, over the last eleven years, I had spent kneeling down in there when Manley wanted to teach me a lesson in submission and obedience.

As the girls were now up, we had Christmas breakfast, callaloo and saltfish, served with fried plantains. Everybody asked for seconds. Afterwards, we sat in the living room and watched the girls tear open their presents.

At twelve noon, Manley was gone. He was more caught up with rushing to meet his friend, than saying goodbye to us. As soon as he left, I sprang into action. The older girls were sent to shower and get dressed in their Christmas clothes. I washed Ruth and Rebecca and helped them to get ready. I bathed and dressed baby Esther.

Back in the kitchen, I filled my trolley with the roasted capon, a dish full of rice 'n' peas and a tray of macaroni cheese. After slaving in the kitchen all night, I was not about to leave my food for Manley. I jumped in the shower while the girls were watching The Grinch, a classic film shown on TV at this time of year. I stole a few more minutes of hot water than I was typically allowed, since I figured Manley was not here to punish me.

When the taxi arrived, we would all get in and we would live happily ever after. Or so I wish! If there was a hard way of doing something, I always found it.

Back downstairs, fully dressed, Mary and Martha were trying to comfort baby Esther. She looked like she is straining to do a poo. Poor pudding had been suffering from bouts of constipation since I couldn't breastfeed her anymore. I gave her another dose of gripe water, hoping that it would give her welcome relief.

Manley must have reached Hertfordshire by now, I thought, looking at the clock. I looked over my INCH list again, like I had done every day; I was ready. The next hour went incredibly slowly. I occupied my mind by watching the film with the girls. It was a foolish film starring Jim Carrey, but we all laugh. Esther was a little better and had finally fallen asleep, so I put her down for a nap.

Adanna called to say I missed an excellent church service. I told her that Manley did not organise a taxi ahead of time.

"Well gal, you should have said!" She replied in her Trini accent. "My cousins own the cab office on the high street, they would have come and got you and the children at a drop of a hat. Next time ah?"

There will be no next time, I thought to myself.

"The baby wasn't too well either, so it was for the best. I am having a good day with my girls."

"Great, Rose. Maurice called me to say they were coming back early, but Manley wanted to stay for fellowship with Pastor Harry and family."

"I hope they stay," I said firmly but a little too quickly.

"How ya mean, Rose?"

"I mean it is a fantastic opportunity for Manley to network and have fellowship with the other ministers," I managed to recover myself.

"Yes, I suppose so. I'll text Maurice and tell him to stay."

"OK, I'll call Manley when I think the service is done. Bye Adanna."

"Rose? Manley left his mobile behind apparently."

I then spot Manley's phone on the mantelpiece. "Thanks for letting me know." I put the phone down, thinking I may have to postpone. The time was 2:30pm. As if I had willed it, Manley's phone rang, it was Manley.

"Rose, I'm calling from Maurice's phone, the service went well. Don't start dinner without me, we're on our way back! Maurice wants to get back to his wife, with the baby on his way and all...Rose?"

"I'm here, where are you now?" I tried not to sound too concerned, but inside I was terrified. He mumbles something to Maurice.

"We're back in London, about half an hour away."

I felt sick to my stomach. From my calculations, the getaway taxi and Manley would arrive at the same time. I told the girls to put their coats on and stand by the front door. They looked so smart with their brand-new backpack's, courtesy of Patti and Antoinette.

"We're going away for a few days."

"Yippee!" The girls squeaked.

"What about daddy?" Martha piped up. Mary looked at me, nonplussed.

"No, just us."

"Good," Mary said.

I peeped out the window to see a black taxi park up outside. The driver, a tall, dark-skinned man is coming up the drive. Mary opened the door.

"Hello, young lady. My name is Dennis. Is mammy there?" Seeing me, he broke into a huge smile.

"Mrs Morgan?"

I nodded.

"The other Mrs Morgan sent me to collect you!" He laughed at his own joke. "Shall I take these bags?" He grabbed the suitcase and trolley.

"Thank you so much," I responded. "Girls, follow the gentleman and get into the taxi."

They all filed out after him as I grabbed my bags, the baby's bag and Esther. It was freezing cold outside.

"Your big girl can hold the trolley in the cab. Let me put the booster seats in for the little ones. Pass me the car seat for the baby and let me strap her in for you." The driver instructed.

I did as I was told but Esther started to scream.

"Nah sah!" The taxi driver said, wrinkling his nose. "I think your baby has done a poo."

"OK," I said, weighing up my options. "I'll change her in the cab."

"No, Mrs. We have a two-hour drive ahead of us. I cannot drive that far with me cab a stink so!"

I checked the time, it was 2.55pm! Manley would be home any minute now. I released Esther from her car seat and took a nappy and wipes from the baby bag. I ran up the path to the house and quickly opened the door. In the living room, I placed Esther on the floor. She was as happy as Larry, having relieved herself of everything she had eaten. Her feces were runny and trailed all the way up her back. I had to use several wipes to clean her up. Manley's phone rang again.

"Yes, Manley?"

"I keep forgetting you don't have your mobile. We're around the corner. Maurice had a brilliant idea. Pack up our dinner, we're going to Maurice and Adanna's to spend Christmas together."

"OK Manley, where's my cell phone?"

"Errrrm in the electric cupboard..." I cut him off. I did not know why, or if the phone slipped out of my hand but it drops unceremoniously into Esther's dirty nappy. Without a second thought, I wrapped up the nappy and made it to the front door, only pausing to collect my phone from its hiding place. I heard Maurice's car before I saw it coming into view. I could hardly breathe as I dumped the soiled nappy in the bin and raced towards the taxi. Poor Esther was not even dressed properly. Maurice's car pulled up behind the taxi. I was about to step inside when two joggers passed me, they look familiar. To my surprise it was Grace and Gabriel!

"Driver? We need to leave right now, right now!" I yelled.

He started the cab, sensing the urgency in my voice. I looked through the back window to see Manley spread eagled on the floor. The angels have purposely bumped into him and were fussing over him.

I did not resume breathing until we reached the high street. Thank God for Dennis, he was a chatterbox. What I imagined a typical black taxi driver was like, with a Jamaican accent to boot. He could talk about anything and everything and I was grateful for the distraction. The girls had fallen asleep by the time we hit the motorway.

Dennis spoke about Jamaican politics, about Portia Simpson-Miller discussing reparations for slavery with British prime minister David Cameron. I remembered the story from watching the news a few months back. Cameron was not going to consider reparations but was interested in building a new prison in Jamaica instead. Dennis was not impressed. He was very articulate and well read. There is so much going on in Jamaica that I knew nothing about. As Dennis proceeded to speak about the famous people he has driven in his taxi, Mary was stirring.

"Yeah, I picked up Naomi Campbell once, you know her, the supermodel? She had just arrived back in London from New York fashion week...she was delightful."

"Hello, sleepy head," I whispered.

"Yeah, she was nothing like how the media portrays her..." Dennis continued talking.

Mary hands me her phone, she looked distressed. My heart sank, there are fifteen missed calls from her father.

Chapter Nineteen

PATTI

"OK, Patti, can you count back from ten for me please?"
"OK what time is it first?"

My nurse Jasmine checked the time on the watch attached to the breast pocket of her uniform.

"It's 4pm, Patti."

"OK, thank you." I can feel the cold liquid entering my bloodstream.

"10, 9, 8, 7..."

My eyes rolled back in my head, and I am out for the count. It seemed like only minutes had gone by when I heard the nurse call out to me again.

"Patti, the procedure is over now, can you hear me?"

I was trying to open my eyes, but my eyelids were so heavy. "What time is it?"

The nurse checked her watch again. "It's just after 6pm, you're in the recovery room now. Are you in any pain?"

The lights were too bright in here, and the room was spinning. I surrendered to the darkness again.

I woke up, and I was back where I started my day, in my private room. It was dark now but when I arrived, it looked more like a hotel room than a hospital. My lips felt dry, and my throat was parched. Out of the darkness, Jasmine came towards me.

"Patti, the surgeon will be along to talk to you about your operation now you're awake. Can I get you something to drink and perhaps something light to eat? I imagine you have been nil by mouth since midnight last night."

I nodded my head.

"By the way, here are your wedding rings. You asked me to hold onto them for you."

She slipped the rings back onto my ring finger.

"Now you're awake, is there anybody I can call for you?"

I paused, Marcus was working away, he would be back on New Year's Day. Yolanda went to her dad's, Veronica was at home, probably cooking to feed the proverbial "five thousand" and Antoinette was spending her first official Christmas with Malakai and Elijah. I shook my head sadly.

"OK I'll be back in a jiffy."

I tried to sit up, with my chest heavily bandaged but it was proving difficult. I slumped back into my pillow and the tears roll down my face. I bet Marcus tried to speak to me before he started work and he was probably worried about me. I missed him, too. Less than a week ago we were celebrating my promotion, dancing, eating and drinking with a room full of people and now I'm here all alone.

I was so busy supporting everybody else and pretending I was Olivia Pope that I had not allowed my family and friends to be there to help me. It was my own fault.

Dr Harris entered my room with the nurse. Jasmine helped me get comfortable and stood nearby while Dr Harris sat at the end of my bed.

"Patti, we removed four lumps from your breast. However, we're going to keep you in overnight."

I was crying again. I should have anticipated that they were not going to discharge me the same day.

"You lost more blood than expected during the procedure and we just want to observe you during the night...if everything's OK by the morning, you will be home in time for Christmas lunch."

Dr Harris stood and talked to nurse Jasmine before leaving. "Patti can have a couple slices of toast now."

The doctor exited the room as gracefully as she walked in.

"Brown or white bread Patti?"

"All please, my stomach thinks my throat's been cut."

We both laughed.

~~~~~

Around seven in the morning, I found myself wide awake and I was feeling a little sore today. I reached for my phone and saw that

I had a few missed calls from Marcus. He must be worried about me by now. I scrolled through my phone and called Veronica.

"Mum? Merry Christmas. Are you back from mass?" I asked

"Yes love, it was a lovely service."

"Where are you? Are Auntie and Uncle Jim coming to yours?"

"No love, she and the man that lives in her house had a row, so they are not coming. You know what the two of dem are like when they have words. I don't want to get in the middle of them. I'm no Kofi Annan!"

I didn't speak, I didn't know where to start.

"Are you OK, Patti? You don't sound yourself."

"Because I'm not myself mum."

"Lord Jesus, what happen now?"

"I'm in Roding Hospital mum. I had surgery to remove lumps from my breast."

I could hear Veronica take a sharp intake of breath.

"Oh, my baby, you should have told me. Does Marcus know?" I ignored the question.

"The thing is, they want to discharge me, but they want to know my family are on hand to help me out for a few days..."

"I'm on my way!"

~~~~~

"Listen, ma daughter just came out of the hospital this morning," Veronica warned the taxi driver "Tek your time over them speed bumps and no driving like you're at Silverstone."

"Yes, Madam," he replied, tapping Veronica's postcode into his sat nav.

I had a small cushion in between me and the seatbelt, and Veronica was holding my hand.

"I have changed the sheets on the bed in your room for when you're ready to rest up? Did you have breakfast in dere?"

I could see nothing but concern and worry on her face.

"Yes, Mum." I was not fobbing her off either, even though historically, I always skipped breakfast, this morning I had porridge oats and a full English breakfast consisting of sausages, bacon scrambled eggs, mushrooms and baked beans, I was paying for it after all.

"What's been going on with you, Patti?"

"I found a lump in my breast in Jamaica, just before the wedding. Long story short, the scan came back with three more. They removed them successfully yesterday."

"And the prognosis?" Veronica looked so sad.

"My consultant suspects a sclerosis lesion of the breast tissue. Normally benign, but they will know more after the results from the biopsy comes back from the lab in January."

Veronica began crying. I squeezed her hand.

"Patti, don't think for a moment that I would not have been there for you if you had told me. You have me, Yolanda, and Marcus. We is you family."

"I know mum, but you're here for me now."

When we arrive back at Veronica's, the house is in darkness and Veronica flicks on the hall lights with flair as though she was switching on the Christmas lights at Oxford Street.

"Tah-dah!" she exclaimed.

I had to blink several times before my eyes adjusted. The hall looks gaudy, like the entrance to Santa's grotto, decked out with tacky shiny decorations and tinsel dangling strategically from the ceiling. Veronica reused the same decorations every year. I surmised that her neighbour Everton must have put them up for her, under her strict instructions, since I couldn't imagine Veronica at her time of life, standing on a step ladder, risking a fall at any moment.

Normally, seeing all this fuss and palaver would upset me. But this festive period, I welcomed the familiarity and nostalgia of the Christmases of yesteryear. It made me feel warm and fuzzy inside. After the sterile whiteness of the hospital walls and the grey dull drive home, I embraced my family home of technicolour, warmth and most of all, a home where I was loved unconditionally.

We walked through to the kitchen diner and Veronica helped me take my coat off. She was chattering away but I was not listening. I was breathing in the Christmas smells, and it was filling me up with precious memories. The kitchen was spotless, and it sparked another childhood memory of growing up as a looked after child in the Scotland's household.

Although the Christmas tree was up all year round, the preparations for Christmas day itself started on Easter Monday, which was a bank holiday. Veronica would clean the kitchen from top to bottom. Then, out would come her beloved food processor from a box she kept at the back of the cupboard. That got a wipe down too. Then these mysterious packets of dried fruit would appear from a carrier bag kept in a bag, which was then sealed in another bag. It was easier breaking into Fort Knox than opening all those plastic bags.

Veronica would take her time and blend the dried currants, raisins and prunes into a smooth paste in her beige iconic ceramic mixing bowl, which every serious baker possessed at the time. Afterwards, she would add Rich Ruby fortified wine incrementally to the fruit, ensuring she didn't waste a drop, combining the liquid until it was absorbed. Lastly, she filled several Tupperware containers with the mixture to steep for the next eight months, occasionally adding rum – Bajan rum, of course – to the fermenting fruits every few weeks. The potency of the mixture alone could have anyone drunk if they took a whiff from the containers.

Years ago, I wrote a report on a woman who was prosecuted for drunk driving offences when she drove her car after eating rum cake at a christening. I chuckled at the memory.

The closer we got to the holiday period, us foster kids would have our chores to do. We literally "picked down the house", a term Veronica used, and cleaned everything. Skirting boards got dusted, doorframes got washed down with soapy water, windows and mirrors got polished with pink Windolene until they shone. Veronica would hang new nets and curtains in every room and soft furnishings like the chair back covers and cushions got removed and were replaced with the best ones reserved for Christmas.

Veronica took pride in dressing her dining room table, which was extended to accommodate the dinner guests. She would spread out a special off-white lace tablecloth and matching napkins with gold ring napkin holders, a gold runner down the centre of the table with a red poinsettia flowers at the centre. Veronica then laid her posh dining set and silverware, and the table was filled with white crocheted doilies to protect the table from coming into contact with Pyrex bowls of hot food.

Barbadian gospel singer Joseph Niles would be singing reggae style carols quietly in the background. Strictly no Baja music allowed, meaning no secular music was to be played on the Lord's birthday. One good thing about Veronica was, the children in her charge always ate first, Christmas day or not.

The table was where I sat now, Christmas 2015, recovering from surgery.

"Who's coming over today, Mum?" I asked.

Veronica joined me at the table, placing a hot mug of sorrel and ginger tea in front of me and a large slice of coconut bread, before sucking her back teeth.

"Stupse! Well child, Cynti and she husband was supposed to come over. A taxi was booked and everything." She pulled out the dining chair next to me and slumped down in the chair. Her demeanour looking pained and discombobulated. "They had a row last night. She wants to come here but he wants to stan' home. She vexed wid he but she ain't coming out without him. You know how cantankerous he can be?"

I didn't know, but I nodded anyway. Uncle was always quiet and reserved. I paused to reflect. "So, if I wasn't here, you would have spent Christmas day all on your own? Oh, mum!" I went to reach out to her, wincing in pain.

"Don't worry yourself, Patti. I good you know." She wiggled in her chair, stiffening her back, trying to look stoic. I could tell she was upset.

The aromatic smells of Barbadian cuisine filled my nostrils to testify that Veronica had killed the proverbial fatted calf for her dinner guests. And if I know Veronica, there was probably a fatted calf still roasting in the oven, alongside roast beef, a turkey and all the trimmings. For now, I was going to finish my tea and cake and go up to my bedroom to get some rest.

"You hear from Marcus?" Veronica rose from her chair.

"No, Mum. It's still early. He'll probably call me later after work."

"Oh," was all she said back. I knew she was thinking what kind of man travels abroad knowing his wife was having surgery. She did not know that I hadn't told him, I wasn't planning on telling her, but the nurses had given me no choice.

I looked up at the clock. It was only 11 O'clock but I felt like I had been awake the whole day. I yawned, thinking to myself, *I hope my ladies are okay.* In a few hours' time, all hell was going to break loose.

~~~~~

I used the handrail, and I took my time to get upstairs to my old bedroom. Veronica helped me into bed and propped me up with extra pillows. *If sleeping was an Olympic sport, I would win a gold medal*, I thought to myself as I sunk into the soft pillows. I wasn't sure how long I was asleep for, but I woke up suddenly, startled by the ringing of my phone. The curtains were drawn even though it was still light outside. I recognised the number it was Charmaine's mum.

"Hello?"

"Hello, Miss Patti. It's Charmaine's mother here. Charmaine asked me to let you know she has left to go to the place."

Her voice was almost a whisper.

"That's very good news," I responded. "Do you have a relative or friend you can go by today?" I was concerned Junior may show up at her home and harass her.

"My brother is in Leytonstone. I am going there for lunch tomorrow..." she trailed off.

"Listen, go there tonight and sleep over."

"OK, OK, but I'm not scared of Junior you know!"

"I know but Junior is a very violent man, and he probably thinks you know where she is."

"OK, I understand."

"In the meantime, I don't care if Jesus comes knocking at your door today, you do not open it for anybody. OK?"

"OK and thank you for helping her escape. I thought to myself one day he was going to kill her."

I checked the time on my phone, and I wondered how Rose is faring. I must have drifted off again, I could hear raised voices in my sleep. It sounded similar to Marcus' voice, and he seemed angry. I must be dreaming.

"Is my wife here? I don't care if she's resting, I want to see her now!"

There was a thudding of someone running up the stairs and along the landing. I opened my eyes, the room was in darkness, then it bursts into light. I was disoriented, thinking I was in my own bed in Gants Hill. It is Marcus, and he looks so angry, but his anger disappeared as soon as he saw the state of me.

"Oh, my God, Patti!" He rushed to kneel by the bed beside me. He tenderly kisses my hands.

"What's happened? I have been calling you since yesterday to tell you I was coming home. I caught the last ferry back to Southampton and I have been on the road ever since. Then I got a call from my brothers...I thought you left me."

He was crying now, and I saw mum retreating and closing the door behind her. It was a while before he composed himself. I told him all about the lump and he kept asking me why I did not tell him. He would never have gone away and left me on my own.

"I'm your husband, Patti. You don't keep those kinds of secrets from me. In sickness and in health, we promised each other not that long ago."

"I'm sorry, Marcus."

"What else is going on, Patti? My brothers are making all kinds of accusations about you."

I exhaled. "Come and sit on the bed Hun, I'll tell you everything."

Marcus was calm, listening to me intently, until I told him about Manley and Junior threatening me. I nervously swivel my wedding ring around my finger as I recalled the encounter. He jumped up, then and paced the room saying, he was going to kill them.

"Did they touch you?"

"No, no, no, Marcus, I'm telling you everything." I rushed to say, "Antoinette and I have been helping Rose and Charmaine to get away."

He stopped pacing to look at me.

"Were you planning on leaving me today too?"

"No babes, why would I want to leave you? I love you!"

I managed to talk Marcus out of confronting his brothers and to just spend the rest of Christmas Day with me. Veronica had spread an old picnic blanket on the bed, and we had our first Christmas meal together. I got a text message from Dennis to confirm he had safely delivered the package. Rose and her family were finally safe, I told Marcus.

"I'm proud of you Patti. I understand why you did not say anything to me. I know what Junior is like, but I have to admit, Manley had me completely fooled." He shook his head.

~~~~~

It is probably the best sleep I have ever had. Marcus spooned me most of the night. And now he was downstairs making me brunch, because it was already midday. I read a text from Yolanda, no doubt Veronica told her about my operation, and she was coming by later. I called Antoinette.

"Christmas Greetings," Antoinette said happily.

"Hey girl, how was your first Christmas with Elijah?"

"Fan-bloody-tastic! We had so much fun, just the three of us! And how was your Christmas? Did you go by your mum's?"

"I'm still here. Listen Antoinette, nothing to worry about but I had minor surgery on Thursday. I had a few lumps and bumps removed but as I said, I'm OK."

"Are you for real, Patti?"

"Yes, but mum and Marcus are looking after me now. Marcus came home early."

"That's wonderful, Patti. But remind me to give you a lash for not telling me you were not well!"

"OK, I'll give you all the deets when I see you next month. Can you put my baby on the phone so I can wish him a Merry Christmas please?"

"His Highness is not here, he left with his father to visit his other grandmother."

"Oh." I was a little disappointed. "What time are they due back?"

"They only just left. Malakai wanted me to go with them, but girl if it requires me putting a bra on to go somewhere today, it is not going to happen. Plus, you know what Malakai's mother is like and I ain't able to deal with her, you hear?"

I have only met Malakai's mother once, but from what Antoinette told me, she's the black version of Mrs Hyacinth Bouquet off the telly in the show Keeping Up Appearances. Antoinette liked nice things, but she was very down to earth, saving her airs and graces for the courtroom. On the other hand, Malakai's family were from old money, upper middle class and fair skinned and his mother had to let people know how rich and connected they were at every opportunity.

"Any feedback from Rose and Charmaine?" I asked.

"Yep, I heard from them both last night and this morning. It sounds as though they both got a good night's sleep. Charmaine is hoping to get a transfer to Primark in Southend."

"Oh, that's really good."

"My girl Charmaine is not messing about. She's already talking about filing for divorce! That Junior Morgan don't know who he's dealing with."

"And Rose?" I asked.

"Very, very early days. But I will support her while you recover, so don't worry, you've done enough for these girls."

That's all I needed to hear.

"How are you spending the rest of the holidays?" I changed the subject.

"In this position hopefully, cooking, eating, playing snakes 'n' ladders with Elijah. The prep for my next case doesn't start until mid-January....hold on a minute, there's somebody at my door. I'm not expecting anybody...'WHAT DA FUCK ARE YOU DOING ON MY KISS ME ASS DOOR? NO, YOU CAN'T COME IN YOU FUCKING BASTARDS!'"

"Where are our children?"

Oh, my days, that man sounds like Manley Morgan! I thought. I heard Antoinette's phone hit the floor. Antoinette started screaming and I bolted upright in the bed.

"ANTOINETTE! ANTOINETTE! ARE YOU ALRIGHT?" I screamed into the receiver.

"Just tell me where they are, and nobody gets hurt."

The line goes dead.

CHAPTER TWENTY

CHARMAINE

"**E**mergency. Which service?"

"The Police, please," Chris responded. I could hear the panic in his voice. He's bricking it.

"Police control room, what is your name?"

"Christopher Collins"

"And the number you are calling from?"

"Zero, Seven, Nine, Six, Nine, Four, Four, Eight, Eight, One."

"What is your emergency, Christopher?"

"I have a CAD number for you."

"OK, go ahead"

"Charlie, Alpha, Delta, four, seven, four, zero, two, six, nine."

"Please hold while that report is uploading... right... I have it now," the operator paused. "It says here that you are a London black taxi cab driver, please confirm your cab number for me?"

"Yes, sure, cab number is two, six, zero, nine."

"Thank you, are Mrs Charmaine Morgan and her children with you now?"

"Yes, madam. And terrified. Her estranged husband clocked us as we were leaving, and he is in pursuit now."

Chris checked the rear-view mirror and reports what he sees. "He's not behind us at the moment but it's just a matter of time."

"Where exactly are you right now?"

"Right now, I'm on Plaistow High Street heading towards Prince Regent's Lane."

"OK, can you give me details of the pursuing vehicle?"

"A black M series BMW. Registration number Tango, Three, Seven, Six, Whiskey, Whiskey, Charlie."

"Thank you, that's great."

"If he catches up and cuts us off before we get to the A13 we're done for, he's a very violent man and we've pissed him off!"

"I understand that, sir. Try to stay calm. Hold the line for me, please?"

I could hear lots of static on the line and other operators talking in the background. I imagined a large room of people dealing with life threatening emergencies as they found calmness in the chaos around them. I also tried to remain calm.

"Christopher, are you still there?"

"Yes, I am."

"We need you to continue travelling East on the A112 and turn left into Newham Leisure Centre. Officers from the traffic team will carry out a routine traffic stop on his vehicle as part of our annual drink drive campaign. Stay there until I tell you to leave."

"Roger dat." Chris hangs up the phone. "I 'ave always wanted to say that you know." He looked at me in the mirror and laughed. "Mi used to love watching *The Bill* when it come pon the telly, back in the day."

I picked up a slight Jamaican accent, reminding me of my dad and I feel instantly comforted. I held my babies closer to me. Thankfully, the motion of the car journey had put them to sleep. When the twins were teething and wouldn't sleep, Junior would strap them in their car seats and take them for a spin around the block. I did not know if it was the heat in the car or the sound of the engine, but it did the trick.

"Sweet Honey Iced Tea!" Chris exclaimed, checking all of his mirrors.

I look behind me too and I could see Junior's car gaining ground behind us. My heart jumped up to my mouth, choking me, so I couldn't breathe. Chris puts his foot down on the gas, running a red light. Junior's car was forced to stop to allow a family to cross at the pedestrian crossing.

At that moment, the road bent, we turned and passed a group of waiting police officers who wave us through. Two minutes later, Junior fell into their trap. When Chris stopped the cab outside the leisure centre, I exhaled.

"What a ting, eh? It's a good job Miss Patti was on the ball with dat CAD report. She rang the police non-emergency number ages ago in case things went tits up! Pardon my French."

Chris passed me a bottle of water and I took long sips.

"Are you alright, Miss?"

"Yes. Thank you, Chris. If I had high blood pressure, it would be through the roof by now!"

"I know right? But I was never worried..."

He so was, but I did not challenge him.

"If it came on top, I would have landed some blows on him ya see?"

Chris started shadow boxing and it made me laugh.

"Thankfully, it did not come to that."

His phone rang.

"Christopher, it's the control room. You are free to leave the centre. The assailant is detained at the scene with several suspected traffic offences. Good luck to you."

"Thank you darling. Over and out!" Chris hung up the call. "OK," he said, re-positioning the glasses on his face. "Let's do this."

The vehicle roared to life, and we were on our way again. Apparently, I was being relocated to Chalkwell, a couple of miles away from Southend, outside of London in the County of Essex. I was relieved, I could finally sit back and start enjoying the journey.

Chris was chatting away, telling me how he met Patti almost 6 years ago. She had lost her debit card on a night out in the West End, and she hailed him with some sob story about having no money. He almost drove off until he clocked her designer shoes and handbag. He took her home and she came good with the fare the following day. They have been friends ever since.

"You weren't at her party last week, were you?" He said taking his eye off the motorway to speak to me.

"No, I couldn't make it," I replied.

"Shame about dat. Patti and her mudda throw the best parties. I ate so much food I thought my belly was going to burst!" He laughed at the memory. "My wife and I danced all night. Did I tell you about my wife, Pam? We've been married for 35 years and never a crossed word. She is the love of my life, and she cooks the best curry chicken in the world."

My tummy rumbled at the thought of food. I was too nervous to eat all of my Christmas dinner and breakfast was a long time ago. Chris rambled on, talking about their trips to Jamaica, spending time with family and friends in Montego Bay and in Kingston. *What a way the man can chat,* I thought to myself. I could not get a word in edgewise.

He told me all about his wife's job in the city and about his children who were doing well. His son was a special police constable with the Met and his daughter was a fashion designer. Two hours later, we turned off the motorway, where everything was a lot more affluent. There were a lot more open spaces, and everything seemed greener, more serene. The children were just as excited as I was to see the sea on our right. We count the boats with their lights twinkling that reflected against the evening sky and I promised them I would take them to the beach in the morning.

"This is as far as I can go," Chris said. "Blokes can't go any further I'm told. See the white house over dere so?"

He pointed to a massive house with a porch lit up with blinking fairy lights. "That's where you will be staying. Let me help you with your stuff."

I glimpsed at the fare all lit up in red and started fretting when I read £121. My head started to throb. The pain began at my temples and travelled to the back of my head. I noticed since my head injury, every time I got stressed out, my head hurts. I had a little money on me, but I would need to find a cashpoint for another £20.

"Don't watch that, Patti and her friend Antoinette have sorted the fares already."

I started to cry.

"Now, now, you have been brave all day lady. It's been a long day, so fix up yourself and get those babies inside outta da col', ya hear?"

He gave me a hug and bent down to speak to the twins.

"You two look after mummy, OK?"

He patted them on their heads and then he was gone.

I dragged our belongings to the door and rang the bell. I was thinking our new lives were about to begin, when my phone lit up with a text message, it's from Junior.

"You ugly, fat, bitch, when I find you, and I fuckin will find you, you're a fuckin dead woman!"

CHAPTER TWENTY-ONE

ROSE

M y birthday on Boxing Day and then New Year's Day passed by in a blur and the older two girls were about to start their new school. Mary was anxious about starting a new school, where all of the other children have known each other since nursery school, but she could hardly go back to her old school. At least she had Martha at the same school, and they could look out for each other. Ruth and Rebecca were at nursery school, while baby Esther attended the crèche, which was on site and was managed by the staff at the refuge.

It was recommended that I have a counselling session with a specialist and I agreed, on the condition that my therapist would be a black woman, with roots in the Caribbean, preferably from London. The Butterfly women's refuge was based in Westbrook Bay, near Margate.

Although it was picturesque and remote, the demographics of the people are so different in comparison to Battersea. For example, if I fancy a plantain or run out of Scotch bonnet peppers, I knew where to go and how much I was expected to pay. Battersea has had its season of gentrification with coffee shops and overpriced sandwich shops, but they are alongside patty shops and Asian newsagents, with their £1 baskets of fruits and veg laying on crates outside on a bed of fake grass.

Westbrook Bay was very different, and I felt isolated in a different way entirely. I was incredibly homesick. l yearned for my church family and my church community. The only black people I saw were some of the other residents. They were a diverse bunch of women from all over London, but that is where the similarities end. They were not my kind of women and I had nothing in common with any of them. I did not like any of the staff members either, considering how it was an all-white staff group. I just got the impression that they were constantly assessing me, and I was coming up short.

The phone calls and text messages made my loneliness one hundred times worse. I had received calls from everybody begging me to come back home, back to Manley. Surprisingly, Sister Loretta left a message offering marriage counselling at the churches expense. My parents were more embarrassed than anything else, praying this was a tiff that would blow over and that I would return to my senses.

During the stressful days between Christmas and New Year, two things surprised me. Adanna reached out and Manley did not. No phone calls, no voice messages, no text messages. He did not even contact me about seeing his children and I think he has instructed his mother not to contact me either, because I never heard a dickie bird from her. I heard from Patti, and I felt bad when she told me she had surgery. I was so angry when I heard about Manley and Junior turning up at Antoinette's home, and the police had been involved.

Up until now, nobody knew how they found her address. I pray God will reveal that person soon. Thank goodness one of her neighbours came to her rescue. I was blessed to hear from Charmaine every day, once in the morning and in the evening on her way home from work. She had resumed working at a local branch of Primark and was thinking about saving up to stay in the area permanently. She could see herself running along the beach when the weather was milder.

During my first counselling session, I met Karen. When she entered the room, she was all smiles and extremely bubbly. I told her my name, even though she probably already knew it. My key worker Sam completed a referral form about me for sure. There was probably more information about me that she knew too. Abi, the Nigerian woman in the room next-door to mine, had already warned me to be careful with what I disclosed to the people here. Everything was on the record, so I reminded myself to be cautious about what I revealed to these so-called professionals, even the black ones. We took each other in as she shook off her coat. She is fair skinned, full figured, sporting a blonde afro under her bobble hat.

"Out there is freezing," she said, blowing into her hands in an attempt to warm them up. "I am a self-confessed hugger I'm afraid." Before I could protest, she wrapped me in an embrace.

I tried to pull away, but she held me in a vice grip. She was taller than me and she smelled so sweet, like peppermint. I was suddenly aware that I might not have smelled appealing right now.

"Any chance of a cup of hot water?" she said, breaking away from me. "I have a couple of herbal teas in this bag somewhere."

I left her rummaging through her large backpack. Rather than grabbing two cups from the communal kitchen, I had already assessed her as worthy of drinking out of my cups. I hurried to my room and rushed back with two cups and a packet of biscuits. There was something quite special about this woman, but I would wait for things to reveal themselves.

She asked me what I would like to do? She had magazines, blank canvases, watercolour paint, chalks and paper of all shapes and colours. It was my very first introduction to art therapy and I do not know what I wanted to do or where to start. The magazines looked interesting. I had never read Pride magazine. The luxury of magazines was not in my budget. I thumbed through a few pages; it felt so good seeing so many beautiful black models looking back at me. The natural hairstyles are so cleverly done and artistic. I wondered if I asked Karen, if she would let me keep the magazine to read later on. As if she read my mind, she said, "You can keep that mag if you like?"

That smile again, so warm and so open. I placed the magazine on my lap so I wouldn't forget it. I caressed the canvases, choosing one to draw a picture. When Karen finished her tea, she joined me at the table.

"Excellent decision. I have some lovely dried rose petals if you want to add texture to your picture. Shall we begin?"

It was more of a getting to know you session, where Karen and I exchanged questions about each other, hers were personal and my questions are professional. Karen's family is from Barbados. She studied locally and lives in London. She has loads of qualifications in her field and years of experience working with men and women experiencing trauma. I figured I was in good hands.

"It must be a big change for you? How's that working out for you, Rose?"

"It's not, if I'm honest." I got silent.

"Listen, Rose, unless you're about to hurt yourself, your children or somebody else, I am not obliged to report back what you tell me. OK?"

"OK," I replied. "I don't like it here. It's safe, it's relatively clean, but it's not home."

Karen listened to me intently.

"For a start, we're all crammed up in one bedroom. My children refuse to sleep in the bunk beds. We all cannot fit around the table at meal times either. I eat standing up or sitting on the sofa. I don't like sharing the appliances like the washing machine or dryer. They even share the iron and ironing board here."

I must have looked so ungrateful, so I wait for her to judge me, but no judgement came. "My girls are having a rough time of it, even my baby is up two or three times in the night, when she had previously slept through. I have taken them away from everything and everybody they knew and love. It's like we're all out of sync."

I gazed across to Karen and she was sticking bits of cloth into her canvas, but I could tell she was listening to every word I was saying.

"I am embarrassed and ashamed."

"Embarrassed and ashamed about what, Rose?"

"About finding myself here at thirty-six years old. About being a statistic, I am the one in four."

Karen looked confused. "The one in four women who experience domestic abuse. It's on the posters all over this room." I said, pointing around the room. "Like I need daily reminding that I am a failure." I became aware that I was shouting.

"Overnight, I became a victim and a single parent to five little girls. Overnight! I have no skills, no income, no job because I am not employable. How am I supposed to love them when I don't even know how to love myself?" We are silent while I tried to compose myself.

Just before the session ended, Karen asked to see my new creation. "Explain what's going on here, Rose?"

I had drawn a self-portrait, at least I think it's me, but my face was obscured, covered with dried rose petals and some of the petals were dead.

"I'm hiding away from the world, behind a shield of petals, and slowly but surely, the petals are falling away. I have spent the last decade hiding, pretending, putting up, making do and shutting up. What happens when the last petal falls away?"

Before the tears fell, Karen was giving me another of her super-duper hugs. This time, I embraced it and sobbed my heart out.

CHAPTER TWENTY-TWO

PATTI

We are over at Mum's house. Veronica was on form! She was at the table "Picking the rice"—old school until the end. I got that when the rice travelled in sacks by ship from places overseas, it was necessary to check and inspect each grain, but nowadays, who's got time for that? When I asked that question, both Veronica and Marcus answered, "I do!" Veronica fist bumped Marcus.

"Turncoat," I said to my husband for siding with his mother-in-law instead of me.

"Well," he reasoned, "with all of this 'fake rice' business in the news recently, you have to resort to these old school methods." I do not want to admit it, but he is right.

"How is Antoinette keeping now?" Veronica whispered.

Marcus was going through to the lounge to watch football. His beloved team Arsenal was playing Bournemouth.

"Very much shaken up, Mum. She thinks someone at her office disclosed her address. She'll eventually get to the bottom of it, but for now, she's taking extended leave, if you remember, she is supposed to take adoption leave in the new year anyway."

"Yes, I remember you saying. Imagine if the little boy was home doh!" Mum chided.

"I know, right? That's the bit Malakai was cross about." I shuffled my chair closer to Veronica so Marcus could not overhear what I was saying. "Like Marcus, Malakai was completely in the dark. Marcus was angry with me for not telling him what had been going on. Malakai was fuming, and he's still not talking to her properly."

Veronica stopped picking the rice to put a couple of dodgy dark grains into a tin cup. I noticed she has quite a few collected and made a note to myself to pick the rice from now on.

"Oh, that's not nice," Veronica said. "Those two are normally so close. So close you cannot put a piece of paper between dem."

"I know, right? Let's hope Malakai thaws out soon."

Veronica scooped the rice into a bowl.

"So, what happened to the two brothers?" Veronica pushed her lips out toward the back of Marcus' head.

Marcus was ecstatic, Arsenal had already scored. He was chatting to one of his mates, probably Shoedoctor Martin who was also an avid Arsenal fan, on the phone, running their own commentary and catching jokes. Don't ask me who scored, because after Thierry Henri left the team in 2007, I lost interest in football altogether. And I did not know one player from another.

I followed Veronica to the sink, where she started to wash the rice under running water.

"Well, you know Malakai wanted to press charges?"

"Oh Lordy," Veronica said, shaking her head.

"Manley received a caution for threatening words and behaviour, Junior was charged with ABH..."

"How many times are they going to let that man put his hands on women before they lock his ass up?"

"Oh, Junior didn't get bail."

"Really now?"

"Nope, he is on remand until the 12th of January. Antoinette reckons he will go to prison for sure this time." I paused and looked around at Marcus, it would be halftime soon. "Manley only got away with a warning because he pulled Junior off of Antoinette."

"Oh gosh! Imagine what Charmaine had been going through all these years with that brute...Marcus, you hear from you mudda?"

Marcus was behind me. Now, I know why she switched up the conversation.

"Yes, we did on New Year's Day. She's OK, doh. Missing my dad. First Christmas without him."

"Of course, I must give she a call sometime soon." Veronica placed the rice into a saucepan of water and lit the stove.

"Remember me to her the next time you speak to her you hear?"

"Sure will," Marcus replied.

Unwrapping his hands from my waist, he heads towards the fridge.

"The beers you like are in the door, Hun"

"Thank you, Mrs Scotland."

"Man, oh, man, I tired telling you to stop being so formal, you can call me Veronica, den!"

"OK, Veronica Den." He laughed and headed back to watch the second half of the football.

"Did you find the paperwork for me, mum?"

"Yes, love," Veronica said reluctantly.

During my short stay after my operation, I let her know that after all of these years of not wanting to find my birth parents, I wanted to look for them now. Of course, Veronica was feeling away about the whole thing, and I tried to explain that it really was not about her. It is about me needing to know my full medical history, especially as the results of the biopsy were due in the morning.

"If it's important to you, then it is important to me. Let me dry my hands."

Veronica wiped her hands with a tea towel and turned the fire under the pot to its lowest setting. She joined me back at the table. I had seen a few case files in my time, but this file was huge. As my foster mother, Veronica would have contributed to putting this file together—it was eighteen years of my life. There were copies of minutes from annual case conferences and professional meetings, court papers and reports from health visitors. All pieces of a very large jigsaw that I hoped, once completed, would lead me one step closer to finding my birth mother.

I wondered if the lumps in my breast were hereditary? From the research I did, if you call google research, there is anecdotal evidence to suggest there was a genetic link.

I shuffled the papers into neat piles. Most of my stitches were dissolvable but I had to get the external stitches removed by the nurse before seeing the consultant for my post op appointment. I knew Veronica, Marcus, and the whole family were worried about me.

"Boomshakalaka!" Marcus boomed from the lounge. He was jumping in front of the TV. He certainly made Veronica and I jump in our seats.

"I would hate to see how he carries on when Arsenal loses!"

"Really, mum, you don't want to know."

"So, did you ever find out who's pregnant, Patti?"

I thought if I concentrated on staring at my birth certificate long enough, she would move on. Alas, it did not work.

"Only Cynti and I are running a book on it at the moment," she paused, "my money is on Antoinette." I stared at Veronica. "Well... miracles happen every day!"

"Who else is in the frame, Mum?"

"Every woman over eighteen and under fifty!"

"Me as well? Are you serious, Mum?"

"Of course! You're newlyweds, so you're having lots of sex! Not so?"

I blushed.

"Whatever Marcus is doing, he's doing it well! Ya complexion looks brighter, and you're less tetchy..."

I opened my mouth to speak and then closed it because she was telling the truth. Even my mother noticed I am walking around less irritable.

"Who else is on the books?"

"Yolanda, Rose, Antoinette, you and Beverley. It has to be one or the two of wanna. Anyway, you can hide and buy land, but you can't hide and work it. Time will tell."

Phew, I had gotten away without telling her about Beverley, but I would tell Marcus. I did not want this to be yet another thing between us. Marcus claimed that he went home to get a change of clothes after his trip, but I think he confronted his brothers about threatening me. When Junior called from Tilbury police station, Marcus swore at him and he ended the call, saying Junior was dead to him. To my knowledge, he has not spoken to Rose or Charmaine, but he always told me to pass on his love and prayers. He missed not seeing his nieces and nephew.

After sorting the papers and clipping everything together, Veronica dished up dinner. We ate basmati rice with stew chicken. Marcus and I left early, citing we had an early start the following morning which was true.

~~~~~

I skipped breakfast again this morning. The anxiety of learning my results was gnawing me from my inside out. This time, Marcus was with me, as supportive as ever. He was attentive, running around the car to open my car door, consistently opening the hospital doors that did not open automatically.

As we walked along the hospital corridors, all I could think of was the worst-case scenario, which was cancer, chemotherapy, radiotherapy, sickness and hair loss. I flicked my shoulder length locs over my shoulder while I still could. What a way to start 2016!

I was happy when I saw the nurse, she took out the main black threaded stitches and she was happy with how I was healing. I came out and sat next to Marcus. He had worry lines etched onto his face but yet, kissed my hand reassuringly.

"Whatever the outcome, I got you, Empress. I love you."

"I love you too, Mr Man," I replied.

We looked into each other's eyes and from a faraway place, I heard the receptionist say, "Miss Scotland, the doctor will see you now."

CHAPTER TWENTY-THREE

CHARMAINE

Antoinette got me a beautiful, lined A4 notebook for Christmas and Patti got me a very decent pen. I have been using it for the past eleven days to write a couple of paragraphs of what I called My Intentions—what I intended to do with my life from now on. It was deeper than just writing a list of resolutions that you break before January was out. I was breaking down the small steps I needed to take to turn my intentions into real actions.

~~~~~

My first intention was to get a divorce.

I almost wrote, "I'm going to ask Junior for a divorce", but I did not need to ask him for shit.

I reached for my purse and put a £1 coin into my swear box. It made a clinking noise when it lands on top of the other coins.

I had booked a session with the solicitor who volunteered at the refuge. When I first saw her, she was signing into the building, then she walked, all business like, to use one of the offices. She looked about no more than 5 feet tall, a pre-teen with her auburn hair and freckles across her face, but she was a tough cookie when I sat down with her to discuss my situation. She would be preparing my petition and sending it to Junior in prison.

He was currently on remand at Brixton Prison, and it was likely that he would receive a custodial sentence for assaulting me and Antoinette. They will also re-sentence Junior for beating up Mandy months ago, too.

By the way, I heard from Mandy. She told me Harvey was discharged from the hospital on Boxing Day, which was the best Christmas present ever, having both babies home with her. She wanted the siblings to meet up and I said I would think about it.

Back to my intentions, it is exhilarating to know that, assuming Junior does not contest the divorce, in less than six months, I could end this sorry episode of my life. If I knew leaving Junior would have felt so good, I would have left his black ass a long time ago!

~~~~~

Intention number two: be healthy.

One of the requirements for staying at the refuge was having to undergo a full medical assessment. I was immediately referred to Southend Hospital for MRI scanning. I reported that I was still having really bad headaches. Although they are less frequent, they have increased in intensity and the painkillers were not cutting it.

We also discussed my sexual health, and I was referred to the sexual health clinic. It was about time I acknowledged the bouts of untreated Chlamydia and tried to find out if it had caused internal damage to my womb. I would also have to be checked for other sexually transmitted infections. For the first time ever, I was not burying my head in the sand. I was adulting and dealing with shit. I reached for my purse and searched for another pound coin.

I had given up smoking. Yes, I gave up before, and went cold turkey, but when I arrived at the refuge and saw Junior's text message, I was shaking like a leaf. The first thing I did was cadge a cigarette off another resident. I pulled two drags off of it and it tasted awful. This time around, I had nicotine patches and I attended a support group. I gathered there was a support group here for everything!

~~~~~

My third intention: promoting my well-being.

I was having counselling, bereavement counselling to be exact. With the benefit of hindsight, I realised I should have been referred by the pastoral lead at my school, especially when I started acting out and bunking off. I went from being top to bottom of my class in weeks, and nobody connected the dots. I had spent the last fourteen years grieving for my dad, mourning for what could have been. The difference was, this time, I was finally getting professional help. I had to admit, I was not keen on my counsellor, she looked nothing like me. She was white, old, and I assumed middle class, but I committed myself to twelve weeks of counselling sessions, twice a week. just to see what would happen.

~~~~~

Intention number four: spend a little, save a lot.

Thanks to Jamal, I got my transfer to Primark in Clacton-on-Sea. It's nothing like the Romford and Westfield shops, but the crew was nice to me, and we have a laugh when we're on a shift. I had yet to accept an offer of going out with the group socially, but I would, once the children were settled. The children were well and enjoying their new nursery, which offered a wraparound service so I could work. My mum was planning to visit us for a weekend soon, staying at a bed and breakfast accommodation opposite the pier. We planned on creating new fresh memories together.

~~~~~

Intention five: to relocate to Essex.

I had no intention of going back to my home in Plaistow and my mum wanted to move to be nearer to me and her grandchildren. I had done my research and apparently, if we could sell our houses for a mint, even in the state my home is in, and buy a house with cash outright, on the outskirts of Southend. I may even have a little paper left over to buy a little run around too.

I aced the theory test last week and I was starting driving lessons as soon as I got paid. It was my intention to be on the road by the Summer, all legal and above board.

~~~~~

Intention number six: keep good people in my life.

Antoinette has asked to sponsor me, I had no idea what that meant but now we spoke twice a day. First thing in the morning and last thing at night. She encouraged me to dream pleasant dreams for myself and to keep writing down my intentions and next steps.

I was eternally grateful to my sister-in-law Patti Morgan. She was instrumental in putting me in touch with the right people who were able to help me get away safely with my children.

Where would I be without Rose? When trying to save herself, she saved me too. She was another person who I tried to speak to every day. I was worried about her and the girls, it did not appear as though she was adjusting very well in Sussex.

Mr Jamal Green...he was such a dear friend. He wants to come and visit me. Apparently, he was catching feelings for me, but I had to make it clear I wasn't looking for a relationship and he said he was OK with that. We planned to meet at Chalkwell beach once the weather improved.

My two children loved the beach. So much so, they have started swimming lessons and they have taken to it like a duck to water; my water babies. They were going to have a shock when they finally dip their toes in the sea and they realised the water isn't heated like the swimming pool, but we will cross that bridge in spring. Tonight, I was updating my journal with my new intentions.

~~~~~

Intention seven: get an education!

The last time I picked up a textbook, Adam was a teenager! I figured if I wanted to train as a midwife, the first hurdle would be for me to get some decent qualifications under my belt. I intended to study towards gaining level 3 in Math and English.

The courses were run by a tutor who came into the refuge, and it was free for all current and former residents, so even, when I was ready to leave here, I could still take the classes. My tutor Kat was so cool and a fitness addict too. I was not enthusiastic about running during the winter months, but I enjoyed her legs, bums and tums class every week.

There was a class this evening, so as soon as I set the twins down at seven, I would be back downstairs with my baby monitor having a right laugh with Kat and the other girlies who lived here. I said girlies but I was probably the youngest amongst them. They were grown ass women who got with the wrong men, too.

~~~~~

I closed my journal and checked the time. I needed to make haste to collect the twins from the nursery. Their key worker wanted to help me make a late school application to the local education department. However, I still got anxious about being summoned into the nursery. It was not that long ago their key worker at the old nursery, was calling me in to say some fuc.... I narrowly stopped myself from swearing again – some rubbish.

Reflecting back now, their previous key worker only had dealings with me, when 9 times out of 10 it was Junior's bad behaviour the twins mimicking. The last time Aronda had called me in, I was mortified learn that Garrison was seen rolling tracing paper into an imaginary spliff. Well that was all in the past now.

We took the scenic route home so the children could throw stones into the icy water and run along the stony beach. They were so talkative and curious and asked me so many questions. After dinner, it was bath and bedtime. I read them a story by Trish Cooke called, *So Much*. They fell asleep halfway through the story and I decided to switch on the night light and put on a cassette which played "Perfect Day" on a loop.

I grabbed the baby monitor and went downstairs to the main hall for class. Kat was on form, and we paired off to do some floor exercises. Another resident was holding my ankles while I tried some sit ups, when we switched places, my head was pounding. I just about made it back to the flat to take two painkillers.

I woke Garrison first, then Geraldine so they could use the loo, then I set myself a hot bath while I put the children back to bed. The bath was luxurious, melting away all my aches and pains as I thought about what I was going to write in my journal. Everything was quiet, peaceful and above all, I felt safe. When I stepped out of the bath, I wrapped myself in a huge bath towel and I repeated the affirmation Patti gave me.

"I am Loveable and Worthwhile! I am Loveable and Worthwhile! I am Loveable and Worthwhile!"

A sharp pain licked my temple and I had to lean against the sink to prevent myself from falling. I feel giddy. When I looked in the mirror at my reflection, my vision was blurred, and the left side of my face was drooping downwards. I was terrified by the monster looking back at me.

I was about to panic when suddenly, my legs gave way, and I tumbled to the floor. The pain was travelling around to the back of my head, and it hurt even more when I tried to move. I tried to reach for my phone, which was on the toilet lid, but to no avail. I could not move, nor could I speak.

My head felt as though a punk rock band was having a rehearsal inside it, and I could feel pins and needles tingling throughout my body. "What the fuck is happening to me?" I scream to myself. The phone vibrated and moved closer to the edge of the toilet lid, I was willing it to fall on the floor, nearer to my reach. That must be Antoinette calling me.

CHAPTER TWENTY-FOUR

ROSE

L ord, forgive me, but I hated it here. I hated everything about
it. Above all, the smell of the place. Despite the cleaning
regime and the use of industrial disinfectant, there was this
offensive smell of people forced to live together; a communal
living smell. It was seeping into the fabric of the walls, and it
lingered on our clothes. It did not matter how carefully I hand
washed baby Esther's clothes, I could smell the odour on her skin,
and I hated it. I hated how my key worker talked down to me like I
did not have any sense. I felt like I was continually being assessed.
It was worse than being watched and judged by Manley.

Speaking of Manley, it had been nearly ten weeks since my exit
and I have not heard a dickie bird from him. Patti called me all the
time to check up on me and the girls, but she was the only 'family'
member that did. My parents told me to go back home to Pastor
and stop following Charmaine and those 'unsaved' people.

Last week, I got a trailer load of calls and text messages from
members of my prayer cell, the bulk of them telling me to go home
to my husband, and my church community as well, who said they
were praying for me. A couple of church members believe I am
possessed by the devil, and I had run off with another man.

It did make me wonder exactly what Manley told them. It hurt
that they believed him over me. Even Adanna and Loretta had
reached out, but I was too embarrassed to return their calls. I felt
like such a failure.

I was going through the motions here. I did not know how I
was going to manage the next few days, let alone the next six
months. Charmaine appeared so chirpy at her refuge, but they
were in a self-contained flat. I was sharing one bedroom with

five girls. I was living out of a suitcase and the accommodation was unsuitable. When the 1:1 sessions ended with Karen, I tried group counselling, but I did not like airing my dirty laundry in that space. I felt depressed when they were calling me a victim and in last week's session, they were talking about 'gaslighting'. When the counsellor gave examples of gaslighting in relationships, it resonated with me deeply. I felt sick to my stomach.

Speaking of dirty laundry, I had to share the kitchen and laundry room with fifteen other families, residents at the unit, and it was driving me crazy. On the weekends, I saw some things that made my stomach turn. A grown woman removed her sopping wet underwear from the washing machine.Who does that? I had always hand washed my baggy in the hand basin, that's just how I was trained. I had been washing my smalls that way since I could smell myself and trained my two eldest to wash their own underwear, with a small cake of blue soap I bought in Jamaica.

Using the communal kitchen at dinner time was also traumatic. The women did not tidy up after they used the stove or the oven. In one camp, some of the women only heat processed food and those who did cook, did not wash their meat before cooking it and they did not use seasoning. The smell made me want to throw up. In the other camp, I don't know where they managed to buy 'bush meat' around here, but the smell was overbearing. It was very inconsiderate.

My strategy during the holidays was to cook dinner straight after breakfast and warm up our food in the microwave. We ate around the small table or sat on the bed. There was definitely a pecking order amongst the residents, and being the newbie meant I was on the bottom rung.

Another islander, Naomi, was the top dog. She thought she was cute because she is fair skinned. She kept going on and on about her ancestors in Jamaica being of Scottish descent and not African. This was much to the disgust of the Nigerian women. She had extra-long manicured false nails painted in bright colours matching her multi-coloured fake hair extensions. She hardly wore any clothes, and her chest was always exposed, even when she was out in the snow. I could almost hear my mother saying, "She gonna catch consumption".

The other women in her clan appeared to hang on her every word, giving her cigarettes on demand and alcohol. The latter was a prohibited substance and in breach of the refuge rules. Naomi was the loudest, always falling out with staff about the high volume of her music. Whenever she was in my orbit, like in the TV lounge, I snatched up my children and left.

The icing on the cake was the state of the iron, the bottom was pitch black. Someone had clearly burnt something and could not be asked to clean it. That is the final straw. My long term plan was to use some of the money to rent a flat in the area. I would work out what I would do from there. In the meantime, I needed to get the girls settled as soon as possible.

Mary in particular had found the move traumatic, and she kept asking questions like, "Why did we have to leave? Why did I have to change schools? Doesn't daddy know where we are?" The younger ones were feeding off of her anxiety too, whining away and being clingy. Even baby Esther was up crying several times a night. I cannot tell you the last time I had a good night's sleep...oh yes, I could, it was in Jamaica and that seemed like a long time ago.

I gazed out of the window, regretting having left my home and feeling guilty about uprooting the girls. I should have kicked Manley out or called the police on him and had him removed. There were several legal resources that I did not explore since I was hell bent on getting away. The snow started to fall again, it looked pretty to watch but I was grateful that I did not have to go back outside until Monday. I regretted leaving my steam iron behind too, but it was way too bulky to carry when we had to flee. I decided to hatch a plan. I could travel up to London, pick up my iron and be back by 9.30pm. Patti had clearly said not to go back but I knew my husband better than he knew himself.

Manley was a creature of habit. Tomorrow was prayer meeting night. He would go by Deacon Maurice's home, and I could be in and out in under five minutes, back on the train in record time.

~~~~~

Yesterday I asked the Somali woman next door to look after the children, she missed her children and volunteered to plait their hair for me. It was Tuesday afternoon, and I made my way up from London Bridge station and I took the bus to Battersea where I shopped, incognito, in the market. I missed my plantain, yams and sweet potatoes. I also got a few packets of saltfish, but I needed to leave some room at the top of the trolley for the iron. I made my way to Avondale Road.

The lamp post that Manley crashed into before Christmas had been removed and not replaced. I crouched down behind a Land Rover which belonged to one of my neighbours and I watched the comings and goings of people on my road. I could not tell if Manley was home since he has written off his car. I wondered if he was working and if so, how was he managing without a car? For the life of me I could not imagine Manley lugging all of his tools on public transport. "Day does runs till night catches it", I think of the old Jamaican saying when the street lights buzzed on, lighting up the entire road, thereby, illuminating my hiding spot.

I could not squat here any longer and risk being seen by one of my neighbours. A black person crouching down by a car would alert them and they would call the police on me for sure. Or worst still, I would be found by Manley, and the outcome of that encounter frightened me to the core.

I did not take my eyes off door number 118, nobody went in or out, and no lights came on. I figured Manley had already left, he may have gone by Maurice's house early. Our bedroom faced the street, and I noticed the curtains upstairs have not been drawn. Perhaps Adanna has been cooking his meals for him. Lord knows Manley could not poach an egg, let alone make rice n peas.

Overnight, Manley went from his mother to me cooking his meals, and he often told me my food did not compare to his mother's. He always ate my food like he was chewing doo doo or with suspicion, like I was trying to poison him. I found it odd that he suddenly wanted to eat Christmas dinner with me and the children on Christmas day.

I guess Maurice did not want to leave Adanna, in the last trimester of her pregnancy, with the boys all day, which meant that Manley had no choice but to come back to London once he finished his sermon.

It was half past seven when I stood up and crossed the icy road. I opened the door with my keys, pleased I did not throw them away when I left, and that Manley hadn't changed the locks. The house was dark, so I waited for my eyes to become accustomed to the darkness. I took it that Manley found his phone in the dirty nappy. I crossed myself, whispering, "Lord, forgive me."

The Christmas tree and the other Christmas paraphernalia has been taken down and packed away. I ran my hand across the counter in the kitchen. Someone, probably one of the sisters in the church, had been in my home. I saw evidence of a home cooked meal, two plates, two sets of cutleries and two glasses are still on the draining board. Someone was clearly cooking for Manley. I left the kitchen spotless. I was really cross when I tried the door leading to the conservatory to find it was open, Manley obviously didn't need to keep the food locked away from me anymore. I helped myself to a couple tins of baked beans, tuna and sweetcorn, placing them in my trolley.

I wondered what story Manley had used to explain away our absence, which woman in the church felt so sorry for him that she would come into another woman's home and cook for him. I had an idea of a few women who would replace me in a heartbeat. Well, God bless them. I wished them all the best with that. I walked upstairs carefully, not wanting to turn the passage lights on. I spotted my iron, it was on the right of the ironing board, evidence that Manley had been ironing his own shirts! This was a chore I picked up as soon as we got married and I had never stopped.

I felt resentment setting in. I really was a servant, a maid and not a helpmate. I did everything in this house and Manley never said please or thank you. I was about to leave when I remembered that I wanted my family Bible. It was a present from Auntie Myrtle.

That's when I heard a noise coming from my bedroom. I stopped in my tracks with my hand on the doorknob. I listened out intently to hear something, anything. I must have imagined it because all I could hear now was my heart thumping loudly in my chest. Then, I heard it again. My Lord! Manley was at home, and he had somebody in the bedroom. What stinking Jezebel was lying on my bed, between my sheets with my husband? I turned the door handle and stood in the doorway.

The fight or flight response was a physiological reaction that occurred in response to a perceived threat to survival. My body does neither, the blood had drained from my body and is pooling at my feet, rooting them to the floor. Manley was on top of a woman making love to her. The street light poured into the bedroom, casting shadows and silhouettes. Manley was clearly enjoying himself as he tenderly moves in and out of her, and I felt jealous. He was never that affectionate with me.

From the long wig the lady was wearing, it has to be Adanna. She was supposed to be my friend! What a nasty woman to be having an affair when she was about to have a baby. I would have to tell Maurice about this betrayal, his wife and his best friend.

Just then, the woman turned her head and saw me. The only thing was, it is not Adanna smiling at me, it is Maurice.

"WHAT IN SODOM AND GOMORRAH IS GOING ON HERE!" I screamed at the top of my voice as I switched on the bedroom light to expose them.

Manley jumped out of bed with his penis still erect and he ran at me like a raging bull. He pushed me out of the door, back to the bannister, gripping my throat with his left hand and punching me in the face with his right fist, his hand still in a cast.

"WHAT" punch "THE" punch "HELL" punch "ARE YOU" punch "DOING" punch "IN MY HOUSE?" Punch. Each punch landed harder than the one before. "HOW DARE YOU COME BACK HERE!" Manley bellowed.

The blows were coming fast and thick. I was gasping for air. I was trapped with my hands pinned against the bannister. I did not know what I feared the most, death by asphyxiation or death by breaking my neck when he throws me down the stairs. This was why Patti stressed that we should not go back to the marital home. And now I knew why.

"Leave her alone Manley!" Maurice said.

He was trying to pull Manley's arm back. "She knows about us now, I'll tell Adanna, and we can start over."

Manley stopped mid punch and turned to look at him. He took Maurice in, naked with a wig on his head, like he was a stranger. He then drew back his arm and viciously elbowed Maurice in the mouth, knocking out his front teeth. Satisfied that Maurice was out for the count, he turned back to me and squeezed my windpipe.

Even through swelling eyes, I could see that the hatred for me was real. I thought of my children as I closed my eyes for the last time. I felt myself flowing up to the ceiling, watching myself being pummelled by Manley. Blood poured from my eyes, nose and mouth.

I heard Manley say that I have turned him gay, and that all of this mess was my fault. He would tell the police that I was sleeping with Maurice and that it was not the first time he had caught me with other men. He said he would tell anybody who would listen that he caught me having sex in the car with Moses.

The last comment triggered me, I could not have him spreading lies about me. I scanned the area around me. I had a helicopter view of my murder, and I knew what I had to do. I willed myself back into my body. The pain was excruciating. I could hardly see anything. I reached out for the cord leading to the base of the iron and pulled it towards me.

With my dying breath, I picked up the iron, and summoning all of my strength, I whacked Manley upside his head. His face imploded on impact. His head was caved in on one side and his left eye had popped out of its socket. Manley released me at once and he crumpled to the floor. The blood loss pooled out of his head and stained the threadbare carpet crimson. I stood in position, with the iron in my hands, gasping for air. I made my way to the phone on the landing.

"What is your emergency?"

"Hello, I need the police and an ambulance. I just killed my husband."

ABOUT THE AUTHOR

Part 2 of the story continues...Patti, Charmaine and Rose form an alliance in Jamaica and agree to support each other when they return to the UK. But with warnings from celestial beings and Veronica dreaming about 'fish', are the women able to bring their plans into fruition and exit their relationships on Christmas Day? By far the riskiest time for any woman in a violent relationship is when she decides to escape. Loving The Sisters is about Love, Sisterhood and Loyalty.

Pamela R Haynes is a retired Senior Probation Officer.

She has previously worked as a domestic abuse programme facilitator and with survivors of domestic violence. In 2018 Pam was awarded Author of the Year and Author of Colour for her debut novel Loving The Brothers and shortlisted for a BLAC Best Writer award 2020. Loving The Sisters is her highly anticipated second novel. On International Women's Day, Pam launched the Author 2 Author Podcast. She interviews Self Published Authors from around the world. Her Podcast was nominated for a Quill Podcast Award 2021 in 4 categories. Pam resides in London on the UK with her family. Follow her book journey on Instagram @lovingtheauthor.

Lightning Source UK Ltd.
Milton Keynes UK
UKHW011524310123
416242UK00003B/65